John Lutz published his first ~~story~~ ... ~~in Alfred~~
Hitchcock's Mystery Magazi... ...ing
regularly ever since. His work includes political suspense,
private eye novels, urban suspense, humour, occult, crime
caper, police procedural, espionage, historical, futuristic,
amateur detective – virtually every mystery sub-genre. He
is the author of more than thirty-five novels and 250 short
stories and articles. His *SWF Seeks Same* was made into
the hit movie *Single White Female,* starring Bridget Fonda
and Jennifer Jason Leigh, and his novel *The Ex* was made
into the HBO original movie of the same title, for which
he co-authored the screenplay.

Also by John Lutz

Chill of Night
Fear the Night
Night Victims
The Night Watcher
The Night Caller
Final Seconds (with David August)
The Ex
Single White Female

Titles featuring Frank Quinn

Serial
Mister X
Urge to Kill
Night Kills
In for the Kill
Darker Than Night
Pulse

SINGLE WHITE FEMALE

John Lutz

Constable & Robinson Ltd
55–56 Russell Square
London WC1B 4HP
www.constablerobinson.com

Published in the US by Pinnacle Books,
Kensington Publishing Corp., New York, 2011

First published in the UK by C&R Crime,
an imprint of Constable & Robinson, 2013

A copy of the British Library Cataloguing in Publication
Data is available from the British Library

ISBN 978-1-78033-959-7 (paperback)
ISBN 978-1-78033-960-3 (ebook)

Printed and bound in the UK

1 3 5 7 9 10 8 6 4 2

For Dominick Abel

Friend, of my intimate dreams
Little enough endures;
Little however it seems,
It is yours, all yours.
—BENSON, *The Gift*

A friend is, as it were, a second self.
—CICERO, *De Amicitia*

1

Across West 74th Street the Cody Arms loomed like a medieval castle that had given birth to and formed the foundation of a thirty-story urban building. The lower four floors were constructed of ornate concrete and brownstone, framing a brass and tinted-glass entrance flanked by stone pillars. Spaced about ten feet apart on the first-floor ledge were leering gargoyles with chipped features that only added to their grotesqueness. They'd once been functional drains to divert rainwater from the entrance, but now a dark brown canopy served that purpose. The gargoyles didn't seem to mind; now they could concentrate full-time on leering at passersby too preoccupied to glance up and notice them. There was iron grillwork over all the windows on the ground floor—for security. It only added to the baroque, lingering elegance of the old apartment building.

In better times the Cody Arms had been the Cody Hotel. But in the Sixties business had fallen off and new owners milked profits without putting money into upkeep. The Cody had declined so far that it was impossible to reestablish its validity as a respectable hotel, so it was sold again to a faceless corporate entity that converted it into apartment units and turned it over to Haller-Davis Properties to manage. Again it was in a state of gradual decline, which was what made the rent there relatively reasonable for this part of town, though still not cheap.

Allie Jones waited for a parade of cabs to growl and rattle past, then hurried across the rain-glistening street and up the old concrete steps to the entrance. She pushed through the door and crossed the tiled lobby to the elevators. There were dark smudges on the yellowed tile floor where cigarette butts had been ground out beneath heels. A faint scent of ammonia hung in the air. Apparently Gray the super, or the janitor service, had made a cursory pass at cleaning and disinfecting something, but not the graffiti on the wall by the mailboxes and intercoms. Boldly scrawled in black marking pen, as it had been for years, was the message LOVE KILS SCREW U. Allie occasionally wondered who had written it and what it meant exactly, though she had no desire to meet the author and ask.

Squeezing her damp bag of groceries tighter, she leaned close to the wall between the elevator doors and pressed the UP button with her elbow. The round white button glowed feebly. Above the paneled sliding doors the ancient brass arrow that had been resting on *15* began its herky-jerky descent to the *L* that signified Lobby.

There was no point in trying the intercom to make sure Sam would have her door unlocked when she reached the third floor. So often was it not working that tenants seldom used it, even when there was no "Out of order" sign taped beneath it. Though there were security precautions at the Cody Arms, people usually came and went as they pleased. With so many tenants, that was simply how it worked out. The street doors, on which any apartment key would work, were often locked after midnight, but just as often forgotten. The elevators were operable only with a tenant's key inserted in their panels, but as long as Allie could remember, the same twisted keys had been in the slots. Once, out of curiosity, she'd tried to remove one and found it stuck in the keyhole as if welded there.

The groceries got heavy, and Allie shifted them to her other arm just as the elevator arrived. It squeaked and groaned as it adjusted itself to floor level.

The doors hissed open and an elderly man and a middle-aged redheaded woman stepped out. They didn't seem to be together and didn't look at each other or at Allie as they crossed the lobby toward the street door. Allie listened to the beat of their heels on the tile floor as the man moved ahead of the woman. He didn't bother holding the door open for her. Neighbors. They probably hadn't so much as glanced at each other in the elevator.

New York was a city of strangers. The Cody was a building of strangers.

That had its advantages.

Such as making possible secret live-in lovers.

Secret was the operative word.

On the third floor, she walked down the narrow, musty-smelling hall to apartment 3H. She balanced the grocery sack on her outthrust hip while she fumbled her key from her purse and unlocked the door. Shifting her weight, she shoved the door open.

"Sam? Me!"

But the answering silence and stale, unmoving air told her she was alone.

2

Allie lay quietly and listened to the night push through the open window: the low, ocean sound of traffic that never ceased in Manhattan. The irrational and impatient blasting of a car horn. A woman's high laughter from nearby down in the street. A distant shout demanding an answer. No answering shout. More laughter. The singsong wail of a siren that seemed to be getting nearer, then faded.

Beside her Sam was sleeping, snoring lightly. They'd made love less than an hour ago, and the stale scent of their coupling still permeated the sheets and wafted occasionally into the fresh night air that was cleansing Allie's bedroom.

She lay very still, not wanting to break the magic of time and contentment. Loving Sam had opened doors and windows in her mind, showed her depths of herself she'd never suspected existed. With it had come the need, the dependency on him that she'd fought so hard against. That, dammit, was something she hadn't expected, at least not in its intensity.

Finally she'd realized he needed her as much as she had to have him, and it was all right to be human, to risk—because he was risking too. The past six months of total commitment to Sam had been fantastic, but nothing like the last two months, after he'd given up his apartment and moved in with her. Those two months had been perfect, a confirmation of their love. It was the kind of thing she used to laugh at in lurid romance novels. Until she found romance.

Sam Rawson was a broker's representative for Elcane-Smith on Wall Street. He'd made a few clients wealthy, and had some of his own money invested and was waiting for it to build. He wanted to be rich; he'd smiled and told Allie it would be for her, however rich he became. She liked to let him talk about options and puts and calls and selling short, and technical graph configurations that foretold the future and seduced its followers with an accuracy and superstition arguably as potent as voodoo. Allie remotely understood what he was saying.

Each day they'd kiss good-bye after breakfast and he'd cab downtown and merge his soul with the markets. Allie, who worked freelance as a computer programmer consultant, would go to her latest job and help to set up systems that would make someone's business easier and more profitable. It often struck her as ironic that she and Sam were both in occupations that helped to make other people rich, while each of them needed to juggle their finances to pay their bills.

Outside in the night, the woman had stopped laughing. A man yelled, "Hey, c'mon fuckin' back!" Allie couldn't be sure, but he sounded drunk.

The woman screamed shrilly (if it was the same woman). Something glass, probably a bottle, shattered. In a softer but vicious voice, the man said, "Teach you, bitch!"

Careful not to disturb Sam, Allie climbed out of bed and padded barefoot across the hard floor to the window. She looked down at the street. A few cars passed, gliding and ghostly. A cab with headlights shimmering and roof light glowing. Other than that, there was no movement on West 74th. No one in sight. Down the long avenue and on receding cross streets, strings of moving car lights traced through the night like low-flying comets in mysterious lazy orbit. Allie stared at the cars, wondering as she often did where they were all going at this lonely hour. What darkside destinations had the people in that beautiful, never-ending procession?

She knew where *she* was going—back to bed.

She retraced her steps across the cool, hard floor. Stretched out on her back, she laced her fingers behind her head and thought how violence always seemed to lurk near beauty, as if eager to balance the universe with its ugliness, like one of those fairy tales with underlying meanness. That was how it was in New York, anyway. Maybe everywhere, only not so close to the surface and evident, not breathing so deeply and not so bursting with corruption and raw life as in New York.

She left the sheet tangled around her bare feet and lay stretched out nude, her arms at her sides, as if waiting to be sacrificed in some primitive religious ceremony, letting the breeze play over her. The cool pressure seemed to be exploring her as sensually as a lover, softly brushing the mounds of her breasts, caressing the sensitive flesh of her inner thighs. She felt a tension deep inside her, like taut strings vibrating, and for a moment thought about waking Sam.

But it was so timeless and peaceful lying there, and they'd made love violently, leaving her somewhat sore. Sleep was the more sensible course.

She reached down languidly and drew the light sheet up around her, deadening the night breeze's sexual caresses.

And fell asleep.

When she awoke the next morning she was cold.

Sam was in the shower.

She lay and listened to the roar of pressured, rushing water, then silence when the shower was turned off.

A few minutes later he emerged from the bathroom with a towel around his waist, his dark hair wet and plastered against his forehead. He was average height and lean, with muscle-corded arms and legs. Thick black hair matted his chest and flat stomach. His face was lean, too, with nose and jaw a bit too long. Thin lips. It was an austere New England face except for his kind dark eyes. He carried himself erectly, with an oddly stiff back, and walked lightly as a dancer, as if suspended by a string attached to the top of his head. Allie knew he weighed a hundred and sixty pounds, but he gave the impression that if he stood on a scale, it would register less than twenty.

He smiled and said, "Awake, huh?"

"What time's it?" Allie asked, not bothering to glance at the clock on the nightstand.

"Ten after eight."

"Damn! I've got a nine o'clock appointment! Why didn't you wake me?"

"Didn't ask me."

True enough; she'd forgotten. Last night hadn't been conducive to reminding one's self about morning business appointments. God, last night . . .

Enough about that.

She swiveled sideways on the mattress to a sitting position, shivered in the column of cold air thrusting in through the window. Sam had removed the towel from around his waist and was using it to rub his tangled hair dry, studying her nakedness with a bemused expression on his dark features. She wondered, if she sat there long enough, would he get an erection?

No time to find out. She stood up, trudged to the window, and forced it shut with a bang that rattled the pane. Someday the glass would fall from the ancient window, shatter on the sidewalk three stories below, and maybe kill someone. She remembered the shouts and the sound of breaking glass last night. No one had died. But even if they had, it probably wouldn't make the news. Things like that happened all too frequently in New York. All those people. All that desperation. Fun City. Nobody seemed to call it that anymore.

Sam said, "You got goose bumps on your butt. It's still beautiful, though."

She turned. He was smiling at her. That narrow, tender smile. She loved him enough just then to consider forgetting about her nine o'clock meeting with the representative of Fortune Fashions. At times it was almost painfully obvious what was and wasn't most important in life.

But Sam had stepped into his jockey shorts and was slipping into his blue pinstripe suit pants. White shirt and red tie waited on a hanger. Working duds. A time for everything, she thought. Was that the Sunday school Bible of her youth echoing in her mind? *To everything there is a season?* Or campus concerts? Bob Dylan, borrowing from scripture? Whatever the source, the sentiment applied. She hurried into the bathroom to shower.

Allie scooped up the tailored jacket that went with her gray skirt. She wrestled into the jacket, wondering if it was tighter on her than the last time she'd worn it. She picked up her small black purse, then her matching black briefcase.

After working the array of chain-locks and sliding bolts on the door, she stepped into the hall first, the procedure she and Sam followed out of habit whenever they left the apartment together. Subleasing and apartment sharing were strictly forbidden and a flagrant lease violation in the Cody Arms. It was essential that no one in the building get a hint of their living arrangement, and they'd worked this knowledge into the fabric of their everyday lives. Apartment space in Manhattan had a scarcity and value that could bring out the worst in neighboring tenants as well as management. In the minds of those around them, there must be no connection between Sam and Allie.

The long, angled hall was empty. She moved ahead, and Sam followed and edged sideways while she did a half-turn and keyed the three locks on the door. It was almost like a dance step they'd perfected. He drifted along the hall to the elevator, punched the DOWN button with the corner of his attaché case, and stood waiting for her to catch up.

She was almost beside him when the elevator arrived. It clanked and growled in hollow agony, groping for the floor level like a blind creature. When its doors slid open it was empty.

Allie and Sam stepped into the elevator and Sam punched the button for the lobby. After the doors had slid shut, he kissed her passionately, using his tongue. When he drew away from her he said, "I love you. Know that?"

"If I didn't," she said, "I do now." She felt a little breathless and disheveled, and was afraid it might show when the elevator doors opened on the lobby.

Neither of them spoke the rest of the way down. What needed saying had been said.

3

Mike Mayfair rotated his wrist to shoot a glance at his watch. It was already nine-fifteen. He was supposed to meet the computer whiz at nine and she hadn't shown. Maybe the cunt should program her own computer to wake her up in the morning.

He stood just inside the hotel restaurant on West 51st, aware of the subtle aromas of breakfast being served, watching pedestrians stream past the stalled traffic outside the window. Horns blared in meaningless cacophony, each solitary blast setting off a flurry of sound. New Yorkers used their car horns more as a means to relieve tension than as warning signals to other drivers or pedestrians. On the other side of the street, a short man with flowing gray hair and beard was holding out an opened display case to show passing potential customers, jabbering his sales pitch. Almost everyone glanced at his glittering merchandise—possibly imitation Rolex watches—but no one stopped and bought. Most of them were on their way to more sophisticated cons.

Where was the bitch? Mayfair wondered, glanc-

ing at his own watch again—a genuine Rolex—
peeking out from beneath his white French cuff.
Nine-twenty. Another ten minutes and fuck her,
he'd head back to the office and see how the new
line was selling out west.

Then the fancy oak door swung open and she
entered the restaurant. She was in a hurry, kicking
out nicely curved ankles and high heels to cover
ground fast, looking worried and a little frazzled
despite her crisply tailored gray blazer and skirt.
She saw him and smiled with something like relief.
Whew! She hadn't missed him. Hadn't blown a
commission. *Blow something else, baby.*

"Mr. Mayfair," she said, gliding over and shaking his hand. She was composed now, though
there was still a slight sheen of perspiration on her
forehead. "Nice to see you again."

He mustered up a smile. "Same here, Miss
Jones. But can we make it Mike and Allison?"

"That'd be nice. I go by Allie, though."

"Fine, Allie." He moved gallantly to the side,
then hesitated before helping her remove her coat.
Never could tell about these liberated women. Had
to shake them hard sometimes before their artifi-
cial balls dropped off. He said, "They're holding
our table."

"Sorry I'm late. Got snarled up in traffic."

"I got here only a few minutes before you," he
lied.

The restaurant's walls were oak-paneled on the
bottom, flocked wallpaper on top with a gold
fleur-de-lis pattern. Wood partitions jutted out from
the back wall, not quite forming booths but pro-
viding a certain degree of privacy. It was a restau-

rant designed for business conversation and expense-account dining, with trendy, overpriced, merely passable food. Just the place to impress out-of-town buyers. After meeting Allie last week at the office of Fortune Fashions, Mayfair had chosen the restaurant in the hope of impressing her.

When they were settled and had ordered coffee, he studied her across the white-clothed table. She wasn't a beautiful woman, but there was something about her. Strong, squarish features, green-flecked gray eyes, wavy blond hair cut short so it could be easily managed. Dyed, it looked like, but what did he know at this point? That full lower lip and the cleft in her boxy chin gave her a determined look. She was a self-possessed, confident woman, but now and then a word, a gesture, allowed a glimpse of soft vulnerability that Mayfair wouldn't mind exploring.

Not that she'd given him the slightest sign she was in the game; but still, you never could tell. For now, it better be mostly business, maybe a cautious feeler now and then.

He said, "You've seen our operation, know some of our needs." *Only some, lover.* "In the fashion business, security's vital. The length of our spring hemline can be as important a secret to us as a new weapon might be to a defense contractor. The fashion world may seem trivial and whimsical at times, but I assure you it's a very serious and competitive place. Few moves are against the rules."

Allie smiled. "You make it sound like a jungle."

"So it is. The business jungle. Debits are as deadly as vipers."

Mayfair couldn't read her eyes. He wondered what she thought of him. Usually he could tell when women liked him. Even now that he was past fifty, many of them still were receptive to him. His features remained boyish until a close look revealed the crow's-feet and sagging eyelids. The deep lines swooping from the wings of his nose to the corners of his lips. His hair was streaked with gray in a way that made him look distinguished, he thought. He'd been lucky there, still had most of it, though it was thinning at the crown. He was dressed today in a dove-gray Blass suit with a maroon tie and matching handkerchief, a white-on-white shirt, and black Italian loafers. Casual, but obviously a man with time and money to spend.

The waiter brought their coffee, placing the cups on the table with dramatic flair, then withdrew smoothly as if he were on rollers.

"Though we're primarily concerned with design, inventory control, and payroll," Mayfair said, "we gotta have a secure system. One that can't be broken into by a computer hack with a compulsion for industrial espionage. Maybe a system only a few key personnel could access."

"That can be done," Allie said. She leaned down far enough for her left breast to brush the edge of the table when she drew a little leather-bound notebook from the briefcase propped against her chair leg. What did she carry in there? Schematics? Spreadsheets? Was she wearing a bra?

He knew this: She was methodical and ambitious and overdrawn at the bank, and the account they were here to discuss was important to her survival.

Mayfair had ordered personnel to check her out thoroughly, and knew more about her than she thought. Knew she'd come to New York six years ago from the small town of Grafton, Illinois, and had no surviving family members. She was alone in the world, and she lived alone in the West Seventies. He also knew that two months ago she'd done an excellent job in setting up a payroll system for Walton Clothiers on Sixth Avenue.

She said, "I'll need some basic figures."

Mayfair pondered again the possible future with this woman who needed his business, what they might do for each other. It was a quid-pro-quo world; always something for something. She had to know that, if she had her own company. Beyond the Fortune Fashions account, what yearnings did she have? What fires that he might quench while finding the satisfaction that his former wife Janice had never given him? What interesting and possibly kinky drives? So many of these hot-shit female execs were intriguing that way. He'd find out about her someday, find out everything.

Then he concentrated on the here and now and satisfied her yearning for statistics, watching the way she cocked her head to the side to listen, the way the muted light played off her blond hair.

Thinking, while he paused so she could catch up taking notes, *Soon, baby.*

4

Allie was optimistic after her breakfast with Mayfair. He'd been all business, which was a relief. He looked like an aging lothario in his tight double-breasted suit and matching tie and handkerchief, his just-so hairstyle that was too young for him. Time held at bay by ego. But except for what might have been a few exploratory remarks, he'd stayed on the subject of the computer system Fortune Fashions wanted Allie to set up, and they'd had hours of involved and fruitful discussion. It was nice to know she didn't have to worry about Mayfair in that regard, sex being an occupational hazard.

The account was a rich one, and when final payment was made, Allie's monetary problems would be solved for a while. Meaning she'd no longer be financially dependent upon Sam; she wasn't sure why that dependency bothered her, but it did. Perhaps because she was emotionally dependent on him, financial dependency as well left her with nothing.

Just before eleven o'clock, when she'd parted

with Mayfair outside the restaurant, the clouds had drifted away and the sun had transformed gloom into light and hope. A dictatorial Hollywood director couldn't have ordered it improved. Why not believe in omens? she'd thought, watching Mayfair wave to her from his cab as it pulled away.

Still buoyed by fate falling right, she wandered around for a while, window-shopping. Then she strode from the subway stop to West 74th through the rare and sunny September day, her light blue raincoat with the white collar folded over her arm.

She realized she was hungry. The breakfast she'd had with Mayfair was delicious but hardly filling. That and a cup of coffee this morning with Sam was all she'd had so far today. I need fuel, she told herself.

She stopped in at Goya's, a restaurant on West 74th three blocks from the Cody Arms. It was a large place with an ancient curved bar and a plank floor. A faded mirror behind the bar reflected shelves of bottles and an antique cash register. The waiters and waitresses all looked like hopefuls waiting for their big break in show business, though some of them were over forty. All wore black slacks and red T-shirts with GOYA'S stenciled across the chest. Allie hadn't been in there before, but she immediately liked the rough-hewn and efficient atmosphere. If the food was good and the prices were right, she knew she'd come back, maybe become one of the regulars.

She ordered a chef's salad and allowed herself a

Beck's to celebrate the way things were going with the Fortune Fashions account. Then she thought about how she and Sam would celebrate when he came home that evening. Sam. Scheming and ambitious as he was in business, he never resented her successes. Liberated man meets liberated woman.

When the waiter brought her salad, she realized he looked familiar. But she didn't ask where she might have met him. Possibly she'd passed him on the street often when he was on his way to or from work at Goya's. New York was like that; people making casual connections over and over, not really recognizing each other because their memories' circuits were overloaded. So many people, an ebbing and flowing tide of faces, movements, smiles, frowns. Pain and happiness and preoccupation. Good luck and bad. Bankers and bag ladies. All in a jumble. Millionaires stepping over penniless winos. Tourists throwing away money on crooked three-card-monte games. The hustlers and the hustled. A maelstrom of madness. A world below the rabbit hole. If you lived here, you took it all for granted. My God, you adapted. And, inevitably, it affected mind and emotion. It distorted.

This man, the waiter, was in his mid-thirties, with one of those homely-handsome faces with mismatched features and ears that stuck out like satellite dishes. He wore his scraggly black hair long on the sides in an effort to minimize the protruding ears, but the thatch of hair jutting out above them only served to draw attention. The impression was that without the ears to support it, the hair would flop down into a ragged Prince Valiant hairdo. He was average height but thin, and moved with a kind of coiled energy that suggested he could probably jog ten miles or wear down opponents at tennis.

When he came back and placed her beer before her on the table, he did a mild double-take, as if *he* thought he knew *her* from someplace.

Then he nodded and went back to the serving counter to pick up another order, probably trying to remember if she'd been in Goya's before, and what kind of tipper she was.

5

Graham Knox had recognized her when he'd served her in Goya's that afternoon. Allie Jones. It was the first time he'd seen her in the restaurant. He'd considered introducing himself to her but didn't quite know how. "Hi, I live upstairs from you and can hear everything that goes on in your apartment through the ductwork," didn't seem a wise thing for a waiter to say—it was the sort of remark that might prompt the flinging of food.

Several months ago, curiosity had goaded Graham to find out what his downstairs neighbor looked like. He'd lurked about the third-floor hall like a burglar until he'd seen her emerge from her apartment. Already he'd gotten her last name from her mailbox in the lobby.

Seeing her up close this afternoon had changed things somehow, made her vividly real and his eavesdropping both more intimate and shameful, no longer an innocent diversion before sleep. But the vent was beside his bed; there was no way *not* to hear what went on in the apartment below.

Even in his living room, when he was working and didn't have the stereo or TV on, sound from her living room carried through the ducts. It wasn't exactly as if he were in the room with her and whoever she was talking with, but he might as well have been in the next room with his ear pressed to the door.

And now he'd seen her up close, and she was interesting. In fact, fascinating. Much more attractive than from a distance. Direct gray eyes. Soft blond hair that smelled of perfumed shampoo. Firm, squared chin with a cleft in it. She had a sureness about her that was appealing and suggested a certain freedom. Not like the rest of us; a woman with a grip on life.

Graham's apartment was cheaply furnished, mostly with a hodgepodge of items he'd bought at secondhand shops. The living room walls were lined with shelves he'd constructed of pine and stained to a dark finish. The shelves were stuffed with theatrical books, mostly paperbacks, that he'd found in used bookstores on lower Broadway. One glance at the apartment might give an interior decorator a month of nightmares, but it was neat, functional, and comfortable. Despite the deprivation, Graham liked it here.

Both apartments were quiet now. Graham was in his contemplative mode, and Allie and Sam had either left or gone into the bedroom.

Graham puffed on his meerschaum pipe and paced to the window, then stared out at the darkening city. Some of the cars had their headlights on, and windows were starting to glow in random patterns on the faces of buildings. New York was putting on her jewelry, hiding squalor with splendor.

Four years ago he'd been divorced; he'd put a genuinely horrific marriage out of its misery before children arrived. Six months later, after quitting his job in Philadelphia to pursue his true calling, Graham had moved to New York and attempted to get one of his plays produced.

Some move! Even the lower echelons of the New York theater world weren't impressed by a real-estate agent from Philadelphia with the chutzpah to fancy himself a playwright. Didn't he know there were a million others in his mold?

With a final glance outside, he turned from the window and crossed the living room to an alcove directly above the one in Allie's apartment. There a thick sheet of plywood was laid over two black metal filing cabinets, creating a desk that supported a used IBM Selectric, a phone and answering machine, stacks of paper, and several reference books. Graham sat down on the folding chair in front of the makeshift desk and got *Dance Through Life* out of the top drawer of one of the filing cabinets. *Dance* was the play he'd been working on for over a year. An off-Broadway company had expressed interest in producing it, if he could satisfy them with some suggested revisions in the last act. He didn't agree with some of the advice, but this would be his first produced play. So he was in the process of following suggestions, doing the minor and, here and there, major revisions, trying all the while to preserve the essence of the play.

He picked up a red-leaded pencil and began tightening dialogue and making notes in the margins. The last scene needed more emotional punch, he'd been told. The theme had to be more clearly defined. Well, he could supply punch and clarity to order, if only they'd produce his play. If only he could see real actors walking through his script, mouthing his lines. Striking life in it onstage.

The evening, his apartment in New York, faded to haze, and he was in Chattanooga, Tennessee, at the Starshine Ballroom, where the play was set. Smoke from his pipe swirled around him as dancers and dialogue whirled through his mind.

He hunched over his typewriter and script, absently puffing on the pipe and absorbed in his work, and forgot about his downstairs neighbor until he'd gone to bed at eleven-thirty. The Scotch and water he'd downed after leaving the typewriter had eased the tension fueled by his intense concentration on the revisions, and he'd almost fallen asleep when he heard the muted ringing.

Her bedroom telephone.

He stared into darkness, not liking himself very much, but telling himself he was a playwright and the study of human nature was his business. It was almost a professional obligation. Arthur Miller wouldn't pass up this kind of opportunity. Would he?

The phone abruptly stopped ringing. Allie had answered.

Graham rolled over on the cool, shadowed sheet.

To the side of the bed near the vent.

Lying on his stomach, he nestled his forehead in the warm crook of his arm and guiltily listened.

6

Allie drifted up from indecipherable dreams, pulled like a hooked sea creature by some sound . . . she wasn't sure what. Then she felt a moment of panic as the jangling phone chilled her mind. She hated to be awakened by phone calls; almost always they meant bad news. The worst of life happened at night.

Oblivious, Sam was snoring beside her, sleeping deeply on his side with one arm flung gracefully off the mattress as if he'd just hurled something at the wall. As she reached for the phone, Allie glanced at the clock on the nightstand. Only quarter to twelve. She'd thought she'd slept longer, that it was early morning. Maybe the phone call wasn't bad news. Maybe somebody who thought everyone stayed up till midnight.

The darkness in the humid bedroom felt like warm velvet as she extended her arm through it and groped for the phone. She pulled the entire unit to her so she could lift the receiver and quiet it as quickly as possible. No sense in letting the damned thing wake Sam.

She settled her head back on the pillow, in control now, and pressed the cool plastic receiver to her ear. Her palm was damp, slippery on the phone's smooth surface. She had to adjust her grip to hold on. " 'Lo."

"I want to speak with Sam, please." A woman's voice. Young. Tense. And something else: angry.

"Who's calling?"

"Tell him Lisa."

"Well, listen, Lisa, Sam's asleep." Something cold and ugly moved in Allie's stomach. Its twin awoke in her mind. "Is it important? About work?"

"Not about work." Was that a laugh? "I don't work with Sam. But it's important, all right."

Allie didn't say anything. She was fighting all the way up from sleep, reaching out for answers and finding only questions. Lisa . . . Did she and Sam know a Lisa? Had Sam ever mentioned the name?

Lisa said, "Gonna let me talk to him?"

"It's almost midnight; he's asleep. Sure it can't wait till morning?"

"It can't wait."

Allie stared into deeper darkness where she knew ceiling met walls. A corner; no way out. "Hold on."

She nudged Sam's ribs and whispered his name.

He rolled over, facing her. She caught a whiff of his warm breath, the wine they'd had with dinner. His upper chest and neck gathered pale light but his face was in shadow. "Whazzit?"

"You awake?"

"'Course not."

"Well, you got a phone call. Woman named Lisa."

"She on the line now?"

"Now. Waiting."

Sam was quiet for a long time. Allie could hear him breathing rapidly. She felt her world sliding out from under her. It was making her sick, dizzy. Too casually, he said, "Tell her I'll call her in the morning."

Allie pressed the receiver back to the side of her head, so hard that it hurt. She gave Lisa Sam's message.

"You're his wife," Lisa said, sounding furious and determined. "I know he's married, 'cause I followed him home from my apartment. Saw you two through the window, then saw you come out together and followed you. Saw how you acted together. Tell him that. Explain to him I know his name's really Jones, just like it says on his mailbox. Tell him he better fucking talk to me, or I'll talk a lot more to you."

Allie listened to her own breathing. "I don't think I will tell him. Anyway, he's asleep again."

"I really think you should."

"Sorry, I don't agree. You've got a lot of your facts wrong, Lisa."

"Not the essential one. Wake up Sam, if he really is asleep. Put him on the goddamn phone."

"No."

Lisa laughed, not with humor. The bitter sound seem to flow from the phone like bile. "You poor, dumb bitch." She hung up. Hard.

Allie lay unmoving, the receiver droning in her ear. The darkness closed in on her tightly, making it difficult to breathe. *Poor, dumb bitch* . . . There had been more than bitterness in Lisa's voice; there had been pity. Allie slowly extended her arm, hung up the receiver with a tentative clatter of plastic on plastic. The buzzing of the broken connection continued in her head, like an insect droning.

After a while she said, "Sam?"

Seconds passed before he said, "Hmmm?" Drowsy. Pretending to be asleep. Maybe it was all a dream. Maybe hope could make it so, glue it where it was broken so nobody would know the difference and nothing was changed from the time they'd gone to sleep.

But Allie knew it couldn't be repaired.

"Lisa told me to say she knew you were married. That she followed you home."

He gave a long, phony sigh, as if this didn't concern him and he resented it interfering with his rest. "Whaddya say her name was?"

"Lisa."

"Last name?"

"You tell me."

Nothing but silence from the darkness on Sam's side of the bed. A jetliner roared overhead like a lion in a distant jungle. The echo of traffic rushed like flowing black water in the night.

She watched him in silhouette. "She'll call back, Sam."

Lying on his stomach, he raised himself up so that his upper body was propped on his elbows, head hanging to stare at his pillow. It was a posture of despair. His hair had fallen down over his forehead and was in his eyes. "Yeah, I guess she will."

Allie said in the calm voice of a stranger, "Who is she, Sam?"

He flopped over to lie on his back. The mattress swayed beneath his shifting bulk; springs squealed. The back of his hand brushed her bare thigh and quickly withdrew, as if he'd touched something forbidden.

"Sam?"

"Yeah." Resigned.

"Who is she?"

"A girl, is all."

Allie was thrown by the simple evasiveness of his answer. He was speaking to her as if she were twelve years old. She didn't like what was welling up in her but she couldn't stop it. She couldn't even put a name to it. "Christ, is that what she is, a girl is all? Is that what you've got to say, like some goddamned adolescent caught two-timing his steady?"

"I'm sorry. God, I'm sorry. But really, that's all she is to me."

"Sam, that's so shabby. So fucking banal."

"So maybe I'm banal. I'm sorry about that too."

He was working up anger now, preferring it to guilt. The hell with him. He wasn't fooling her.

"How long you two been being banal together?" she asked.

"This isn't an ongoing relationship," he said. "Something happened one time. Only one. Damn it, Allie, I wish it hadn't happened. I sure didn't plan it. Neither did she."

"God's plan, huh?" she said bitterly.

"More like the devil's," Sam said. "A moment of weakness on my part, and it led to something. I thought that kinda thing only happened to the clowns on soap operas, but I was wrong."

She said, "I don't believe things like that just happen, Sam."

"But they do. Then the people involved regret it but can't change the past. Please, Allie, try to understand this. Try not to be—"

"Try not to be what?" she interrupted.

"I dunno. Naive, I guess."

She sat up, and switched on the lamp by the bed. Sam twisted his head away from the light, shielding his eyes, as if he might decompose under the glare like Dracula caught in the sun. Allie knew it was the truth that was making him come apart.

"You *have* to do that?" he asked. "Turn on that damned light?"

"What do you mean by naive? That I trusted you?"

Now he did roll onto his side to face her, his head resting on his upper arm so that his cheek was scrunched up. His eyes were still narrowed to the light. "No. But I don't want you to think an accidental affair with another woman means anything important." He scooted toward her, touched her hip gently with his fingertips, making her suddenly aware and ashamed of her nakedness. She pulled away violently, startling him. "Allie, please!"

Allie kept her distance. "She said on the phone she thinks you're married. Talks as if you lied to her, led her to believe she was the only one in your life. The way you've been lying to me."

"The point is, it doesn't matter a gnat's ass to me what she thinks."

"Sure, I can believe that."

"Oh, c'mon, Allie. You're mad right now, not thinking straight. Not putting this in perspective. And I don't blame you. But it was a onetime affair of the glands, not the heart. And it's over, I swear it! It meant no more than a shared dance that can never happen again."

"Lisa would disagree with you, I bet."

"Maybe. But so what? I only care what *you* think, Allie. That's all that's important to me in this crazy world. Honestly. You believe me, don't you?"

"No."

He made a sound almost like a moan. "I don't know what I can do about that. I only wish I could do *something* to make you see the facts. The Lisa thing just sort of happened and then ran its course and no longer matters. Please, Allie, accept that as the truth, because it is."

"You're not denying it, only repeating that it doesn't matter."

"I don't like lying to you. Never did. I admitted I slept with Lisa Calhoun. If you need to hear it again, I'll admit it again. I can't see why you don't realize the rest of what I'm saying's true."

"I don't *need* to hear it, Sam. Not anymore."

"Well, yeah, I guess not. Allie?"

She knew his wheedling, little-boy voice. Right

now it sickened her. Sam was about to ask her forgiveness. She couldn't handle that. She reached
out an arm and hurriedly switched off the lamp.

"That's better, Allie." He'd assumed she wanted
to go back to sleep, that their discussion was over
at least until morning.

She said, "Get out, Sam."

"What?"

"Out. Now."

"Hey, I know it's your place, but it's midnight."
He switched on the lamp on his side of the bed,
then glared at her so she could see he was furious.
He hadn't expected this, his look said. Didn't deserve it. She was being damned unreasonable, and
all because of some insignificant one-night stand
that had come to light. "Where do you expect me
to go at this hour?"

"Find a hotel. Come back tomorrow for your
things. Or the next day. Or don't come back at all.
I don't care, Sam, not anymore."

He appeared puzzled for a while. Injured. Then
he tried a smile. It was male mastery time. But he
was acting out of desperation and she knew it. "I
don't believe you," he said, like a line from a
movie, as if the script was on his side and their des-
tiny was in the last reel.

She wasn't sure if she believed herself, but she
looked away from him. "Get out."

Sam clutched her arm and she slapped his
hand away. She was startled by how loud a sound it
made.

He stood up, naked, his maleness wilted between his legs. He located his jockey shorts and

danced into them, yanking them tight. *You'll hurt yourself that way, Sam.* He found his pants.

She turned away from him, watching his madly writhing shadow on the wall as he stormed around, wrestling angrily into his clothes. A button clattered on the floor, bouncing and rolling.

Then the shadow was still. He'd worn himself out; she could hear his deep and rapid breathing, like right after sex.

Calmly, he said, "All right, Allie. I'll send for the rest of my stuff."

Allie felt something pointed and sharp swell in her throat; she was afraid if she tried to answer him she might sob. She lay very still, listening to the night sounds of the city, to Sam's ragged breathing.

She heard him leave the bedroom. Heard the thump of his rubber heels as he crossed the apartment to the door. The metallic snick and rattle of the locks being worked on the door to the hall.

The door slammed.

Allie lost it. She pressed her face deep into her pillow and sobbed.

At four-thirty A.M. she gave up on trying to sleep and climbed out of bed. She switched on the lamp and put on her white terry-cloth robe.

She padded barefoot into the living room and to the alcove where she had her desk and IBM-clone computer. It felt good, settling down before the computer; this was a world she knew, a dance whose steps were no mystery. She flipped the computer switch and booted the system.

At first she'd considered working on the Fortune Fashions job, but she realized this wasn't the time for that. In the green glare of the monitor screen, she sat idly toying with the keyboard, trying to relax her whirling mind. Computers and Allie were compatible. Right now, she envied them. Computers thought, in their basic way, but they didn't feel. Allie didn't want to feel. She wanted to see herself from a distance, so she could analyze and convert emotion to cold fact. An IBM clone—that's what she wanted to be.

She keyed in her household budget program and looked over the figures. Made a few calculations and studied the results on the screen.

The computer played fair with her and gave her the hard truth. Without Sam, if she wanted to stay in the Cody Arms and pay her bills, she'd need help, even with the Fortune Fashions account.

There was a way to obtain the right kind of roommate, she knew. She'd considered it before Sam had moved in with her.

Allie keyed in the word-processor program. She typed "Wanted, roommate to share apt. W.70s," then her phone number.

Tomorrow she'd look at the classified pages of some newspapers and decide where she might place the ad. She wanted to do this right; didn't want to attract the wrong kind of people. She'd read the ads in some of thé underground papers. Desperate singles, divorcees, shut-ins, and gays. People looking for sex partners who shared their particular perversions. There was a loneliness there, a sadness she didn't want to touch her.

She spent the next half-hour composing and printing out rental application forms.

She couldn't leave the computer; it was like a friend she could rely on, one that wouldn't deceive, or switch allegiance. There was comfort in predictability.

When the windows were beginning to brighten with the dawn, she switched off the computer, went back to bed, and finally slept.

7

Allie slept until almost noon, then awoke to the sinking realization of what had happened. Lisa. A woman named Lisa. She felt a hollowness when she thought about Sam, and beyond that a deep resentment and anger. Love could do a quick turn to hate, sudden as a tango step, and she didn't want that. She chose not to have that kind of corrosiveness inside her. The task would be to exorcise him from her mind, a necessary knack if she wanted to continue her life.

For a few minutes she lay in bed, getting used to the new Allison Jones in her state of existence without Sam. Then she rolled her tongue around her mouth, making a face at the bad taste, and struggled out of bed.

Slightly stiff from sleeping so late, she staggered into the bathroom and brushed her teeth with the final surrender of the Crest tube. She picked up Sam's toothbrush from the porcelain holder and dropped it, along with the distorted corpse of the toothpaste tube, into the wastebasket. Then she turned on the shower and adjusted the water temperature. She stood for a long time beneath the hot needles of water, waking up all the way and working up courage to face what was left of her Saturday. Of her life.

After toweling dry, she put on black slacks and a baggy white T-shirt with SIMON AND GARFUNKEL CENTRAL PARK CONCERT lettered across the front; she d bought it the day after she'd attended the concert several years ago, and the letters were faded. Simon, who was still hard at it, probably had a song about that. He was doing fine without Garfunkel; she could make it without Sam.

She stepped into the comfortable soft leather moccasins she wore on weekends and wandered as if lost through the apartment, pausing here and there and running her fingertips over the furniture, as if to reassure herself it was real.

Jesus, she thought, how maudlin. She walked over to the office-alcove, ripped the fan-fold paper from the computer printer, and read the classified ad she'd composed before dawn. It was simple and to the point. Effective. She'd been thinking clearly enough when she considered advertising for a roommate to share expenses.

It occurred to Allie that she might have a problem, telling potential roommates they'd have to live surreptitiously in the apartment, be coconspirators in an arrangement that fooled neighbors and management company. On the other hand, apartments in Manhattan were so expensive and difficult to obtain that most renters would find the required discretion only a minor inconvenience. It might even appeal to the more adventuresome. Beating the system was a New York way of life, a point of pride as well as a means of survival in the cruelest of cities.

She got her purse from the bedroom, folded the computer printout in quarters, and poked it in behind her wallet. Then she thought for a moment, pulled the wallet out, and counted her money. Twenty-six dollars. She thought about how much she had in the bank. Depressing. Even with the Fortune Fashions retainer, within a month she'd really be feeling the pinch. Something had to be done, and soon; if the wolf wasn't at the door, it was prowling the corridors.

Allie had slept through breakfast; she realized she was starving. Considering the scarcity of edible food in the refrigerator, she could treat herself to eating lunch out despite having to watch the flow of pennies.

She locked the apartment behind her carefully. Woman alone now. Then she disdained the elevator and took the stairs down to the lobby too fast, as if to assert her physical capability and spirit.

Breathing hard, she trudged outside and walked until she found a newsstand, where she bought three likely papers in which to place her classified ad. An obese man beside her bought a magazine with a cover illustration of a nude woman seated on a yellow bulldozer. He followed Allie half a block before falling behind her rapid pace and giving up. She glanced back and saw him standing near a wire trash basket, leafing through his magazine. Possibly he meant no harm, but New York had more weirdos per square yard than any other city.

She tucked the newspapers more firmly beneath her arm and returned to West 74th. It was a little past one when she entered Goya's.

The restaurant did a good lunch business of neighborhood regulars and tourists. She had to wait for a table, and then was ushered to a tiny booth wedged in a corner. On the table were a napkin holder, salt and pepper shakers, a Bakelite ashtray, a half-full Heinz catsup bottle, and a two-dollar tip from the last diner. Allie found herself staring at the creased bills, thinking that theft, on a larger scale than this, was a way out of her financial difficulties.

She shook that thought from her mind when the waiter arrived and stood by the booth. Stealing was stealing, a risk and a moral compromise she was unwilling to explore.

The waiter said, "Something to drink?"

She looked up. It was the same guy who'd taken her order when she was here the day before, the one with the intense, familiar face, the black hair and satellite-dish ears. Homely in the way of Abe Lincoln, or dogs you wanted to take home and feed. There was something clumsy and rough-hewn about him; a long way from Sam's smoothness and grace. He laid a closed menu before her with ceremony. Like a good book he was recommending.

"I'll order now, drink and all," she said, and looked at the grease-spotted menu. It was a computer printout, she noticed. The microchip was everywhere.

The waiter said, "You're Allison Jones."

She looked away from the menu, up into the homely face. Dark, earnest eyes gazed back at her, amiable despite their intensity, not devious or threatening.

He smiled and said, "I live in the apartment above yours over at the Cody Arms. I've seen you around. Got your name from the mailbox." He extended a hand and she shook it without thinking. "I'm Graham Knox."

The guy seemed friendly enough, not putting moves on her. "Glad to meet you, Graham."

He said, "The double burger and the house salad are good."

"I'll have them, then, with fries and a large Diet Pepsi. I'm hungry today."

He scribbled her order in his notepad and scooped up the tip from the table in the almost unnoticeable manner of waiters everywhere. He smiled his lopsided smile and said, "Back soon."

And he was. Goya's kitchen must have cooks falling all over themselves.

He placed her food on the table and straightened up, dangling the empty tray in his right hand. "We're neighbors, Allie, so anything you need, you let me know."

Oh-oh, where was this going? She gave him her passionless, appraising stare. The same one she'd given the obese man with the sex magazine when their gazes met. *Turn it off, buddy, whatever you're thinking.*

"Not that kind of anything," he assured her, smiling. He had long, skinny fingers that played nervously with the edge of the round tray. His nails were gnawed to the quick. "Don't get me wrong."

Okay, so he wasn't interested in her that way.

Now she wondered, was he gay? She mentally jabbed herself for being so egotistical and unfair. Any man who wasn't interested in going to bed with her on first meeting wasn't necessarily gay. And there was something about this man she instinctively liked, but in the same platonic fashion in which he seemed to see her. "Okay, Graham, thanks for the offer. And if you ever need a thumbtack, knock on my door."

"Not many people at the Cody would say that. Most of us don't even know each other and don't want to meet."

"New York," Allie said, dousing her French fries with catsup. *New York, like a disease.*

"Most big cities, I'm afraid."

"Maybe, but it's special here."

"Could be it is. Well, I better get moving—orders are piling up. Come in sometime when we're not busy and we'll talk."

She nodded, holding the catsup bottle still, and watched him smile and back away, moving among the tables toward the serving counter.

Did he want something? Or was he simply as he'd presented himself? Was she being cynical? Everyone didn't have an act, an ulterior motive and an angle, even in New York. She had her choice now: she could stop coming into Goya's, or she could become a friend, or at least an acquaintance, of Graham Knox.

She sampled the salad with the house dressing, and bit into the double burger. Graham was right, they were both delicious. And among the cheaper items on the menu. She decided what the hell, she could use a casual friend who didn't clutter up her life with complications. Allie sensed that was all Graham wanted to be to her, someone she could talk to, and someone who'd listen if he felt compelled to talk. She almost laughed out loud at herself, thinking she could trust her instincts about people. She and Lisa.

Allie wolfed down the rest of the salad and hamburger, then ate what was left of her fries more slowly.

Afterward she ordered another Diet Pepsi and sat sipping it through a straw while most of the lunchtime crowd drifted outside. A vintage Beatles tune, "Strawberry Fields Forever," came over the sound system. Softly. People came here to eat, not listen to music. It was one of Allie's favorite Beatles numbers, so she leaned back, closed her eyes, and let it play over her mind. And she was thinking of Sam, trying not to cry.

When Stevie Wonder took over, she opened her tear-clouded eyes and saw that Graham was staring curiously at her from the other side of the restaurant, like a confused terrier.

Allie nodded to him and he looked away. Not ill at ease, but as if he didn't want to cause her embarrassment.

She slid her cool glass to the side and examined the classified columns of the newspapers she'd bought, laying each one flat on the table, not caring about the spreading damp spots from puddles left by her glass.

She decided to call her ad into the *Times*. The other ads in their "Apartments to Share" column seemed respectable enough—not placed by creeps or swingers trying to make contact. Abbreviations abounded in the small print: Single white female was, in the lexicon of the classified columns, "SWF." Also being sought to share "Apt W Pvt Rm" were "Yng Prof'l Fem," "GWM," "SBF," and "SBM prof nSmkr." Allie took these to mean "Young professional female; gay white male; single black female; and single black male professional, nonsmoker."

She decided to make the wording of her ad more economical and change it to read "SWF seeks same."

Graham took the order of a middle-aged couple who'd just entered the restaurant, then walked over to Allie. For the first time she noticed that he had an oddly bouncy sort of walk, jaunty, with a lot of spring in his knees. A tall Groucho Marx. He used his sawed-off pencil as a pointer. "Refill on the Pepsi?"

"No, thanks, I'm going in a minute."

He tucked the pencil behind his ear, then thumbed through the torn-off order slips stuck into the cover of his note pad. He laid Allie's check on the table with practiced precision, as if dealing her a card faceup. "You can pay the cashier up by the door. See you next time, Allie."

"Right." She watched him bustle away, the busy waiter, showing her he wasn't the sort to get smarmy and make a pest of himself.

Allie chewed on the crushed ice in her glass for a while, thinking about how life could change so drastically and unexpectedly. A phone call in the night, and the center of her universe had shifted. A simple phone call, and a relentless momentum had taken hold. Everyone's fate was so precariously balanced, even if people didn't seem to know it.

She paid for her lunch and left a tip, nodding to Graham Knox as she pushed open the door to the street. In the bright sunlight outside the restaurant she stood still for a few minutes, as if trying to decide which direction to take.

Then she walked back to her apartment and phoned in the ad.

8

Allie's classified ad appeared in the Wednesday *Times*. Seated in bright sunlight at her kitchen table, steaming coffee cup before her, she read it to make sure it was worded correctly, then found herself scanning the news. The city's murder rate was up (a bloodless statistic listed along with the birth and divorce rates and per capita income). A woman's body had been found in her apartment, dismembered and decomposed. Yesterday a man's body had been discovered hidden in the bushes in Central Park, only a few hundred feet from Fifth Avenue. Someone had struck him in the back of the head with a sharp rock, perhaps during sexual intercourse, and severed his hands. New York was a tumult of souls seeking fulfillment bright and dark, where sanity and madness converged often and sometimes violently. Allie grimaced. A nice place to visit, but you wouldn't want to die there.

The rest of that week her phone rang almost continuously. Most of the people who answered her ad were eliminated almost immediately by the amount of rent, or the apartment's precise location, or the fact that Allie preferred a nonsmoker without a pet. Or for various personal reasons.

After the initial winnowing process, five seemed promising enough to interview.

Allie set up appointments and had each person who arrived fill out the rental application form she'd composed and printed out on her computer. It asked for present and previous addresses. Occupation, salary, reason for wanting to move, approximate work/sleep schedule. Whether friends would be entertained in the apartment and if so how often. Any hobbies or activities that might cause problems.

Afterward, mulling over the interviews and rental applications, she reflected that no matter how much information you gleaned about someone, you were still taking a chance on any prospective roommate. It figured to be that way. Even people who'd known each other for years and then married sometimes found out when living together day in, day out that they hadn't *really* known each other. She felt a cold weight in the pit of her stomach. She hadn't really known Sam, and she'd lived with him for two months.

Allie finally settled on Hedra Carlson, a twenty-nine-year-old temporary office worker with a hesitant smile and a shy manner. Hedra wasn't the perfect applicant, but she certainly was the best bet out of those who'd responded. And Allie, smiling inwardly, realized the real reason she'd chosen Hedra was that the diffident and quiet woman was the least likely of any she'd seen to leave dirty socks on the floor and hair in the shower drain. So it came down to personality rather than employment records, pastimes, or schedules. To DNA, maybe. With Hedra as a roommate, Allie would be giving up as little of her independence as possible. Simple as that.

As soon as she'd informed the ecstatically grateful Hedra by phone that she could move in immediately, Allie tore the other applications in half and dropped them in the wastebasket. They hadn't proved very useful, since this business of choosing a roommate had reverted to emotion and a certain positive feeling about the applicant. But that was okay. Maybe in something like this, unknown territory, instinct was the most reliable compass; the floating needle in the heart.

Allie had already shuffled the items that had been stored in the second bedroom, spreading some throughout the apartment, transferring most of them to her insecure though padlocked storage area in the basement. At a used-furniture store, she bought a four-section folding screen to isolate the alcove she used as her office. The screen was quite a find. It had a few stains on it, but it was gray silk and adorned with a delicate black Chinese willow design. She thought it added something to the décor while concealing her desk and computer.

Hedra moved in by degrees over the next few days. She didn't have that many possessions, and the one short trip by a moving company to bring in a bed, dresser, chair, and several boxes went smoothly. Allie was sure no one who mattered had seen which apartment the movers actually entered and left.

The smoothness of the move seemed a good omen. The first night with Hedra in the apartment, Allie slept soundly, not once waking to lie restless and wondering about money and the near future. Something in her life was going right. Maybe there was balance in the world.

Friday, in the sun-drenched kitchen that smelled of burnt toast, the roommates had their first breakfast together. After asking politely, Hedra had turned on the radio at low volume. WRNY was playing soft rock from the seventies—Jefferson Airplane, the Beach Boys. God, the Beach Boys! Harmonizing about innocence and surf and sand, nothing deeper than a dime. Allie was glad Hedra liked the Beach Boys.

The agreement was that each roommate would have an assigned set of shelves in the refrigerator, and each would prepare her own meals. Allie, dressed for a meeting with Mayfair, sat before coffee and two slices of toast with grape jam. Hedra, still in her robe, was swigging Coca-Cola from a can and munching a cold slice of the sausage-mushroom pizza she'd had delivered last night. Pizza, especially with mushrooms, was something Allie didn't like to look at so early in the morning, but she decided she could stand it, considering Hedra was paying half the rent and utilities.

Gazing across the table at Hedra, Allie wondered for the first time if the woman's appearance had a great deal to do with why she'd settled on her for a roommate. Hedra was average height and slim, but without much of a figure. Her face was oval with small, even features and pale green eyes too close together beneath eyebrows that could use shaping despite the current unplucked, natural fashion. Hers was the sort of face you'd expect to see when opening a Victorian locket. The set of her eyes lent her an apprehensive, searching expression, as if she were afraid one wrong move would lose the entire game. She would have been somewhat attractive if she'd only done something with her medium-length brown hair. She wore it pulled back tightly with a center part, but hanging loose on the sides, like a Sixties folksinger. She wasn't the type to duck into Bloomingdale's and get made over. There was an inherent plainness about her, a subservience. Hedra, Allie knew, was no threat.

Hedra used a finger to tuck a strand of cold cheese into her mouth. "I'm sure this is gonna work out, Allie." Her voice was soft and carefully modulated. It suggested the same apprehension as her eyes. Had she ever in her life really been sure of anything?

Allie the practical said, "You going to work today?"

Hedra giggled, her hand covering her mouth, for a moment looking like sixteen-year-old concealing braces. Surprising Allie. "You sound like my mother."

Her mother! Jesus, loosen up, Allie told herself. Back away and breathe. She smiled. "Yeah, I guess I do. Sorry. I was just making conversation, not checking up on you. Hey, for all I care, you can stay out all night for the prom."

"I'm way past those years," Hedra said. "Never was much of a dancer anyway. Do you dance?"

"I used to," Allie said, remembering nights out with Sam. "I love to dance."

"I never actually went to a prom. Did you?"

"Twice. Back in Illinois. In a green world I barely remember."

"Musta been nice."

"No, not really. A little nerd named Pinky tried to rape me in the backseat of a sixty-five Chevy."

For a second Hedra seemed shocked. Then she said, "Well, those things happen."

"I guess. It wasn't really much of an attempt. Not the sort of thing you go to the police about."

"Oh, you should have reported him."

Allie laughed. "Then half the girls at the prom should have signed complaints against their dates. I mean, there's attempted rape and then there's attempted rape."

"I can't see much difference."

Allie took a bite of toast. Swallowed. Now who should lighten up? Next they'd be discussing the social ramifications of date rape. "Well, maybe you're right, but it was the consequence of teenage hormones, and a long time ago."

Hedra shot a frantic glance at the wall clock, as if suddenly remembering there was such a thing as measurable time. "Golly, almost eight-thirty. I am working today. Gonna be a receptionist for a while at a place over on Fifth Avenue. I better shower and dress." She stood up and placed her dishes in the sink, carefully not clinking them too hard against the porcelain. "You *are* done with the bathroom, aren't you?"

"Sure. All yours."

"I'll do my dishes when I get home," Hedra said. "Yours, too, if you want."

"I'll take care of them this time," Allie said. "I'm

coming home around noon to do some computer work."

"I won't be here . . . home till this evening." Hedra yanked the sash of her robe tight around her thin waist and carefully tied it in a bow, though she was on her way to the shower.

She paused in the kitchen doorway and turned to look at Allie. "I think this is gonna work out just great, you and me. No, I don't just think it, I'm positive of it!" She was like an enthused ingenue in a movie.

Allie put down her half-eaten crescent of toast and started to agree, but Hedra was already gone. Deferential ghost of a girl, wanting to be somewhere else.

She has a real problem with her shyness, Allie thought. A shame, because she wouldn't be nearly as unattractive as she seemed to believe, if she'd learn to dress effectively and use makeup to advantage.

But maybe she fancied herself the intellectual type. Those boxes she'd had brought in might have been stuffed with books. Or maybe, looking and acting as she did, she attracted the sort of men she liked. Who knew about men? Joan Collins? Madonna?

Not Allie.

Goddamn you, Sam!

Hedra was humming what sounded like a hymn in the shower when Allie left to meet Mayfair.

9

Hedra said, "I envy you, Allie. I mean, your looks, your clothes, guys always calling and leaving messages on your answering machine."

"My answering machine?"

Hedra looked away from Allie's gaze. "I can't help hearing you check for messages now and then. I'm sorry, Allie, I don't mean to be nosy."

In the two weeks since Hedra had moved in, this was one of the few evenings they were spending together in the apartment. It was storming outside, and the wind was slamming sheets of rain against the window, rattling the panes. Hedra was sitting in the small wing chair next to a lamp. She'd been reading a mystery novel, something with "death" in the title, while Allie was slumped on the sofa, idly watching the *MacNeil/Lehrer News Hour*. Hedra traded paperbacks at a secondhand bookshop, she said. She had a small and ever-changing collection of dog-eared mysteries lined up on her bedroom windowsill. The fear on her pale young face prompted a pang of pity in Allie.

"Listen, I know you're not nosy," Allie said. "Two people in the same apartment, we're gonna know something about each other's lives. No way around it. I suppose we'll have to trust one another. And what's this about my social life? You've been out with someone at least five times in the past two weeks." Which was not only true but a conservative estimate. Each time, Hedra had gotten dressed up, even combed her mousy brown hair to fall below her shoulders, and left to meet her date before dinner. She'd explained to Allie that this way he wouldn't attract the neighbors' suspicions by picking her up at the apartment. Allie appreciated her discretion, though she didn't think it necessary to carry it to that extreme. What was this guy going to do, hop out of a limo with a bouquet of roses in each hand?

Wind and rain crashed at the window, as if determined to get inside. Gentle Jim Lehrer was lobbing kindly, probing questions at an Alabama prosecuting attorney who thought an island penal colony should be established off the U.S coast to incarcerate hardcore criminals. Lehrer was making comparisons to Devil's Island while the prosecuting attorney was talking about a land east of Eden.

Hedra settled back in her chair and closed the novel. She fidgeted with it so violently Allie thought the lurid cover might tear. "Truth is, Allie, I haven't really been going out on dates. I got a job working nights, typing reports at a company over near Lincoln Center."

Huh? The girl could surprise. "Then how come you lied to me?"

Hedra dropped the novel; she jerked when it thumped on the floor, but she didn't bother to pick it up. "I was jealous of you, I guess. The way you're so assertive and active and all. I didn't want you to think I was some wallflower wimp, so when I took the temporary night job, I decided to tell you I was going out to meet a man instead of a typewriter."

"There was no reason to lie," Allie assured her. "I don't consider you any kind of wimp, Hedra. And your private life's none of my business."

Hedra blushed; it was obvious even in the yellow lamplight. The wind drummed rain against the window. Sounded as if the storm had claws and was clambering to get in. "There's another reason I said I was meeting a man. I didn't want you to think . . . you know."

Allie didn't know. Not at first. Then she laughed. "I never doubted your sexual preference, Hedra, or I wouldn't have chosen you for a roommate."

Squirming in her chair, Hedra said, "It's just that I have trouble meeting men, while you seem to have trouble holding them off. Oh, I mean, I can see why. You have such confidence and style and all."

Allie was getting tired of Hedra's unabashed admiration that bordered on idolatry. It was the one thing in their otherwise smooth relationship that bothered her. "Hell, I'm no beauty contest winner, Hedra. Not even a runner-up."

"Beauty comes from inside," Hedra said solemnly.

What could Allie say to that? So does a fart?

From the corner of her eye she saw that Lehrer was talking with the U.S. Attorney General now. What would the Administration think about resurrecting Devil's Island American style? Well, it was a possibility. She stood up from the sofa. "It's a crummy night outside. I'm gonna make a cup of tea. You want one?"

"Yes, please. No—wait, I'll help you."

"No, you won't. Stay put."

The command had come out sharper than Allie intended. The subdued roommate sank back into her chair and seemed prepared to stay in that position for days.

In the kitchen, Allie filled two cups with water, placed them in the microwave, and set the timer for three minutes.

While she was waiting for the water to boil, she wished again that Hedra would stop idolizing her for what she no doubt considered an outgoing if not downright hedonistic lifestyle. Not that Allie wasn't somewhat complimented by Hedra's open admiration. Who wouldn't be? But at the same time it made her uncomfortable. This wasn't part of the deal. She didn't want to be anyone's big sister.

It was true that word of her and Sam's breakup had gotten around, and unctuous, curly-haired Billy Stothers from Sam's office had phoned her several times for a date. Allie had gone out with him once, to a boring off-Broadway play and then a late dinner and dancing.

Stothers hadn't tried to bed her that night; he was the patient sort. But he bored the hell out of her with his stock, predictable lies, and she was trying to dissuade him, but nicely. Which prompted the spate of messages on her machine. Actually Stothers and Mayfair had been the only men who'd phoned during the past two weeks.

Sam was lurking like a persistent interloper in the far reaches of her mind, always with her. How long would that last?

The microwave timer chirped, and Allie removed the cups and dropped tea bags into them. Waited. Removed the soggy bags and added cream. She carried the two steaming cups into the living room.

MacNeil/Lehrer's all-purpose theme music was on; the program was over. The air in the apartment was warm and sticky, but the storm made tea seem appropriate. A cozy and proper beverage, tea. Veddy, veddy English.

"You didn't have to do this for me," Hedra said, accepting her cup.

"I know," Allie said, irritated by all this subservience. She'd just heated some water and dropped in a bag; she hadn't donated a kidney. "So maybe next time you make the tea."

Hedra smiled. "I'd like that. Sort of earn my keep."

Hedra, Hedra, Hedra . . . Allie switched off the TV and settled back down on the sofa. "You're paying half the rent and utilities, remember?"

"Oh, sure. But I can't forget this was your place to begin with. I mean, I know how hard it is to get any apartment in this part of town. I appreciate your taking me on as a roommate."

"So you've told me."

"Yeah, I guess you get tired of me telling you."

God, she was even apologizing for that. "It's okay, Hedra. But be assured I believe you."

Hedra sipped her tea and said, "Just right." She set the cup on the upholstered arm of the chair, balancing it there with a light touch of her right hand. Allie felt guilty about losing her patience. Hedra was, in many ways, a more agreeable roommate than most. She was certainly preferable to a loudmouthed egotist who'd try to take over and run things. *Or a lover who'd throw away your heart like a used Kleenex.*

Allie said, "It's nice having you around, Hedra. I mean that."

"I . . . well, thanks, Allie." She was actually pretty when she smiled, a kind of animated Mona Lisa. "Oh, I forgot to tell you, a guy was by here looking for you yesterday morning after you left. Said his name was Sam."

Allie almost spilled her tea, which was too close to the rim. She hadn't drunk any, waiting for it to cool. "Sam, you said?"

"Right. Something wrong?"

"Sam's the man I was living with here. Before we decided to part. I decided, actually."

"Oh. You were . . . ?"

"We were lovers."

"I'm sorry about the breakup, Allie. Those kinda things happen."

"All the time," Allie agreed. But not to me. Not so suddenly. With a phone call in the night that knocked the entire world out of kilter. Damn it, she was straightening that world and Sam had no right coming around and trying to complicate things. He'd sent Billy Stothers to collect the rest of his belongings before Hedra had moved in; there was nothing of him left in the apartment, and Allie wanted nothing left of him in her life. That was the only way to stay off the roller coaster. He'd deceived her once and he would again, if she weakened and gave him the chance. He was booze and she was an alcoholic—one drink and she was lost.

"Did you tell him you lived here?" Allie asked.

"No. He didn't ask, so I didn't have to lie. And he didn't seem to suspect. Probably figured I was just a friend waiting for you to get home."

"I doubt it," Allie said. "He knows me and my finances."

The wind and rain took another whack at the window, rattling the glass, almost breaking through. Or maybe the noise seemed louder because the TV was turned off. Who the hell needed *Wall Street Week*? "Sam seems nice," Hedra said.

"Seems." Allie sipped at her tea. It was almost cool enough to drink without burning her tongue.

Hedra said, "He left a message. Told me to tell you he was sorry he missed you and he'd be back."

Allie said, "I was afraid of that."

10

As soon as she swung the door open, Allie was sure someone was in the apartment. The air hadn't the usual stale stillness of a room unoccupied since morning. Something had stirred it not long ago. There was no discernible sound, yet the silence wasn't complete.

She stood paralyzed on the threshold. Hedra was working all day at her temporary receptionist job. Sam. Maybe Sam had forced his way in. Her glance darted to the locks on the door. She found them intact and without scratches on the surrounding wood. But it was possible Sam had an extra key made before returning his. He'd deceived her in other ways, why not that?

Damn him! Damn him!

She took a stiff step inside and glanced around the living room. Everything was normal, the television and stereo—candy for burglars—were still in place.

Sam.

Had to be Sam.

Anger rose in her and supplanted fear. She

moved farther into the apartment and quietly shut the door.

She slipped off her high heels and laid them gently aside, then padded in her nyloned feet across the floor toward the short hall to the bedrooms. She peered into Hedra's room and found it unoccupied, the bed, unlike Allie's, neatly made in almost military fashion. It was possible to bounce a quarter off the spread and watch it glance off the ceiling, Allie thought. Hedra the good soldier. She'd delight the most demanding drill instructor.

The faintest of sounds was emanating from Allie's bedroom. Someone moving around, the soles of their shoes lightly scraping the floor. Odd. Almost as if they were dancing.

Allie edged forward, her heartbeat quickening. She reached out her right hand and touched the wall as if for balance. Should she be in here? she wondered. Should she be doing this? Of course, damn it! This was her apartment. *She* lived here, not Sam.

At the door she paused and drew a deep breath. Then she stepped boldly into the room. "Sam—"

Not Sam.

Hedra.

She was standing very erect in the middle of the room. Before the full-length mirror mounted on the closet door.

Hedra's body twitched and her head snapped around. Her eyes and mouth grew round as she saw Allie. She said something like "Whaa—" More a rush of breath than an exclamation.

She was wearing Allie's expensive blue dress from Altman's, with the silver belt, silver shoes, and even Allie's dangling silver earrings with the cubic zirconia stones. Transformation. Night-on-the-town time.

Allie stood rooted in surprise, not knowing what to say, and wondering what was happening. Hedra's slim body hunched over violently, as if she'd been punched in the stomach. She wobbled back a few steps in Allie's high heels, like a little girl playing dress-up, and groaned, "I thought you were going to lunch . . ." As if Allie had cheated by returning home.

Allie said, "The lunch was canceled. I thought you were working today."

"Didn't need me today." Hedra's lower lip quivered. Her face was flushed with embarrassment. If Allie handed her a shovel, she'd try to dig a hole in the floor so she could climb in and hide. "I'm sorry. God, I'm sorry about this . . ."

A hot rush of anger welled strong in Allie. Then it quickly waned. She's about to cry, she thought, staring at Hedra. Oh, no! I don't want to fucking see that! Or hear it! She's about to collapse into a sobbing jag that might last for an hour.

Then pity forced aside the anger, and she crossed the room and placed her hand on Hedra's quaking shoulder, on the smooth material of her own dress. She thought selfishly for a moment that she didn't want tearstains on it. Hedra shrank away as if Allie were preparing to strike her.

Allie managed a cardboard smile. "S'okay, Hedra. Okay. We're only talking about a dress here, not international espionage. No harm done."

"My God, I mean, I was trying on your clothes. I don't know why I did it, what possessed me. Honest."

"I believe you." She patted the shoulder, still vibrating beneath her touch. "Now *you* believe *me*. It's all right; it really is."

The flesh at the corners of Hedra's lips arced down and danced; tears still glistened and threatened in her injured-animal eyes. "It's just that I envy you so. I mean, how you seem to make your own way so confident and all. You're always sure of yourself and I'm always in doubt. It sounds crazy, but I thought, well, maybe if I put on the dress you look so great in . . ."

"That some of it would rub off?" Allie finished for her. "A kind of personality transfer?"

Even in her humiliation Hedra had to smile. "No, not exactly. But I guess, well, yeah, maybe *something* like that. I just wanted to try on the dress and see how I'd look, is all."

"Then it's simple as that," Allie said. "No point getting uptight and Freudian about it."

"I guess not," Hedra agreed, after seeming to consider for a moment whether to let Freud in on this.

Allie moved away from her and sat down on the edge of the mattress. The bedsprings sang. *Sam.* "Don't envy me, Hedra. My life's not as good as it seems from the outside. I have doubts, problems. Just like you do. Big problems sometimes."

"Only sometimes, though. And you solve them."

"Not always."

Hedra frowned, puzzled. "You mean Sam?"

"Yeah, him."

"That'll work out eventually."

"I don't want it to work out."

"You want it to be over? Permanently?"

"It *is* over. And as permanently as I can make it."

"You're really sure?"

"Most of the time."

"Well, the way you look, Allie, men'll never cause you to suffer forever. I seem to have big problems *all* the time. And it shows and just makes things worse for me."

"It doesn't show as much as you think. You're attractive and smart, Hedra; you need to believe in yourself more." *Christ, I sound like Dear Abby,* she thought.

Hedra ran a hand over the silky front of the dress. "That's easy enough to say."

"Yeah, I know what you mean. But you're a kind of Pygmalion determined to make *yourself* over, and that's all right. Shows there's lots of hope and plenty to work with. You'll be okay, Hedra, I can sense it."

"Sense it? Actually?"

"Actually. And it's not like me to be wrong, is it?"

Hedra giggled. "I suppose not. Oh!" She suddenly unbuckled the silver belt, then reached around and unzipped the dress. As if she'd abruptly remembered her transgression and wanted to set things right, like a child seeking parental forgiveness.

Allie sat and watched her strip to panties and bra. She really didn't have a bad figure. Better than it appeared in the drab and poorly cut clothes she favored. "Leave on the earrings, Hedra. Maybe I've got another dress you'd like."

She turned and stared at Allie with disbelief. "You don't mean, after this . . . ?"

"You didn't steal or destroy anything," Allie reminded her.

"I'd never purposely destroy anything of yours," she said with all the fervor of a Girl Scout uttering a sacred oath.

Allie got up from the bed and walked to the closet. Wire hangers whined on the steel rod as she separated her clothes and found an inexpensive beige dress. It was styled very much like the blue one Hedra was now fitting with precision back on its hanger. Less full, longer hemline, but similar. "Try this one on," Allie said, and withdrew the beige dress from the closet with the kind of flourish she'd seen salespeople use in exclusive boutiques.

Hedra was impressed. "You mean it?"

"Mean it," Allie assured her.

Within a few minutes Hedra was wearing the beige dress, pivoting in front of the full-length mirror. Her movements were exaggerated yet controlled, almost like a dance.

She moved away from the mirror, smiling, and slipped into her brown shoes with the medium-height heels that had been lying near the bed. Took another look in the mirror, then spun neatly in a tight two-step so the skirt billowed. "What do you think, Allie?"

"I think it looks terrific on you." The dress *was* flattering. "Better than on me."

"No, that could never be."

"You're good for my ego, Hedra, even if you're not very realistic."

"I hope I'm good for something," she said timidly.

My God! Allie thought. She said, "You need a drink. In fact, I need a drink." *Do I ever!*

"Now?"

"Especially now."

"Okay, Allie. Let me get this off." She contorted her arms, elbows out, to grope behind her back for the zipper.

"No, leave the dress on. It's yours."

"But I can't afford to pay for it."

"I don't want you to pay. It's a gift."

"You're kidding!"

"I'm not kidding, damn it!" Too sharp again.

Hedra didn't seem to know why Allie was suddenly irritated. She lowered her arms and said, "Thank you, Allie," and almost curtsied.

Allie said, "I'm not royalty, Hedra."

"What do you mean?"

"Never mind. Let's go. The glass coach is waiting."

No coach. Not even a cab. They walked through the gloomy gray afternoon to a restaurant and bar over on Broadway near West 76th. Before they entered, Allie noticed that the lighted time-and-temperature sign on the Apple Bank said it was one o'clock, but she wasn't at all in need of lunch. The bedroom encounter with Hedra seemed to have killed her appetite. Intense emotion did that to her, be it anger or pity.

There was piped-in music in the bar, heavy-metal rock, but it wasn't loud. The restaurant was through a low arch; Allie could see several people seated at red-clothed tables, eating lunch.

She and Hedra sat in the bar, at one of the small wooden tables against the wall. Allie looped her purse strap over the back of her chair, close to the wall where no one could snatch it, and looked around.

The place was darkly paneled, with a lot of high shelves lined with fancy beer mugs. Spicy cooking scents wafted in from the adjoining restaurant. Half a dozen people were perched on stools at the long bar. About a dozen more sat at tables. Allie's gaze drifted back to the mugs. A few of them looked like antiques. She wondered if they were worth something to collectors. The bar owner might not know, might be ignorant of such things.

Not likely, she told herself, not in New York. Everybody but tourists seemed to know the price of everything in the city. Except for the slowly exacted price they were paying for living here.

A tired-looking barmaid plodded over to their table. She stood poised with her order pad, waiting, looking indirectly and dispassionately at them as if she didn't know or care if they were genuine human beings or cardboard cutouts. She finally said, "Yeah?" then took their order.

Allie had two martinis. Hedra drank a Tab, then a martini. She seemed to enjoy the olive more than the drink. A matched pair of guys in gray business suits interrupted their loud conversation about the Jets long enough to size up the two women. One of the men had bad teeth and ap-

peared drunk. Allie looked away before Hedra
did. She saw in the mirror that the other man
winked at Hedra.

Swiveling in her chair to face Allie, Hedra said,
"No thanks."

"They didn't offer," Allie said.

"They would if we gave them encouragement."

"Most likely."

Football talk began again. Louder. Then the
subject was changed abruptly to the stock market.
Probably to impress anyone who might overhear.
Be a bear, said the guy with crooked teeth. The
one who'd winked at Hedra was bullish on more
than America.

Hedra glanced again in the men's direction.
"Couple of creeps."

"Maybe not," Allie said. "You never know."

"Nobody knows for sure about anything," the
philosopher Hedra said.

That was the truth. When they got back to the
Cody Arms, Sam had just come out and was jogging down the steps.

11

Sam saw Allie and Hedra and took the last few
steps slowly, then came to a complete halt outside
the Cody Arms and stood still, like a wind-up toy
that had run down. He was wearing gray sweat-
pants, a blue pullover shirt, and his maroon Avia
jogging shoes. He needed a haircut badly. Allie
thought he might have lost a few pounds. Not in a
healthy way, but as if he'd been sick. She stifled a
thrust of concern for him, watching his eyes dart
from her to Hedra and then back.

He said, "I was out for a run, and I thought it
might as well be in this direction so I could see
you."

Allie said, "About what?"

He frowned. "Is that where we are? It has to be
about something?"

" 'Fraid so, Sam."

He stared at Hedra until silence began to build
on itself and someone had to speak.

Finally Allie said, "This is Hedra Carlson. Hedra,
Sam Rawson."

Allie saw him give Hedra a quick up-and-down

glance, show mild surprise as he recognized the beige dress. She'd worn it one weekend they'd spent in the Catskills; he'd removed it from her in a way she couldn't forget. Sam shook Hedra's hand gently. "You an old friend of Allie's?"

Ill at ease, Hedra said, "Not so old. I mean, we haven't been friends all that long. But we're friends."

Sam showed his amiable smile. "Wait a minute! We met the other day when I came by the apartment to see Allie. You were visiting. Waiting for her inside. Remember?"

"Sure. Now I do."

He adjusted an elastic sweatband on his right wrist. It was blue and white, lettered YANKEES. "I told you my name, but you forgot to introduce yourself."

"I'm, uh, sorry."

"Anyway," he said, "I think it's great Allie's got a close friend like you. Wear each other's clothes, that sorta thing. New York's not the kinda place where you usually have somebody close."

Allie'd heard enough. "Sam, we're in kind of a hurry."

"Oh?"

"I thought you were out jogging."

"On my way to run in the park, actually. So I thought I'd drop by. But you weren't home. You are now."

"Not quite, Sam, but I'd like to be. Nice seeing you."

She moved around him and started up the steps.

Suddenly he had her elbow in a firm grip. Desperation flowed like electricity through him into her. "Allie, listen, please!"

Hedra said, "I'll just run on upstairs."

Sam said, "Pleasure meeting you, Hedra. I'm sure we'll see each other again."

Allie yanked her elbow free, sending a jolt of pain up her crazy bone. She wasn't the crazy one here. "I'm going with her, Sam."

He shuffled in a half-circle and blocked her way. There was an agonized look on his face. "Allie, I only wanna talk."

"And I *don't*." But she knew she did. *Goddamnit, she did!* "Wait for me, Hedra."

Hedra was standing at the top of the steps, a confused expression on her face. In the beige dress and high heels, her legs looked very shapely from the sidewalk. Sam stared at her for a moment, as if he were seeing Allie in the dress. His teeth were clenched and his breath hissed like steam escaping under great pressure. Allie could smell liquor on his breath. Had he seen them in the bar? Beaten them back to the Cody and set up this scene?

No, she decided, it was possible but unlikely.

It began to rain then, slanting under the entrance canopy. Not hard, but steadily enough so another few minutes of standing outside and they'd all be soaked. Windshield wipers on passing cars started their metronome action. Some of them had their headlights on, wary yellow eyes lessening the chance of collision in the lowering gloom. The wet street became opaque glass, reflecting the late-afternoon traffic in muted colors.

A trickle of rainwater broke from Sam's hair

and ran down his forehead. Finally he stood aside and gave Allie room to go up the steps. She moved past, barely brushing his arm.

She took each step with deliberation, keeping the sway of her hips to a minimum, knowing he was watching. Behind her, the swish of tires on wet pavement was like harsh and secret whispering. Hedra reached out a firm hand as if to help her achieve the final push of a climb up a mountain. And maybe that's what it was—climbing up out of Sam's influence. Maybe.

She grasped Hedra's hand, squeezed it as if to say "Thank you," and pushed ahead of her, through the door into the cool, dry lobby. Sanctuary.

"We'll talk later, Allie!" Sam called up the steps.

She didn't answer. A raindrop clung to her eyelash; she brushed it away impatiently with the back of her hand.

As they were rising in the elevator, Hedra said, "An awkward situation, but you handled it fine, Allie."

Fine? Allie interpreted it differently. "Did I?"

"I mean, you seemed so calm. So in control. More so than I coulda been; that's for sure."

"Didn't seem that way to me, Hedra. I wasn't so calm on the inside."

"That doesn't matter. You're here, and you and Sam aren't having the conversation he was demanding. You didn't let yourself get bullied. That's the important thing."

"No, it isn't," Allie said. "The important thing is that now Sam's sure we're living together."

"Huh? How could he be? He only saw me in the

apartment that one time, and he supposed I was a friend waiting for you to get home."

"Don't believe what he says."

"But what could he prove?"

"I don't mean he could *prove* anything," Allie said. "But he doesn't have to."

"What do you mean?"

"If he wanted, he could notify Haller-Davis I have a roommate and get us both evicted."

"Would they believe him?"

"They'd send someone to look over the apartment, and they'd see there are two people living there. No way you can conceal that from somebody looking for it."

"What if we didn't let them in?"

"They'd sneak in with a passkey. Then they'd serve an eviction notice, and it'd be up to me to prove I was living alone. They'd know I couldn't do that." Allie wasn't sure that was exactly how the eviction would go, but she *was* sure Haller-Davis could and would force her out.

She remembered how Sam had noticed the beige dress, how he'd said he recognized Hedra from when she'd answered the knock on the apartment door. He was letting Allie know that *he* knew: Hedra was her secret roommate. She didn't like that at all. There was no way to predict what might happen; divorces, from affairs as well as marriages, could take unexpected bitter turns.

The elevator arrived on their floor and the doors rumbled open, admitting a press of warm air from the hall.

A vision of the countless street people she passed every day invaded Allie's mind. The ones the rest of the human race avoided thinking about, even avoided seeing, with a convenient selective blindness. She might become one of them. Sam had it in his power to do that to her. A Svengali in jogging shoes. That was what really ate at her, the knowledge that he *could* do it.

Absurd! she told herself. I'm self-supporting and every bit as capable as Sam. My life's in my own hands.

Hedra stopped halfway down the hall and stared incredulously at Allie. "Sam wouldn't really turn you in to the management company, would he?"

"I don't know," Allie said. "A month ago I wouldn't have thought so, but he's full of surprises. All men seem to be full of surprises."

"Not to me."

Allie smiled. "I know what you mean, Hedra." But she didn't.

In the apartment, the phone rang and Allie absently answered it, still thinking about Sam.

"Allie?" A man's voice. Not Sam's.

"Yes?" There was only silence on the line. "Hello?"

A steady buzzing erupted in her ear. Whoever was on the other end of the connection had hung up.

12

At Fortune Fashions, Mayfair sat at his wide desk, before his IBM computer, and went through the routine taught to him by Allie Jones. His fingers pecked at the gray keys with dexterity now, sure of themselves. She'd done an excellent job of setting up the programs. Inventory, payroll, graphics for sales and manufacturing projections, all reduced to relatively simple commands. She was about fifty percent through the project, she'd told Mayfair. Which meant it was time for him to do what he'd intended from the first moment he'd seen Allie Jones. And why not? You were vice president of a company like this, certain perks were implied.

Allie had too much time invested to give up the Fortune Fashions account now, and she stood to lose too much money. Without a doubt she'd be vulnerable to pressure. And she'd recently broken up with whatever guy had been balling her; Sam something, he thought she'd called him. So Mayfair figured she was ripe enough to fall. Ah, timing was so important in life.

Not that he'd explain the facts to her in such

crude terms. He was too practiced for that. But in varied and subtle ways, Mayfair would let her know that now *he* had enough knowledge to call some other programmer in to finish what Allie had started. Even his secretary Elaine must be getting proficient with a computer by now. The basic software systems were online, so no problem there. Allie had gotten a small amount of money up-front. Gradually, over a week or so, he'd make it clear that if she wanted to finish the Fortune Fashions job and see her big payday, he, Mayfair, was part of the arrangement. It wasn't so unusual; she'd probably done some job-related screwing before. Part of landing accounts, he was sure, a piece of the deal from the beginning, or there wouldn't have been a deal. An attractive woman didn't need a computer to figure that one out. Let's face it, software was software.

The door to the anteroom swung open, allowing traffic noises from the street ten stories below to infiltrate Mayfair's plush and virtually sound-proof office. The thick carpet and drapes, the flocked wallpaper and deeply upholstered furniture, seemed even to absorb sound produced from within the office.

Elaine, tall and gaunt as a model, dressed in a Fashion Fortunes fall outfit, swished in and gave a perfunctory nod to Mayfair. They had run through a hot and frantic affair five years ago, but they seldom talked about it now. At the time, Elaine had known sleeping with him was a prerequisite for employment. Somewhat the same dilemma that would now face Allie.

Elaine had been married then, but so what?

That shouldn't have caused such a problem. He hadn't asked her to go off on a guilt spree and spill her guts to her husband, who went crazy and came looking for Mayfair at home. At fucking home with the wife and kids, no less. Jesus, what a scene? What a night!

Mayfair had forgiven Elaine for that error in judgment, and even helped to find her an apartment to begin the single life she still led. So it turned out to be the best thing that ever happened to the bitch. She was having a ball now, dating different guys all the time, accepting gifts from them. Not a hooker, though. A secretary. Mayfair almost smiled.

The scene with Elaine's husband had hastened his own inevitable divorce. His wife Janice and the kids were living in Buffalo now. Everybody seemed better off. Mayfair was certainly happier. He supposed that indirectly he could thank Elaine for that.

He leaned back in his padded swivel chair and studied her as she bent over a lower file drawer. She still had the wasp waist and trim ass, the nice legs.

Elaine straightened up and smoothed her skirt. Her calf muscle bulged as she swiveled a foot back into one of her high-heeled shoes that had worked halfway off. Sexy. She was holding the file folder she'd been seeking.

She turned around and aimed her heavily made-up eyes at him. "Allie Jones coming in today?"

"She's scheduled," Mayfair said. Allie was tutoring Elaine in the use of the computer. Elaine was in the fold and would stay there. Mayfair would point this out to Allie to let her know the company's need for her expertise had decreased. In fact, she herself wasn't actually *essential* at this juncture. But he'd hint that there was no problem; she might increase her value in other ways.

About ten o'clock Allie and Elaine would isolate themselves in a corner of the anteroom, Elaine at her new computer while Allie sat next to her in the red and brown Danish chair pulled over from where it was usually angled against the wall. Patiently, professionally, Allie would explain to her what she was doing right, what she was doing wrong. Tutor and student got along well; both were bright and adaptable people.

He smiled. It wouldn't be long before they had something else in common.

She was getting ready to leave the apartment and ride the subway downtown to Fashion Fortunes when the phone rang.

Allie put down the earring post she'd been trying to work through her pierced ear, turned away from her dresser, and answered it with an absent "'Lo."

Her face became serious. Then bone white. She squared her jaw and slammed down the receiver so violently she pinched a finger between it and its cradle.

A psycho. Whoever had called her had to be a psycho to say the things she'd heard on the phone, to even imagine what he'd said he'd do to her. *Go someplace and masturbate, buddy! But leave me alone!*

She remembered the phone call she'd received earlier, the man who'd hung up on her. Might both callers have been the same person? It was possible, but she knew the odds didn't necessarily favor it. The city was full of sick people who regarded telephones as a means of erotic stimulation, Allie told herself. Any single woman in this city could expect that sort of phone call now and then. It was as much a part of life in Manhattan as being approached by panhandlers or getting cursed at by cabbies.

Yet there was a familiarity about both calls that chilled her. The man—or men—had used her name. Casually called her "Allie." Not "Allison"— "Allie." Old chums. More than chums.

She grimaced and wiped her hand on her skirt, as if contact with the phone had soiled it.

Jones was such a common surname that she'd used her first name in the phone directory instead of merely her initial, as was the custom of most single women who wanted or needed to be listed. Allie had been uneasy about it at the time, and would have preferred an unlisted number precisely so she could avoid the kind of sick and random call she'd just received. But because of her business she needed to be accessible. An unlisted number might cost her accounts and income. She couldn't afford it.

Returning to stand before her mirror, she told herself whoever had phoned almost certainly wouldn't call again. Probably a sicko hunched over a public phone and running his finger down the directory pages, calling whichever female names appealed to his perverted sexuality. Maybe right now he was making the same kinky suggestions to some woman whose name began with *K*, a woman he'd never met. No need to worry about a sorry individual like that, whose sex life depended on Ma Bell. Allie made herself smile out at the world from the mirror. A philosophical, confident smile.

But as she attempted again to work the earring post through her earlobe, her hand trembled so that it was almost impossible to do.

13

Other than a massive Hispanic youth in shorts and a black muscle shirt, Allie was the only customer in Goya's. Apparently the restaurant didn't do much morning business. On the other hand it was past nine o'clock; she'd slept late, then decided to eat a quick breakfast out before her appointment at Fortune Fashions with Mayfair's secretary. She'd pushed the obscene phone call as far from her thoughts as possible.

Goya's was cool. The air conditioner and ceiling fans were toiling away despite the briskness of the morning. The young guy in the shorts and sleeveless shirt ought to be shivering instead of sitting there calmly sipping what looked like a Pepsi and gazing out the window. His leather jacket was slung over the back of the chair next to him.

Graham Knox, the skinny waiter with the jug ears and bushy black hair, took Allie's order, then returned a few minutes later with her bagel with cream cheese and coffee. He seemed to be fighting back a grin as he placed the order before her on the table. Good cheer was like pressure beneath the skin of his face.

He began to walk away, hesitated, then turned back. A neat pivot. He said, "I know simply being your neighbor gives me no claim on your time, but . . . well, I've gotten some good news and I guess I just have to share it with somebody. Business is slow and you're here and we *are* neighbors, so you're it, Allie. You mind?"

Allie set the bagel back on its plain white plate. What was this about? Had Graham hit the lottery? "I don't mind at all. I like hearing good news, even somebody else's." She smiled, which Graham took as a signal to put on his lopsided grin. He looked like an amiable puppy when he did that. Allie liked this sincere and friendly man with the protruding ears and intent dark eyes.

He did an embarrassed little dance. "It happens I'm a playwright, and I've been working on a script for over a year. *Way* over a year, actually. And finally it sold. It's going to be produced." He waited a beat or two, then he shrugged, as if, on second thought, having a play produced was no big deal and he shouldn't have mentioned it. "Anyway, that's my good news."

"It's great news!" Allie said. "Congratulations! I mean it."

"The title's *Dance Through Life*. It'll be onstage at Creative Playhouse down in the Village. Know the place?"

" 'Fraid not. I love live theater, though. Especially off-Broadway."

He widened his grin. "This is far enough off Broadway you'll need binoculars and a guide to find it."

"Don't be silly. That is a hell of an accomplishment. God, to come to New York and actually have a play produced. You realize how many people try that and fail?"

"Oh, believe me, I do."

"I'll go see it when it opens."

"Really? I'll make sure you get free tickets— good seats. For you and your—" He suddenly clamped his mouth shut. "I mean—"

Allie knew who he meant. Hedra. But how had he found out about her?

He glanced around like a conspirator in occupied territory. The big Hispanic kid stared back at him with flat, wary eyes, as if suspecting he was the subject of derision. "It's all right by me if you have a roommate," Graham said softly. "What am I, the police? I noticed her in the Cody lately, saw her a few times with you. Then one day I heard you two talking as you got off the elevator, and you or she said something that revealed she was living with you. That's a major taboo in the Cody. I got out of sight in a hurry so you wouldn't see me. Didn't want to let you know that *I* knew."

"How long have you known?"

"Oh, a couple of weeks. It's okay, though, your secret's safe with me. Honest!"

"I believe it is, Graham." What choice did she have? "But don't mention it to anybody else. Please!"

"My word of honor on that, Allie. In this frig-

gin' city, I never know when I might have to adver-
tise for a roommate myself to share expenses."

"Not you, Graham. Not a successful playwright."

She was afraid she'd sounded patronizing, but
he didn't seem to think so.

He wiped his hands together as if drying them
on an invisible towel. Blushed. "I wouldn't say successful. At least not yet. And there's not that much
money in it. Besides, *Dance* might fold after a
week. Maybe after one performance. It happens."

"Don't jinx yourself." Allie spread cream cheese
on her bagel, took a bite, and sipped her coffee.

He began to back away, embarrassed. She realized for the first time that he had a crush on her.
Well, that was all right. A natural enough phenom-
enon that happened between men and women.
Mature, normal people didn't let it upset their
lives, didn't act on those low-level emotions and
let them develop into more than friendship, into
something that seized control.

Then she remembered the obscene phone call.
Graham?

No! Ridiculous. *I won't let life in this city poison
me.* Graham Knox was the nicest and least threatening male she'd met in months. She wouldn't let
urban paranoia destroy a burgeoning friendship.

He said, "I better get busy or I'll be fired and
have to write like crazy." He picked up a catsup
bottle from the next table, then walked another
table down and picked up a second bottle. A third.
Where was he going, into the kitchen to water
down the stuff so there'd be enough to last

through lunch and dinner? "Hey, I mean it about those tickets, Allie."

"You better. I want opening night."

"No, let's make it a few performances later. When all the bugs are worked out."

"Okay, you're the playwright."

The lopsided grin. "Enjoy your breakfast."

"Already have."

After she'd eaten, while she was digging in her purse to pay the check, Allie realized she'd forgotten a disk she wanted to program into the Fortune Fashions computers. No problem. She could hurry back down the street to the apartment and pick it up, then still make Mayfair's office on time.

When she opened the door, she was surprised to find Hedra home. As soon as she saw Allie, she stood up from where she was sitting on the sofa. Her hands hung awkwardly at her sides, fingers working, kneading air.

"Thought you were at work," Allie said, striding to the alcove where her computer was set up.

Behind her Hedra said, "I was just about to walk out the door."

Allie found the floppy disk she was searching for, slid it into a protective hard plastic cover, then stuffed it into her purse.

When she walked out from behind the silk folding screen that formed a fourth wall of the alcove, she said, "I had an interesting conversation with a waiter down at Goya's."

Hedra adjusted the belt of her brown skirt. The

skirt's hem hit her at an unflattering angle, Allie noticed. "It's too easy in this city to have interesting conversations with waiters."

"This one turned out to be a nice guy."

"Far as you know from talking to him over the soup. You shouldn't mix with strange men that way, Allie."

"He's one of our neighbors."

Hedra frowned. She had more makeup on today and looked almost attractive. Allie recognized the eyeshade and lipstick. Colors like her own makeup. "He lives here?" Hedra asked. "In the Cody?"

"Right."

"Like I used to," Sam said, walking in from the kitchen. He was using a spoon to scoop low-fat yogurt from a plastic container. Dressed for business today: dark blue pinstripe suit, white shirt, red tie. It was an outfit the dress-for-success books said was supposed to inspire trust.

Allie realized her mouth was open. She looked at Hedra, who couldn't meet her eyes and seemed to be studying the toe of her black loafer. Hedra mumbled, "I tried to let you know . . ."

Allie glared at Sam. "What are you doing here?"

"Came to see you, but Hedra said you'd left."

"Hedra—"

"Don't blame her," Sam interrupted. "I sorta forced my way in."

"I wasn't gonna blame anyone but you for being here," Allie assured him. Anger gathered deep in her. "If you think you have the run of this place just because you can notify the landlord I have a roommate, think again, Sam."

He gave her his smile that could melt cold steel. Usually. "I only wanted to see you. I still love you, Allie. I can't help it."

Hedra coughed nervously, then said, "I better get moving or I'll be late for work."

Neither Allie nor Sam spoke as she grabbed up her purse and a light coat and went out, moving jerkily and too fast.

"I'm leaving, too," Allie said.

"I'll go with you down to the street."

She knew she couldn't stop him from doing that. Not unless she wanted to leave him here in the apartment by himself. "You sure will. You don't think I'd leave you here alone, do you?"

"I don't suppose you would," Sam said.

Allie locked the apartment door behind her while Sam stood in the hall, watching. There was the slightest hint of a smile on his face, as if he'd just heard a good joke and it lingered in his mind.

Hedra had already gone down in the elevator. Allie and Sam waited silently while it rose slowly back to the third floor. It seemed to take long enough to rise three hundred floors.

Allie heard the cables thrum as the elevator adusted to floor level. The doors slid open. Sam stood back like a gentleman to let her enter first. She felt like waiting until the doors were about to close, then stepping into the elevator so he wouldn't have time to follow. The old rattletrap didn't have the kinds of doors that opened automatically if someone stuck a hand between them. But she knew that was foolish and would accomplish nothing in the long run.

Alone with him in the elevator, she reached

around him to press the button. Gave it a twist with her thumb.

Sam said, "I'm asking for your forgiveness, Allie."

She was silent, trying not to let his nearness affect her in the cramped space. She could smell his familiar aftershave, feel the warmth of him. The doors slid closed and the elevator hummed into motion.

Neither she nor Sam said anything until the elevator doors opened. Allie started to step out, then realized they weren't at lobby level. She looked at the floor indicator light, saw she'd pressed the wrong button on Three. The elevator was on the thirtieth floor. Sam was smiling faintly, as if he suspected she'd done it with subconscious purpose as some kind of Freudian slip. *My God, might he be right?*

She very deliberately stabbed a finger at the LOBBY button, and the elevator began its descent. She felt a hollowness in her stomach, as if they were plunging straight down the shaft at dizzying speed. Down to the center of the earth.

He said, "Other women forgive other men for less."

"We're not other women and other men."

He gave a humorless soft chuckle. "*Somebody* has to be. How else could Gallup and Harris take all those polls?"

"I never took part in a poll."

"My life's not good without you, Allie."

"You don't seem to have any trouble finding stand-ins."

He clenched his fist and stared down at it, as if what had happened to his hand troubled him. Then he banged it into the elevator's steel wall. "So I'm a fucking sinner! Who are you, Mother Teresa? Isn't a human being allowed one mistake? For God's sakes, are you shooting for the ministry? *I need* you, Allie!"

Allie's heart was slamming. The abruptness of his outburst had startled her. The unexpected violence, and the heat of his words. Words that penetrated like darts because they recognized an imperfect world and made undeniable sense.

He was staring at her, his deep dark eyes angry and injured. She didn't know quite how to react. She heard a voice something like hers say, "What now, Sam? You grab me and kiss me into submission like in the movies? Or give me a good shake until I see reason? Get what you want by force if it isn't given willingly?"

"I don't play the game that way and you know it."

He was right, of course. She did know that about him. "Game, huh?"

The elevator stopped on *10*. The doors opened to an empty hall, then closed again. They continued their descent.

"Don't twist what I say, Allie."

"All right, I suppose that wasn't fair. Mother Teresa apologizes."

He wiped a hand down his face in slow motion, a gesture of remorse. "I shouldn't have lost my temper."

"No, but maybe I shouldn't blame you."

He bent down and kissed her gently on the forehead. "I'm sorry, Allie. So sorry." She didn't move. Felt him bend lower as he braced with one hand against the elevator wall. His lips were against hers. She was suddenly tired of resisting, and all this time she hadn't realized she *was* resisting him. Perhaps that was the most exhausting kind of self-denial.

Allie parted her lips, felt the probing warmth of his tongue. She felt herself catch fire.

He shifted position and his arms were around her, pressing her to him.

The fire spread throughout her body. Jesus, she didn't want this! Yet she wanted it fiercely! So fiercely! She was ashamed of herself but couldn't help it, couldn't stop needing Sam. This was the kind of crap that happened in romance novels, not in *her* life.

They were no longer plunging through the core of the building. They'd been at lobby level for some time while the elevator adjusted position. The doors hissed open on the empty lobby, to faint sounds of traffic and the outside world.

Allie pulled away from Sam. She stared at the world beyond the street doors, and suddenly she didn't want to go any farther. She was held by a force stronger than her pride. Sam pulled her close to him again, as if she were as weightless as she felt. She heard him say, "Can you phone wherever you were going and say you'll be late?"

She nodded, her cheek pressed against his white

shirt and red tie. Trusting him. Wanting him. She nodded again, more vigorously, so he could feel the motion of her head against his chest even if he couldn't see it.

She reached around him and pressed the UP button.

14

Sam played it light and easy, continuing to live at the Atherton Hotel over on West 44th Street. He told Allie he wished he could move back into the apartment with her so things could be the way they had been, but it wasn't necessary; things could be even better this way. He took her out a couple of times a week, to restaurants, for walks in Central Park, for easy jogs along early-morning deserted West Side streets, nurturing what he'd coaxed back to life. He hung around the apartment some weekends, but not in any way that created tension. If he sensed he was interfering with even normal domestic activity, he left. Allie was sure he was going out of his way to demonstrate to Hedra that he posed no threat to her secret living arrangement with Allie.

The two of them—the three of them—became close friends, learned how to coexist with minimum friction. Allie and Sam were falling back into their old relationship, bodies slipping into familiar orbit. Hedra was dressing more stylishly, going out more often in the evenings. Allie never asked where she went, suspecting that sometimes her reason for leaving was to make the apartment available for her and Sam. And Hedra never pried into Allie's affairs.

Allie received a few more obscene phone calls. Not only obscene, but puzzling, and with that eerie familiarity that made her stomach drop.

But all in all she was happy in her reconstructed world. The roommate arrangement was working out.

However, other things in Allie's world were not. Hedra was a comfort when Allie needed her most. Sam was in Chicago, at something called a new-issue seminar, when Allie entered the apartment sobbing without inhibition, seeking shelter and thinking she'd be alone.

But there was Hedra, standing near the door and wearing Allie's blue coat with the white collar; she was doing temporary office work nearby for an orthopedic surgeon, had come home for lunch, and was about to leave.

When she saw Allie's agony, the pained look that came over Hedra's face almost made Allie momentarily forget her own problem and feel sorry for Hedra. Then she realized it was pain reflected—*her* pain.

Hedra's hand was on her arm, fingers gently kneading. "So what's the matter? What's going on, Allie?" Her voice was throaty, urgent, and weighted with concern.

Allie pulled away from her, from the surprising intensity of her compassion, and was immediately sorry. What the hell was she thinking, drawing back from a friend's attempt to console her? She

paced in front of the window, trying to organize
her thoughts, then came back and sat down on
the sofa. Listened to the refrigerator droning in
the kitchen. Something was vibrating inside it;
glass singing on a wire shelf. It was a subtly piercing sound, like an accepted and ignored scream.

"Allie . . . ?"

Allie swiped at a tear on her cheek and said,
"Goddamned Mike Mayfair!"

"Mayfair? What happened?"

Allie made an effort to even out her breathing,
not look like such a crushed idiot. The universe
was still in place, the earth revolving. Talk, she
told herself. Talk about this latest kick in the gut
and it might not seem so devastating. "He made it
clear to me that if my services for Fortune Fashions were to continue, I'd have to supply certain
services for him."

"Huh? Oh, I get it . . ."

"And Mike Mayfair's *not* going to get it. I made
a pact with myself when I moved to this shit-hole
city. My body, the essential me, wasn't for sale. I
wouldn't let myself be devoured by what's outside
that window. And, dammit, I still feel that way!"

"Maybe you oughta tell Sam about Mayfair."

"That'd only cause more trouble, and it wouldn't
really change anything."

Hedra crossed her arms and studied Allie as if
peering through flesh and bone and observing
the wheels of her mind, coolly assessing this situation that had broken their lives' tranquility. It gave
Allie an odd feeling, glimpsing this unexpected,
calculating side to Hedra. As if the family pet
turned out to know how to balance a checkbook.

"The company hired you and the job's not finished," Hedra said. "So don't they still need you?"

"Not much. Not at this point. I did too good a job. The systems they need are online and simple enough so that even Mayfair's secretary can run and expand the programs. Even Mayfair himself. It'll take some time, and there'll be minor fuck-ups, but the truth is they can get along fine without me."

Hedra bit her lower lip so hard Allie thought blood might appear. Hedra said, "Well, I think it's . . . *just rotten!*"

That made Allie feel better, almost made her smile. Hedra being Hedra again. But it didn't tell her anything she hadn't known. Rotten. That was Mayfair, all right.

Hedra stared at the floor and ground her high heel into it, as if trying to bore through wood and plaster to the apartment below. "You were counting on the money from this assignment, weren't you?"

"Hell, yes. That's the card Mayfair was trying to play. He was smooth and he made it all seem halfway respectable, but it came down to prostitution and we both knew it. What we were talking about was ass for cash."

"What'd you tell him?"

"Christ, Hedra!"

"I'm sorry. I meant what'd you *say* to him?"

"Nothing at all. I simply left."

"Best thing, maybe."

"I passed up some solid accounts because the Fortune Fashions job was so lucrative, and now here I sit with empty pockets and empty time."

"Empty pockets?"

"Well, they'll be empty soon."

Hedra gave a careless backhand wave, as if shooing away a mosquito instead of financial devastation. "I can carry us for a while. And Sam'll help, I'm sure."

"Yeah, I'm sure, too. If I ask him. But I don't know if I want that."

"That *isn't* prostitution, Allie. Not with Sam."

Allie worked her shoes off and let them drop to the floor. One landed on the soft throw rug, the other *thunked* on wood. "I guess it's not," she said. She began massaging her foot. In her anger after leaving Mayfair, she'd walked blocks along Seventh Avenue before hailing a cab; her legs were tired and her feet were sore and felt clumsy and heavy. Her soles tingled as if she'd been marching barefoot on sandpaper. She leaned back and closed her eyes. "God, I really feel shitty, Hedra."

"Anybody would, after what happened." There was a hitch in Hedra's voice; she seemed about to cry. "I don't like seeing you like this."

"I know you don't," Allie said, her eyes still closed. "I don't like it, either."

Hedra spoke from the blackness. "If you want, I can get you something."

Allie wasn't sure what she meant. "No, I'll be okay. But thanks."

"You sure?"

"What do you mean by 'something'?" Allie asked.

"You know. A pill."

Allie opened her eyes and met Hedra's guileless stare. "What kind of pill?"

"Just something to make you feel better, that's all."

"What kind of pill?" Allie repeated.

"I dunno, it's something like Demerol. You heard of Demerol?"

"Sure. In hospitals." Allie stared at Hedra, who was outlined against the bright haze of light streaming through the window. There was something unreal about her, as if she were someone's strayed shadow rather than solid substance. Here was yet another side of Hedra. "It's none of my business if you do drugs, Hedra; I'm not preaching. But it's not for me and thanks anyway."

The figure silhouetted against the light writhed with discomfort. "Wait a minute, Allie, it's not like I'm a drug fiend. It's just that I got used to taking certain drugs when I was in the hospital in St. Louis."

"I didn't say you were an addict."

"No, I guess you didn't. Guess you wonder what I mean, though, about being hospitalized and all."

Allie sat quietly, waiting, knowing Hedra felt compelled to tell her about this. Allie had been wounded and brought down to earth. The weak could safely confide in the weak.

"I was just a kid," Hedra said, "and a car hit me when I was on my bike. It tossed me twenty feet and injured my spine. The doctors couldn't figure out exactly what was wrong; injured backs can be like that. Anyway, I was in the hospital for a while, and they had me on this drug and that drug for pain. They were doing that to a lot of people in those days if they couldn't diagnose what was wrong; I even saw a TV documentary on it once.

Well, eventually the pain just went away by itself, but I was in the habit of taking drugs when I felt bad. I still do it, but it's not as if I'm hooked or anything. There are millions of people like me, using drugs the way I do sometimes, to help them over the rough spots."

"I suppose there are," Allie said. "But it's a habit I never fell into. Where was your family when all this was going on?"

Hedra stepped out of the light and Allie was shocked by the dismay and rage on her face. "My family situation was never good. I try not to think much about those people, after the way they let me down. Heck, the way the brain can block out bad stuff, I hardly even remember them. Except for my father's hands, and the things he did with them. That's the way I see him now, just a pair of big powerful hands with dirt under the nails. I can't even picture my mother at all."

Her mood passed abruptly, as if a dark cloud blown across her mind had dissipated. Her mental sky was clear and blue again. She smiled. "Oh, well, it's all in the past. Doesn't matter anymore. It's today that matters. And tomorrow. Don't you think?"

Allie nodded. The end of the month would matter, when the rent had to be mailed to Haller-Davis. She said, "When you don't have any remaining family, like I don't, sometimes you think even bad family's better than nobody at all."

"Oh, you're so wrong, Allie."

"Maybe. I guess it depends on the seriousness of the problem."

The phone jangled and she jumped at the

noise. Lord, she was wired. Tempted to gulp down that pill.

"Easy," Hedra said, "I'll get it."

She crossed the room and lifted the receiver. Said, "Hello. No, but she's right here. Just a minute." She held the receiver out for Allie. "For you." She cupped her hand over the mouthpiece. "Maybe it's that Mr. Mayfair calling to apologize."

"He's not the type," Allie said, hoping Hedra was right. She got up from the sofa and padded in her stockinged feet to the phone, pressed the receiver to her ear, and said hello.

A male voice said, "Allie, I'm gonna tie you to the bed and whip your ass till you come. Make you eat shit with a rough wooden spoon. Listen, bitch, I'm gonna . . ."

The voice faded to silence as Allie lowered the receiver in her trembling hand. Let it drop the final few inches to clatter into the cradle. Her breathing was ragged, her throat tight.

She tried to remember the voice of whoever had made the other obscene calls. She couldn't know for sure if this caller was the same man.

"Who was it?" Hedra asked.

"A crank call."

"You okay?"

"Sure." She turned around and faked a smile that didn't fool Hedra, then felt it go brittle on her face.

"Oh! That kinda call, huh? Think it was that Mayfair jerk?"

Despite her loathing for the man, Allie was unable to imagine him making such a call. "No, not his style."

"Don't be so sure," Hedra said. "Remember, the creep asked for you by name."

That was what Allie couldn't forget.

Hedra walked over to the window, her hands jammed deep in the pockets of Allie's coat as if she were cold.

Staring outside, she hunched her shoulders and shook her head. She said, "It takes all kinds, Allie. And they don't wear indentifying labels."

15

He looked like a computer-game figure weaving through a maze. Allie watched Graham Knox's slender body maneuver among the crowded tables at Goya's as he brought her the hamburger and Diet Pepsi. Though he actually moved gracefully, there was that inherent and somehow appealing awkwardness about him that seemed to stem more from the tentative, intense expression he habitually wore than from physical motion. He always seemed preoccupied and puzzled by some inner conflict.

"You're busy tonight," she said as he placed her order on the table. The charred-beef scent of the hamburger wafted up to her. She wasn't sure if it made her feel hungrier or slightly ill.

"And you have something on your mind."

Allie was amazed. "How'd you know?"

Graham gave his canine-like lopsided smile and wiped his hands on the small white towel tucked in his belt. "I'm sort of a student of human nature. Gotta be, in my profession." A Beatles song, "Lucy in the Sky with Diamonds," began blasting from the speakers. The decibel level of conversation in the restaurant rose to challenge it. The result was a maelstrom of noise. Graham leaned down close to her, his mouth near her ear. "You need to talk, Allie?" She felt his warm breath, like the life-breath of a lover.

"You shared your good news," she said, "I thought I might share my bad—tempered with some good news, though."

"The bad news isn't *too* bad, I hope." He glanced at his watch, one of those with a moon phase dial on it to make it more complicated. "It's just past seven o'clock. The rush is almost over, and I can get off around eight. Wanna combine talking with walking?" He made it sound like a trick of coordination.

Allie thought a walk was a good idea; the noise might not abate in the usually quiet Goya's. And it was a beautiful late September night, warm and clear. "I'll eat slow," she told him.

"I can sneak you some dessert, on the house. Give you an excuse to hold down the table. Unless you're on a diet."

She smiled sadly. "No, I'm not in a dieting mood."

Graham touched her shoulder in sympathy; she noticed his fingers were long and tapered. He retreated through the melee of noise and laughter, toward the swinging doors to the kitchen, his lanky frame swaying among the tables with practiced precision and efficiency. From behind, he appeared not at all awkward or tentative. Someone in a far corner called to him. He waved a hand to confirm that he'd heard. Somebody somewhere turned down the volume of the canned music. The Beatles were finished with "Lucy" and were singing now about "Sergeant Pepper."

Allie blocked out the voices around her, the laughter and the clinking of glasses and flatware. She gnawed on her hamburger and listened to the music. John Lennon. Christ! How could anyone shoot John Lennon?

Graham had brought her a scoop of vanilla ice cream with fresh strawberries over it. Allie was often amazed by how available fresh produce was in the concrete world of New York. Fresh flowers, too. As if there were a garden on every cloud-high roof.

After dessert and coffee she felt better. Her guilt at eating so many calories was assuaged by the fact that the strawberries and ice cream were free. She suspected even Richard Simmons would accept free dessert in a restaurant. He would if he saw those strawberries, anyway, and his appetite was heightened by other unfulfilled yearnings.

Now she and Graham were walking west on 74th Street, toward Riverside Park. There was a light breeze blowing in off the Hudson. The night was cool and, despite the exhaust fumes, the air smelled remarkably fresh for Manhattan. The sidewalks were crowded with people who seemed to be dawdling, enjoying the unseasonably fair weather; even traffic seemed to be moving slower, car windows cranked down, drivers' elbows jutting out in vehicle after vehicle as if an amalgamation of flesh and metal formed each machine.

Graham walked on the street side, slowly so Allie could keep pace, and listened intently with his head bowed as she told him about Sam.

"There's something doubly good when somebody you love is out of your life, then reenters it."

"Second time around and all that," Graham said. He didn't sound happy about what Allie had told him. "Sounds as if you really love this Sam."

"I don't seem to have much choice, Graham."

"Sure, I understand. Lucky Sam. He smart enough to know he's lucky?"

"I think so."

"You'd better know it."

She couldn't help remembering Lisa. "That's not an easy thing to know for sure."

"Yeah. Well, that's the human condition. What keeps people like me from ever running out of material to write about. Anyway, tell me the bad news you wanted off your chest. If I sound more eager to hear it, don't blame me."

She told him about Mayfair and losing the Fortune Fashions assignment. Then she told him about the obscene phone calls in which her name was used.

"You tell Sam about any of this?"

"Just some of the phone calls."

"Why not about Mayfair?"

"I'm afraid of what he might do. Men like Mayfair are everywhere; Sam getting embroiled in a fight or a lawsuit wouldn't change society—or get the account back."

"I suppose not. It's the phone calls that are really bothering you, right?"

"You know me like a good friend, Graham."

"That's because I am a good friend." They stopped and stood on the corner of West 74th and West End Avenue. "Didn't you say your full name's in the phone book?" Graham asked. The breeze riffled his dark hair, mussing the wings over his protruding ears.

Allie nodded.

"Then I wouldn't worry so much about the phone calls. Just some pervert who chose you because he spotted the complete listing in the directory and knew he could shake up a woman by using her first name. It's probably not as personal as you think. Or as you *feel* it is. You'd be surprised at the number of obscene phone calls made every day in this city. Every hour."

"What bothers me," Allie said, "is that my address is in the directory along with my number. This sicko—if it is only one man—knows where to find me."

"Yeah. Well, I can see where that makes you uneasy, and that's exactly what a bastard like your caller wants you to worry about. But believe me, the kind of nut who phones women and makes sexual references almost always does it because he's too intimidated to confront them face-to-face. These are usually the last people who'd show up at your door and try something."

"'Almost always,' huh? 'Usually'?"

"Those words apply to virtually everything, Allie."

True enough. But she didn't agree with him out loud.

John Lutz

"What'd Sam say about the phone calls?" he asked.

"Pretty much what you said. He doesn't think they're anything to worry about. That's what most men would say; they don't feel the vulnerability in that kind of situation."

"Can't help that," Graham said. "We're not afraid of mice, either."

They began walking down West End. A raggedy man wearing incredibly wrinkled, oversized gray pants, and a green wool blanket draped over bare chest and shoulders, approached them and in an almost unintelligible mumble asked if they had any spare change. The breeze carried his odor of stale perspiration and urine. Graham shook his head no and said, "Sorry." Allie wondered how it would feel to be rejected that way by an indifferent world. To live on the streets of a city as cruel as Manhattan. Delusion might be essential to deflect the pain.

She watched the beggar veer toward a well-dressed couple waiting to cross the intersection. Trying to muster pity but feeling only fear, she said, "It must be a bitch, having to exist like that, struggling to survive through each day."

Graham said, "It is, but he asked the wrong people for money. You're out of work, and I've only been paid the first half of the advance on my play."

"We don't have to justify not giving a beggar money," Allie said, a bit surprised at the vehemence in her voice.

"Yes, I'm afraid we do."

At a newspaper and magazine kiosk, Allie paused to buy a *Village Voice*. She enjoyed reading the weekly paper, and it also contained help-wanted ads, maybe for computer programmers.

She abruptly yanked the *Voice* out from beneath the rock that was weighting it down on the stack of papers, and handed over a dollar bill for the paper to the grizzled old woman inside the kiosk, but after taking a step and starting to shove her wallet back into her purse, she stopped, realizing something was wrong.

She squeezed the wallet with probing fingers.

Opening it, she checked the plastic card and photo holders. She pried apart the leather compartments, her movements quicker and less controlled.

"They're gone!" she cried.

Graham was staring at her, puzzled. "What's gone?"

"My Visa and MasterCard."

"You sure?"

She examined the wallet again, more slowly and carefully. "Positive. And something else is missing. My expired Illinois driver's license."

"Expired, is it? Good. Somebody might be surprised if they try to use it to cash a check. You sure this stuff was in your wallet at the restaurant?"

"Not absolutely sure. It might have been gone and I didn't notice. The wallet felt different to me just now, not as bulky. I haven't charged anything in over a week. Shit! The cards might have been gone for days!"

"Don't panic, Allie, you can only be held responsible for fifty dollars on each card, even if the thief uses them to travel to Europe. It's a law."

"I know. Still . . ."

"And they've probably only been gone a short time, or you'd have missed them earlier."

Allie didn't answer, trying to remember how the wallet had felt in Goya's when she'd gotten out money to pay for dinner. She hadn't actually taken the wallet out of her purse, letting it rest inside so it and the folding money would stay out of sight below table level. Couldn't be too careful.

"Better get on the phone," Graham said, "and report the cards missing. They'll cut credit on them and issue you some new plastic with different numbers."

"I don't understand how I lost them."

"You probably didn't lose them. Credit cards are stolen every day."

Every day. Like obscene phone calls to single women. "But no one's had the opportunity."

"Haven't they? Thieves can be damned clever. And no woman guards her purse every minute she's out."

"I suppose you're right."

"Maybe the creep who stole your credit cards and driver's license is the same guy who phoned you. Maybe that's how he settled on you to pester. If so, it'll lose its thrill after a while and he'll stop."

"You sound sure of that."

"I told you, I'm a student of human nature. But if it'll make you feel better, maybe you should go to the police. Report the obscene calls and the stolen cards and license. Might not help, but it can't hurt."

"I'll think about it," Allie said. "Meanwhile, I'd better notify somebody about the missing cards. Whoever stole them might be off on a shopping spree right now. Buying one of everything at Bloomingdale's."

"I've gotta admit, that sounds like fun."

She responded with morose silence.

"Maybe they're only lost, not stolen," Graham said to comfort her. "That wouldn't be so bad."

Allie thought inanely that nothing could be worse than being lost; she'd been lost for a while and knew.

She tucked the folded *Voice* under her arm, clutched her purse tightly, and she and Graham began walking at a fast pace back toward West 74th. Their heels clopped out a relentless rhythm on the hard concrete.

The night no longer seemed friendly.

16

When Allie reached the Cody Arms she happened to glance up as she crossed West 74th and saw a shadow flit across the drawn shade in Hedra's bedroom window. Again. It was moving rapidly, arms flailing. Allie suddenly realized someone was dancing madly in Hedra's room, whirling, shaking her head, hair flying.

She went upstairs and let herself into the apartment. As she walked silently down the hall to her bedroom, she heard the floor creaking in Hedra's room and saw darkness pass across the lighted crack beneath the closed door. Allie moved nearer and put her ear close to the door. There was no music inside the room, only the *swish swish scuff scuff* of Hedra frantically dancing.

Allie knocked on the door. "Hedra? You okay?"

The noise on the other side of the door ceased abruptly. Then Hedra's voice said, "Sure, Allie. I was practicing a new dance step, that's all."

Allie hadn't even known Hedra danced. She stood there a while longer, but Hedra said nothing more. The light washing from beneath her door suddenly disappeared.

As long as she's all right, Allie figured, what she does in her own room is her business. That was part of the understanding when they'd become roommates. Still, there was something about the absence of music and the uncontrolled wildness of the dance that gave Allie the creeps. On the other hand, a backlighted figure moving in silhouette could be deceptive.

Apparently Allie's roommate had danced enough that night and had gone to bed. Allie decided that was a sound idea. She turned away from the blank face of the door and went to her bedroom.

Allie woke the next morning to the sound of a sanitation truck grinding away at garbage that had been piled high at the curb. Loud metallic clanking, then high-pitched whining and rending was followed by the coughing roar of the truck engine, then the squeal and hiss of air brakes. Now and then one of the workers handling Manhattan's throwaways would shout frantically or bark loud laughter. It was an adventure, picking up trash.

She opened one gritty eye and studied the dust motes swirling in a sunbeam bisecting her bedroom, then slowly shifted her gaze to the red digital numbers on the clock by the bed. Eight-thirty. Still early.

Then she realized, late, early, it made no difference. She had no appointments. Nowhere to go.

No work and no immediate income.

She heard tap water run for a moment in the kitchen, then Hedra stride across the apartment and open and close the hall door, leaving for whatever job she was working.

Allie remembered last night's discovery that her I.D. and credit cards were missing from her wallet. She would look up the card numbers on her monthly statements, then she'd call the credit companies and inform them of the missing cards. Their numbers would soon be listed among those stolen, among hundreds and perhaps thousands listed on the hot sheets for salesclerks and cashiers to scan while infuriated customers waited in checkout lines.

New plastic would be sent, but Allie would be left without much cash and with no credit until her replacement cards arrived. She realized, with an edge of subtle panic, that getting new charge cards might take a while. It was almost as if an integral piece of her were missing; plastic had become essential in her life.

She rolled over to lie on her back and gazed listlessly at the ceiling, listening as the metallic mayhem of the trash pickup moved down the street like a raucous carnival. Finally the noise drifted faint and echoing from the next block.

As she ran her tongue around the inside of her mouth, she realized she was parched and thirsty. She'd lain in bed for a long time last night before falling asleep, and she hadn't drunk anything since dinner at Goya's.

Still, she was more tired than thirsty. She watched a tiny insect on the ceiling make its gradual, indirect way to the corner near the window. It stopped, started, slowly detouring around cracks in the plaster, moving through life with the care necessary for survival. Finally it disappeared in deep, angled shadow. Into safety? Or danger?

Allie sighed, stood up, and plodded barefoot from the bedroom. The floor was hard and unyielding beneath her soles. She could feel the individual cracks between strips of wood. She returned to the bedroom to get her slippers, but she couldn't find them. Hedra had been wearing them last night; maybe they were in her room.

But the slippers were nowhere in sight in Hedra's bedroom. Allie peeked beneath the bed. Nothing there. Not even dust. She walked to the closet to see if compulsively neat Hedra had placed the slippers in there.

A moment after she opened the closet door she stepped back in surprise. The clothes. Hedra's clothes. They looked so much like . . . they *were* Allie's own clothes.

Allie turned and hurried to her own room. She flung open the closet doors.

Her clothes were there, as they'd always been.

She sat down on the edge of the mattress, gazing at the rows of dresses, blouses, and slacks on hangers. There were a few variations in color and material from Hedra's closet, but not many.

Wherever possible, Hedra had bought exact duplicates of Allie's clothes.

Allie sat very still on the edge of the bed, wondering what it meant.

Later that day she phoned Sam and told him about it. He seemed more amused than alarmed.

"What the girl wears is her business," he said, "and you know how she idolizes you."

"She does idolize me," Allie said. "More than I find comfortable."

Sam laughed. "You deserve it. Have I ever told you that?"

Allie had to smile, remembering. "Yeah, you've told me."

"Meant it, too."

"Seeing Hedra's clothes this morning, after losing my credit cards last night, is what's got me rattled, I guess."

"You lost your credit cards? As in Master and Visa?"

"Yeah. I don't know how."

"Get the cards back?"

"No, they might have been stolen."

"Better phone in the numbers."

"I already have. I notified the police, too."

"Well, your liability's limited when you lose credit cards, and maybe they'll turn up."

"I can't use them if they do; I have to wait for replacements. That'll take a while."

"By the way, Allie, I've got some bad news."

Her heart took a dive. "Bad news? Dammit, Sam, that's not what I need this morning."

"Christ, not that bad." He laughed. "I only meant I have to be away for a couple of weeks. A conference in Milwaukee, then a junk-bond seminar in Los Angeles. Can you live without me?"

"I'm not sure."

"Well, I can't live without you. Not for more than a few weeks. I'll phone you."

"You'd better," she said.

"Try not to worry so much, okay, lover?"

"Sure. That's probably good advice."

Loudly, only half-jokingly, he blew a kiss into the receiver.

When she hung up on Sam, the phone rang almost immediately. She thought it might be Sam, calling her back to say something he'd forgotten.

But as soon as she picked up the phone she knew it wasn't Sam.

No voice on the other end of the connection, only heavy, uneven breathing.

Then, "Allie, baby? Sweet Buns? I know it's you. Soon we're gonna—"

She slammed the receiver into its cradle.

17

Disgusting habit, Detective Sergeant Will Kennedy thought. And I'm disgusting for indulging.

He snubbed out his cigar in the ashtray, knowing even then that he'd soon light another despite his doctor's advice to stop smoking. Sitting at his desk in the squad room, he peered through the noxious haze hovering above the ashtray. A woman was standing at the wooden restraining rail that ran parallel to the booking desk. She leaned forward, her pelvis against the rail, and spoke earnestly and rapidly, as if she wanted to get her story out in a hurry.

Kennedy watched Sergeant Morrow listen to her in his patient, speculative way, then say something and point in Kennedy's direction. The woman smiled at Morrow, and walked purposefully toward Kennedy.

Davis, who was working undercover in Narcotics and looked like a street punk, blatantly leered at her. It didn't matter, Kennedy figured, she'd think he was a suspect and not a cop. The other detectives and a couple of uniforms contented themselves with sly glances in her direction. This was a busy precinct, but there was always time to appreciate beauty in the midst of police work. For the contrast.

As she got closer, Kennedy pretended to notice her for the first time and glanced up, smiling warmly. She was in her early thirties, average height and build, short blond hair, good eyes, firm, squarish jaw, and a mouth that looked as if it had smiled plenty but which now was a grim red slash. She was wearing a lightweight raincoat, powder blue with a white collar and oversized white buttons. High heels, good ankles. Not a stunner, but an attractive woman up close as well as viewed from across the room.

She stood in front of his gray metal desk, leaning forward as she had against the railing. "Sergeant Kennedy?"

"Me," he told her.

"The desk sergeant said I should see you about my . . . complaint." She was obviously nervous, not used to being in places like this. A respectable citizen in a bind.

He nodded and motioned for her to sit in the chair alongside the desk. Kennedy was a large, shambling man of middle age who knew he presented an avuncular, soothing image to women. He was six feet tall and close to two hundred and fifty pounds, with bushy, raggedy gray hair and sleepy blue eyes. Well into his fifties. Not a handsome man or a sexual threat. A slow and amiable old bear, that was Kennedy. If he hurt anyone, it would be accidental. He fostered that impression and capitalized on it. Being underestimated could be a great advantage.

The precinct house was warm and felt uncomfortably humid because of the rain that fell silently on thick windows reinforced with steel mesh. It even *smelled* damp. Fetid as a swamp. Though the ceiling didn't quite leak, there were ancient water stains on it that always appeared wet. The air was so thick and sticky it seemed to deaden sound and coat bare flesh like oil.

When the woman had unbuttoned her coat and settled down in the straight-backed chair, Kennedy said, "Get you a cup of coffee? Maybe a soda or glass of water?"

She seemed surprised by his hospitality. "No. No, thank you."

"You mentioned a complaint, Miss . . . ?"

"My name is Allison Jones, and I live at One Seventy-two West Seventy-fourth Street."

He smiled. "And you sound like a very nice and well-prepared twelve-year-old reciting in front of the class. Relax, Miss Jones. Like the PR ads say, your police department cares. This old cop does, anyway."

"Not so old," she said, smiling back as the tension loosened its grip on her. The set of her shoulders changed beneath the blue coat, became less squared and then slumped wearily. But the rigid cast of her jaw and mouth remained grim. She was wrapped tight and ticking, this one.

"Thank you, Allison Jones. Could be there's some good years left in me at that." He picked up a ballpoint pen and idly rotated it between

sausage-like powerful fingers, wishing he could
smoke the damned thing. Despite his huge, rough
hands, he had beautifully manicured nails. He
wore a plain gold wedding ring, though Jeanie
had been dead almost ten years. Ah, Jeanie! He
said, "Now, dear, what seems to be troubling you?"

"Well, phone calls, among other things."

"Oh? Of an obscene nature, do you mean?"

"Yes. Very obscene."

"In what way?"

"The man—if it was the same man—talked
about doing things to me."

Kennedy cautioned himself. Gently now. "What
sorts of things, Miss Jones? What I mean is, could
you be more specific?"

"Tying me up, gagging me, whipping me. Making me . . . do things I never would do."

"Of course not."

"Bondage, it's called," she said flatly.

"Yes, I know." He stared sadly for a moment at
the ballpoint pen almost lost in his big hand.

"You get a lot of complaints like mine?"

"Oh, yes. We see everything on this job. Soon
lose the capacity to be shocked, I'm afraid."

"He talked as if I'd enjoy sadomasochism."

"He might well have believed that. The sick sort
of man who'd make such a call generally has some
very twisted ideas about the fair sex."

"Not just twisted," Allison Jones said, "positively
kinky."

Without a change of expression, Kennedy studied her more closely. Was she enjoying this? Getting her kicks by reporting phone calls that never
occurred? It happened. All sorts of people wan-

dered into precinct houses and reported all sorts of crimes, real or imagined. And for reasons only the psychiatrists ventured to guess, most often wrongly. This woman certainly didn't seem that type, but Kennedy knew better than to classify by appearance and mannerism. He remembered an apparently typical young mother who'd murdered her two children as casually as one might destroy unwanted kittens.

Allison Jones seemed suddenly aware that he was assessing her. She frowned and stirred in her chair. Crossed her legs the other way. He heard taut nylon swish.

"This sort of thing's been happening," Kennedy said quickly. "Keeping us poor civil servants busy." As if she were the twentieth woman that day to complain of obscene phone calls, and not the fifth or sixth.

"It doesn't usually happen to *me*," she said sharply. He decided she was probably telling him straight.

"The caller might never have laid eyes on you," he told her. "He could've punched out your number at random. That's how most of these characters operate. The odds are greatly against it being your number, so you assume he knows you personally in some way and you lose sleep over it. Just what anonymous callers want; they feed on fear."

"That's so sick."

"Oh, it is."

"And another thing, he called me by name."

"Ah!" Kennedy seemed to make a special mental note of that.

"There's something else," she said, leaning forward. And she told him about stopping to eat at Goya's, the walk with Graham Knox, and the disappearance of her expired driver's license and credit cards.

He tapped the pen several times on the gray metal desk, leaving tiny dark slashes, then noticed what he was doing and rubbed the desk clean with the heel of his hand. There was cigar ash on the desk; he brushed that away. "And did you notify the credit people of the loss of your cards?"

"Of course. Soon as I realized they were gone. It's the phone calls *and* the cards being stolen that I guess has me spooked."

"You sure the cards were stolen, not misplaced?"

"Almost certain."

"Almost?"

"I'm almost certain the sun will set tonight, Sergeant Kennedy."

He smiled. "Now, now, no need to get testy."

She nodded and tried a return smile that barely broke the surface. "You're right. I'm sorry."

"The city's full of sick and tortured people who use the telephone for reasons not dreamed about by Alexander Graham Bell. It's probably nothing that should cause you undue concern."

"But what about him calling me by name?"

"Well, I'm assuming you're listed in the directory."

"Yes. My full name, since I have such a common last name. But he didn't say Allison, he said Allie. And that's what I'm called, Allie."

"Could be he guessed that. It must be the most popular nickname for Allison."

"But what if he *does* know me?"

Kennedy put down the pen and leaned back in his chair. The buttons on his shirt threatened to pop. "Well, that's possible, but I'll tell you, Miss Jones, it's been my experience that men who talk dirty to women on the phone usually don't carry the matter any further. The psychiatrists could tell you why. I can only tell you the pyschiatrists are right. These men are often sexual and social misfits who are too afraid of women to talk to them face-to-face. That's why the miserable wretches use the phone."

"That's what Graham said."

"The Graham who was with you when you noticed your credit cards were missing?"

"Yes, and he's my neighbor. He's also a playwright. And as I told you, a waiter at a restaurant near my apartment."

"Well, Graham's right about obscene callers." Kennedy sat forward slowly and placed his elbows on the desk, rested one hand on top the other. "Tell you what. If it happens again, we can have the phone company put a tap on your phone."

"Tap?"

"It's a tracer, actually. It would enable us to find out what telephone any future obscene calls came from. But again, in my experience, these men usually call from public pay phones. And they don't often use the same phone twice."

"Then a tracer probably wouldn't do much good."

"To be candid, no good at all, most likely."

"What about my stolen credit cards?"

"You should make a complaint on that one. At

least give us the account numbers. But I need to be honest with you, there isn't much chance they'll be recovered. People who steal credit cards, if they're pros, either sell the cards immediately or charge everything they can on them before they might be reported stolen. On the street, stolen credit cards depreciate by the hour. Whatever's going to be done with them is done fast, then they're often destroyed." He clucked his tongue. "Some sad society we live in, isn't it?"

Allie Jones smiled and shook her head in futility. "Have I wasted my time coming here, Sergeant Kennedy?"

"Maybe not. You never know. I'd advise you to fill out the forms, report the credit card theft. The cards might turn up on somebody we bring in. It's happened."

"All right, then," she said. "I'll do that."

Kennedy ran the appropriate form into his typewriter and one-fingered out the information as she answered his questions. She was alert and efficient. From working with computers, Kennedy thought. He was uncomfortable around computers, didn't understand them. What were microchips, miniature potato chips?

When he was finished he read over what he'd typed. After making a few sloppy corrections with Wite-Out, he ratcheted the form from the typewriter and had Allison Jones sign it.

He said, "I promise we'll call you right away if there's any progress on this."

She thanked him and stood up. There was something about this troubled young woman that intrigued Kennedy, evoking pity and concern. Did she resemble Jeanie? Maybe. A little. And it was the cruelest of cities out there, a crouching monster that waited patiently for as long as it took and then devoured its victims.

"Miss Jones," he said, "is there anything else bothering you?"

She gave him her slow and appealing smile. "It shows?"

"Afraid it does."

"Not a police matter," she said. "It's just that my life hasn't gone very well lately. My job, my . . . Well, never mind that."

"What about your, ah, romantic life?"

She seemed to consider telling him something, then decide against it. "My love life's fine, Sergeant, believe me. But that's irrelevant."

"We can't be sure about that."

"We'll have to be."

Testy again.

"My personal problems are more job-related. Financial." She straightened and shrugged as if none of it mattered. "It's how the world works sometimes," she said.

"Isn't that the truth for all of us?" He stood up halfway, leaning on his desk, and shook her hand. It was limp and cool. "Hang on," he told her, squeezing the narrow fingers reassuringly. "Things'll take a favorable bounce. They always do, eventually."

She said, "I'm sure you're right. Thanks for reminding me."

He watched her walk from the squad room and out the large oak doors to the street. Then he sat back down heavily. The chair groaned beneath him. His hemorrhoids flared. God, his health was deteriorating like the South Bronx.

"What we got there?" a voice said behind Kennedy. His partner, Hector Vasquez.

"Obscene phone calls, stolen credit cards."

"Nice-looking woman," Hector said. "The sort that'd attract that kinda call."

"Isn't she, though?" Kennedy picked up the complaint form Allie Jones had signed and considered it. Stolen credit cards were seldom recovered.

"Better file that so we can get going," Hector urged. "Lieutenant wants us to drive over to Queens and pick up that prisoner."

"My hemorrhoids are on fire," Kennedy said. "I don't want to drive to Queens."

"I sure feel sorry for you," Hector said with mock sympathy, "but that's how the world works sometimes."

"Funny," Kennedy told him, "that's just what she said, about how the world works sometimes. Her words exactly."

"Whose words?"

"Allie Jones's. The woman who just left."

"Forget her and come on," Hector said, "unless you wanna receive an obscene phone call from the lieutenant."

Kennedy braced with his hands on the arms of his chair and levered himself to a standing position. He tucked in his wrinkled white shirt around his ample stomach and wrestled into his tweed sportcoat. After even that brief effort, he was breathing hard. Better watch the blood pressure, he told himself. Lose some weight. Really lay off the cigars, like the doctor advised, or someday he might be waddling after a suspect and collapse and die from a heart attack.

But he knew he wouldn't change the way he lived. Or the way he'd probably die. Suicide by cigar.

He filed the complaint form and trudged after Hector.

18

Allie walked home from the precinct house unsure of how she felt. Around her the wet pavement had a mirrorlike effect. The rain had become a cool, persistent mist that found its way down the back of her collar. She moved through it as if it were the atmosphere of dreams, unconcerned about getting wet or catching cold. The tires of passing cabs *shiiished*. Windshield wipers *thunk, thunked*.

Though she felt better after having told Sergeant Kennedy about the phone calls and missing credit cards, she was sure the police couldn't help. Reporting a crime was a long way from seeing that crime solved. Kennedy himself had as much as said that. He seemed to see the city as a festering, vile creation out of control. The good guys were overwhelmed.

When finally she reached the apartment, she found Hedra concerned about her. "For Pete's sake, Allie, what are you doing out wandering around in the rain?"

"I went to the police station."

"You *walked*?"

"Took the subway there, but I decided to walk back."

"The doctor'll be your next stop." There was a mothering quality to Hedra's voice; a different Hedra, with Allie in trouble.

She hurried across the living room and helped Allie shrug out of the blue raincoat. After shaking the coat so that hundreds of drops of water caught the light and glittered like scattered diamonds, she hung it in the hall closet, well away from the other coats. Hedra had always liked the blue raincoat and took special care of it, though she hadn't bought one like it, probably because the coat was four years old and the style was no longer in the stores.

"I told them about the obscene phone calls and the stolen credit cards," Allie said.

"I gathered that. Why don't you get out of those wet shoes and sit down. I'll fix you a cup of hot chocolate."

"Thanks, but I don't think I want anything."

"Don't be ridiculous; you'll catch pneumonia or worse." She rested a hand on Allie's shoulder and pushed and guided her to the sofa, like the stern guardian of a recalcitrant child.

Allie let herself be pushed. She was tired, she missed Sam, and a cup of hot chocolate *would* taste good and damn the calories.

While Hedra was clattering around in the kitchen, Allie sat and stared at the rain that was falling hard again and reflecting distorted light as it flowed down the windows. It was a perilous world out there beyond the glass. She'd been blind, preoccupied since she'd come to the city, and hadn't realized how very hostile and dangerous it was.

Hedra was back with the cup of hot chocolate for Allie and one for herself. She sat down next to her on the sofa. The steady patter of the rain made the apartment seem smaller, cozier. "So what'd the cops say?"

"They were nice, but not very helpful."

"They're busy," Hedra said. "Too much crime in this city. Too much evil."

"That's more or less the impression I got. Obscene phone calls, stolen credit cards—these things happen every hour, so they don't get excited about them. They concentrate on more important crimes. Until the person who got the phone call becomes one of the important crimes."

"Don't worry so," Hedra said. "Nothing's gonna happen to you." She sipped at her chocolate. She'd put marshmallows in both cups. Thoughtful. "By the way, Allie, I hope you don't care about me wearing your sweatshirt." She used her thumb and forefinger to stretch the gray material of the FORDHAM shirt she was wearing. Allie had bought it at a street bazaar two years ago. "I looked through my closet and didn't have much to lounge around in. I'll wash it for you when I'm done with it, I promise."

"Doesn't matter," Allie said. She took a long, painful swallow of the scalding chocolate, burning the roof of her mouth. Lowered the cup and wiped melted marshmallow off her upper lip, leaving her hand sticky. She looked up at Hedra. "I opened your closet door, Hedra. I saw how you bought so many clothes exactly like mine."

Hedra's lower lip quaked.

Allie said, "Don't do that, Hedra, please. Both of us can't be basket cases."

"You mad?" Hedra asked.

"Not exactly mad. Puzzled."

"Well," Hedra said, "I saw how good your clothes looked on you, and I figured if they only looked half as good on me, it'd be an improvement."

Allie sighed. She didn't feel like coping with this unabashed admiration, not right now. "Don't buy any more duplicates, Hedra. Borrow whatever you want from my closet."

Hedra beamed as if she'd been pronounced royalty. "Thanks! And you're welcome to borrow anything in my closet." Her expression sagged. " 'Course, you're not likely to wanna wear any of my stuff."

Concerned, mothering Hedra was gone; deferential Hedra was back. Allie didn't know what to say. She finally mumbled, "Lucky we're about the same size."

"Lucky," Hedra agreed. "Want some cold milk in that chocolate to cool it down?"

"No, thanks," Allie told her. "I'll wait for it to cool. Then I think I'll rest awhile."

"Sure, rest'll make everything seem better."

Allie seldom went out of the apartment during the next week. Sam phoned several times and sensed her despondency. He tried to cheer her up, told her he loved her and would be back soon. After talking to him she usually felt better, for a while. The few acquaintances who called her soon caught on that she wanted to be left alone. Oily Billy Stothers, probably on the make with Sam out of town, called several times, but he stopped when she made it plain that she preferred loneliness to his company.

And she couldn't help it; she found herself wondering about Sam, so far from her arms. Was that part of the reason for her depression? The Lisa factor?

She was alone most of the time. Hedra went out every day to a temporary office job. She had to dress well for it, she'd said, and usually left the apartment wearing a duplicate of something of Allie's. Allie sometimes lent her clothes. She didn't care; she had no place to wear her nice clothes now. The ads she'd placed in the classified columns brought her no business, and the résumés she'd sent around garnered no replies. Work was scarce for computer programmers; colleges were churning them out by the thousands. And she was sure Mike Mayfair, his male vanity bruised, had spread stories about her so that prospective clients would be scared away. She should hate Mayfair, but that required effort. The acidity of hate was in her, but not the energy.

Sometimes she thought she was becoming a hermit, not going out, not concerned about her appearance, not taking care of herself. What made one a recluse by definition? Leaving shelter only once a week? Twice? Did recluses have roommates? From time to time she wondered if she might be lapsing into a clinical depression. Endorphins in decline.

After watching a Donahue program on agoraphobia, and seeing a woman interviewed who for years had been terrified to leave her apartment, Allie became frightened. She'd never been the type to pull the walls in around herself, yet that was what she was doing. What was happening to her? *Come back, Sam!*

She put on her old Nikes, struggled into her jacket, and immediately went out. Breathed deeply. Walked for miles.

She fell into the habit of walking every day, and every day brought Sam's return that much closer. He'd phoned and told her the conference would be longer than originally planned, and to expect him when she saw him.

Surprisingly, money was no worry. Hedra had been assigned a lucrative job filling in for an executive secretary at a catering firm who was on extended maternity leave. It made Allie miserable at times, gave her a feeling of guilt and uselessness, knowing Hedra was paying for rent and groceries. But she told herself that when things got brighter she'd pay Hedra back and add generous interest. What she wouldn't do—couldn't do—was borrow from Sam.

Some days, like this morning, she couldn't stop thinking about Sam. She had him on her mind from her first moment of wakefulness, and lay staring at the ceiling, slipping in and out of sleep.

She and Sam were in Mexico, where they'd often talked about going, and were lying on the beach in soft white sand. A huge full moon drifted lazily on the black waves, like a lost and luminous beachball. The breeze off the ocean sighed warm secrets. New York was far away. Sam said he loved her and her only, and loosened the top of her wet bathing suit. Ran his fingertips over her pulsing nipples. Then her stomach and the insides of her thighs. Parted the suit from her crotch, brushing her lightly with a knuckle.

Whispered, "Lisa . . ."

She awoke trembling. Her eyes were juiced with tears that threatened to flow any moment. Her legs thrashed of their own accord. She had to get up.

Out of the bed.

Walk.

Outside, in the vibrant and beautiful morning, she felt better. She cut over to Broadway and walked for block after block, taking long strides, as if trying to exhaust something accompanying her so it would eventually give up and turn back.

But whatever it was, it strode side by side with her and drew its energy from her desperation.

Finally, when a muted sun had climbed much higher in the lead-gray sky, she began wending her way home.

On the corner of West 74th and Amsterdam, a man wearing baggy Levi's faded the exact color of the sky, and a red windbreaker with the sleeves turned up, approached her. At first she thought

he was gazing beyond her, at someone else. But
no, he was definitely looking at her. She glanced
away but knew it hadn't been in time. Make eye
contact on a teeming Manhattan street and anything can happen.

"Hey! Allie Jones?"

She stared into his face. A short guy in his
mid-thirties, with curly, sandy-colored hair and uptilted green eyes. There was something vague and
a little wild about those eyes, a touch of dangerous
disorientation. His flesh was freckled and ruddy,
and though there was a fullness to his cheeks, his
legs and the torso beneath the Windbreaker were
very thin, almost emaciated. The wrists protruding from the turned-up sleeves were bony and
fragile. Allie knew she'd never seen him before.
She said, "Sorry . . ."

He looked scared and unsure of himself for a
moment, then said, "Listen, I'm ready." His words
were slightly slurred.

"Ready?"

"You know. To do what we talked about." He
glanced around. Grinned. They were coconspirators. "What we decided at Wild Red's. I wasn't as
shtoned as you might think. Hell, I always said I'd
try anything at least once, then give it a second
go-round. That's always been my motto, you might
shay."

Confused, Allie backed away. "You and I never
talked about anything."

She might as well not have spoken. He ran a
bony hand through his already ruffled hair. Something ugly and desperate moved across his face.
His nostrils twitched, in that instant reminding

her of a pig. "Thing is, any fuckin' condition's okay with me. Whatever action turnsh you on, lover, even if it's rollin' in shit."

"Goddamnit, I don't *know* you!" Allie almost screamed.

That startled the man and he shuffled away from her, studying her with his opaque green eyes. He seemed to be dazed, as if he might be drunk or on drugs and peering at her through an internal haze. "Hey, maybe I made a mistake, thought you was shomebody else." He sprayed saliva when he talked, tattooing her face with it.

"But I am Allie Jones."

Out of patience, he said, "Well, shit!" as if he'd never figure this out. He clenched a fist angrily and extended it toward her. She didn't think people outside of comic strips actually did that. She was ready to run, but he didn't advance. There was something hypnotic about the way he was looking at her, something twisted and intimate.

Then he seemed to relax. His fist came unclenched. He dropped his hand to his side and let it dangle, as if to say she wasn't worth the effort of striking her.

Stunned, Allie could only stare as he turned and walked away, weaving in and out among shifting currents of pedestrians to lose himself on the crowded sidewalk.

She dragged her fingers across her cheeks, feeling repulsive wetness, and stood staring after him, ignoring the streams of hurrying New Yorkers who were ignoring her. Several people bumped into her and walked on.

She wiped her damp fingertips on her jacket. *"I
don't know you!"* she said again.

No one acknowledged in any way that she'd
spoken.

Everyone was careful not to make eye contact.

19

"All kinds of scuzzballs in New York," Hedra said when she'd returned home from work and listened to Allie. She'd brought with her the scents of outside: exhaust fumes, tobacco smoke. "This guy must have got you mixed up with somebody who looks a lot like you, huh?"

Allie was sitting in the wing chair in the living room, legs drawn up, chin resting on her knees. She'd been in that position for hours. Her chin ached dully and there were white spots on the insides of both knees where it had dug into the flesh. She hadn't eaten anything, and had drunk only half the Diet Pepsi Hedra brought her. She said, "No, he called me by name."

Hedra shrugged. "That one I can't explain." She walked to the window and gazed outside. There was something about her walk. It wasn't the slump-shouldered, tentative shuffle that had been Hedra's when she'd first moved into the apartment. Yet it was oddly familiar. Disturbing. Maybe it was simply the dress; she was wearing Allie's yellow dress—or a duplicate—with the pleated skirt.

Allie's shoes that she'd borrowed, though they had to be half a size too large. Did she wad Kleenexes in the toes?

Then it struck Allie and she shivered. It wasn't the dress or shoes, but the way Hedra was standing with hand on hip. The lean of her body. Even the tilt of her head. Allie saw familiarity in Hedra because of her, Allie's, own characteristics. Oh, she knew this person in front of her. A composite. A thousand flat images in countless mirrors, a thousand glances into reflecting display windows as she walked past; it was as if they'd all come to life in Hedra.

Hedra, envying Allie. Mimicking her.

Allie, understanding at last, said, "Hedra, you don't really want to be me."

And Hedra turned. Allie almost expected to see her own face. Hedra's features were twisted in self-pity and guilt and fear. The breeze sifting in through the window had toyed with her hair and given her childish bangs. She seemed to shrink inside the dress, a small girl caught playing grown-up with Mommy's clothes.

Allie was incredulous. She knew the meaning of Hedra's reaction. "You've been impersonating me . . . !"

Hedra took two unsteady steps toward her, then stopped cold, as if she might fall down if she continued. "God, no! Nothing like that . . ."

"What, then? Who was that man? Who's been calling me?"

"I don't know. Honest! It was because of the coat, I guess."

"Coat?"

"When I was at a singles bar down in the Village I had on your coat—the blue one with the white collar and big white buttons. I mean, there aren't a lot of coats like that. You must have been wearing it today when that creep came up to you on the street."

Allie *had* been wearing the blue coat. Fascinated, she lowered her legs and placed her bare feet flat on the floor. She sat and waited for Hedra to continue, wanting to hear it but afraid of what Hedra might reveal. There was something here she didn't understand. Something elusive and primal that skittered across the back of her mind on a thousand delicate legs and left her frightened.

"Anyway," Hedra went on, "this real cute guy came up to me at the bar and we started to talk. Then we had a few dances. I mean, there was some real chemistry there, but I didn't wanna lead him on too much, wanted to take it slow. I guess, tell you the truth, I was a little scared. It's just the way I've always been around men. So when he asked me my name, it took me by surprise, and I didn't wanna use my real name so I just blurted out the first one that popped into mind, and it was yours. I didn't figure it'd hurt anything."

"What did this guy look like?" Allie asked.

"Tall, with black hair going a little thin on top, but with a kind face and a terrific build. Really great shoulders. Like an athlete. I wouldn't be surprised if he was one."

Not the scrawny, sandy-haired animal who'd accosted Allie. Allie said, "So who was the kink I talked to today?"

"I don't know. Me and Brad—that was this guy's

name—were joined by some of his friends and he
introduced me. It was too late to back out then; I
had to keep on being Allie Jones. We went to another place, and another. More of Brad's friends
joined us. I didn't like them, hardly any of them,
especially the women. And some of the men were
absolutely scary. You know, the extreme kinky
kind you run into every once in a while at clubs
and singles bars."

Allie knew, from her early days in Manhattan.
She never wanted to revisit that scene. But now,
thanks to Hedra, it had left its dim and boozy con-
fines and visited her on a sunny street, bringing
with it its own sleaziness and darkness.

"Anyway," Hedra said, "we went to this one guy's
apartment and drank and talked, and one of the
geeky women suggested group sex. Just got up
and took off her blouse, danced around, and said
something about us all doing some dope and having some *real* fun."

"And what'd you do?"

"Well, for God's sake, Allie, I got outta there!
Soon as I saw that, I was history."

"What about Brad?"

Hedra frowned and bit her lip. "He stayed."
Anger reddened her cheeks, brought out pinched
white patches around her nose and the corners of
her lips. "I never want to see him again, Allie! No
matter what he does. He's not anything like he
pretended to be."

Wolves in sheep's clothing, Allie thought, mon-
sters in people's flesh. Terror shot through her. "It
might have been more than coincidence that I was
approached by that weirdo so close to the Cody.

Did you tell any of these people your—my address?"

"I didn't think so, but I might have. I don't remember a lot of that night clearly; I was . . . I'd drunk more'n I should have."

"Had you been taking pills?"

"No, no, not pills or any other kinda dope. 'Cept for liquor. And only mixed drinks, that's all. But a crowd like that, maybe somebody put something in one of my drinks. Maybe somebody'd doctored the drinks of the girl who started dancing topless. She wasn't acting quite normal. Her eyes were funny. I dunno, bunch of sickos get together that way . . ."

Allie described the man who'd approached her on Amsterdam and West 74th, then she asked Hedra if he'd been one of the group of Brad's friends.

"Yeah, I think so. I remember him because he was so thin, and he had this nasty kinda leer and kooky eyes. He kept looking at me like he could see through my clothes."

My clothes, Allie thought. But what difference did that make? "Remember his name?"

"Carl something, I think. I'm not sure. It's hazy." Hedra suddenly looked horrified. "Allie, you *do* believe me, don't you?"

Allie wanted to believe, and did believe at least enough to feel the relief of having some explanation about her encounter with the pervert on the street corner, who for Christ's sake had known her name. It was easier to believe than to doubt, and what Allie was hearing was damning enough, so there was no reason for Hedra to lie. Besides,

Hedra had this Calvinistic compulsion to confess, to purify herself. Truth in her would work to the surface like a splinter in a festering wound. Allie was so tired, so worn down. God, all she wanted to do now was sleep, secure in her understanding of what had happened.

Softly, she said, "Of course I believe you."

Hedra approached and laid her trembling hand on Allie's shoulder. No, not Hedra trembling. Allie realized *she* was trembling; Hedra's hand was steady. Hedra, wearing a sapphire ring given to Allie by an old boyfriend in college. "I'll stay away from that place and those kinda people, Allie."

"I know you will."

"There'll be no more encounters like today, no more nasty phone calls. Not if I can help it."

"Why, that's right," Allie said. "That explains the obscene phone calls, too."

"Sure it does." Hedra's hand caressed and petted. "Everything's gonna turn out okay, Allie, believe me. We'll go out for breakfast tomorrow morning before I leave for work. At that deli down the street. All right?"

Hedra comforting Allie, calling the shots.

"All right," Allie heard herself say. Through her weariness she realized that things weren't the same. An important balance had shifted.

Somehow, inexorably, Allie had become weaker and it was Hedra who'd come to dominate their relationship. Mimicking Allie. Dressing like her. Sometimes even wearing Allie's clothes. *Becoming* Allie Jones. A strong Allie Jones.

Imitation was the sincerest form of flattery,

Allie had often heard. But this was, in some strange way, more than mere imitation. It made her think of that old science-fiction movie *Invasion of the Body Snatchers*.

Allie didn't care. Not right now. Maybe in the morning.

Maybe.

Now, tonight, she was tired and wanted only the sweet oblivion of sleep. The bliss of total surrender.

Hedra said, "I think you should go to your room and lie down, Allie."

Allie went.

20

Allie slept deeply until the next morning. The clock radio blared and yanked her awake at eight o'clock. Mick Jagger and the Rolling Stones blasting about spending just another night with somebody. Somehow the volume of the radio had been turned up. The Stones might as well have been wailing and gyrating right alongside the bed, Mick jackknifed at the waist to lean insolently over Allie and scream in her ear.

Allie suddenly remembered one of the few responses to the résumés she'd sent out. She had an appointment for a job interview this morning. Not a very promising appointment, but nonetheless a straw to grasp.

She scooted over, reached out, and slapped the plastic button on the side of the clock radio. In the buzzing silence that followed, she lay motionless and let herself gradually wake up.

Her mind reached complete wakefulness before her body. Did she really want to get dressed and be interviewed for a job she most likely wouldn't get? Of course she did, she tried to convince herself. After all, wasn't that the reason she'd sent out résumés? Her legs were ignoring this internal debate; they felt too heavy and comfortable to move. The rectangle of sunlight lying over them seemed to have the warmth and solidity of a lead-lined blanket. Another fifteen minutes of rest won't matter, urged a deep, persistent part of her brain.

Her mind drifted, went blank.

An explosion of sound caused her body to levitate off the mattress.

But almost immediately her pounding heartbeat slowed. She'd pressed the snooze button by mistake and the Stones were back in the bedroom. That got her up in a hurry and she switched off the clock radio. She was a Stones fan, but she wanted no truck with them at eight A.M.

She noticed a sheet of yellow paper, a Post-it, stuck to the top of the radio. At first she thought it was her own handwriting, a reminder she'd left for herself. Then she squinted and read:

> *Sorry, I didn't have time for breakfast—had to leave for work. Decided you needed sleep anyway.*
> > *Love,*
> > *Hedra*

Allie peeled the note off the radio, wadded it, and tossed it aside. She'd allowed herself plenty of time to make her ten o'clock appointment. After taking a shower, then blow-drying and combing her hair, she stood in front of her closet and chose a subdued blue skirt, navy-blue high heels, and a white blouse to wear for the interview.

When she was dressed, she glanced out the window at the gray morning and saw that it was raining. Not heavily, but with a gloomy regularity that suggested it might rain for the next twenty years, and certainly it was coming down hard enough to make a wreck of her hair. She clattered to the entry hall in her high heels and checked to see if there was an umbrella there.

No umbrella. And her blue coat she'd intended to wear—the one Hedra favored—was gone.

Maybe coat and umbrella were in Hedra's closet.

Allie went to Hedra's bedroom door and knocked lightly, to be sure the unpredictable Hedra hadn't returned.

No sound. No sign of life inside.

She eased the door open and saw that the bed was made. Its white spread was smooth and pristine as layered icing on a great rectangular cake. She turned away, walked down the hall, and peered again into living room.

She noticed that the lamp near the sofa was glowing feebly in the morning light. Had Hedra left before daybreak, or had she simply forgotten the lamp last night? Maybe she'd stayed up all night, hadn't slept. Well, she was a big girl, and what she did with her time was none of Allie's business.

Allie still didn't want her hairdo destroyed.

She *tap-tap-tapped* on her high heels back into Hedra's bedroom and stared at the smooth expanse of bedspread. She'd never seen a bed that looked *so* unslept in, as if it were a display in a department store window.

Allie opened Hedra's closet door and there were the familiar clothes that Hedra, and not Allie, had worn lately. A sachet gave the closet a fresh scent of sun and flowers despite the rain outside.

The blue coat wasn't there. Neither was an umbrella.

Allie's attention snagged on something else, though. There were three cardboard shoeboxes on the closet shelf. She told herself that one of them might hold a collapsible umbrella, but she knew she really was simply curious about what the boxes contained.

She got them down from the shelf one by one and opened them, moving slowly and methodically, listening; she knew it wasn't unusual for Hedra to come home unexpectedly any time of day or night.

The first box contained only a few pieces of inexpensive jewelry. It looked familiar to Allie, and she realized the pieces were near or exact duplicates of jewelry she herself owned. Some of it, she was sure, was her jewelry, such as the gold chain Sam had given her for her last birthday. It had a very distinctive link pattern; Allie was sure Hedra wouldn't have been able to find a duplicate.

The second box held nothing but folded tissue paper, and beneath it some old newspaper clippings. Allie glanced at the top clipping. It was a recipe for blueberry cobbler. That struck her as odd; she hadn't figured Hedra for someone who liked to spend time in the kitchen. The clipping slipped from her fingers and fluttered to the floor.

When she picked it up she noticed that on the back of the recipe was a grisly news item about the discovery of a dismembered murder victim.

When she opened the third box, Allie stood staring at what was inside.

A blond wig. Exactly the shade of her hair. She gingerly drew it from the box and held it up. Then she moved over so she was in front of the mirror. She raised the wig slightly so it was at the level of her head. The wig was tangled and needed to be combed out, but it was cut precisely in the style in which she wore her hair. Something about seeing it reflected next to her own hair made her shiver.

She sat down on the edge of the mattress. She glanced at Hedra's dresser. The cosmetics lined before the mirror were almost exact duplicates of those on Allie's dresser. Lying near an eyebrow pencil that was her shade were either Allie's purple-tinted sunglasses or glasses just like them.

"Jesus!" Allie said softly. Her own voice startled her.

She got up, reached for the end shoebox, and placed the wig inside. She stared at the mass of blond hair again. Looking at it caused something icy to wriggle up her spine. It was so much like a part of her image in the mirror, like a part of *her.* This was too much, *too much!*

Then Allie saw the time on the clock radio that was like hers. Nine-fifteen. She had to hurry if she was going to be on time for her interview.

She looked again at the wig in the box and put the lid on gently, as if there were a fragile creature inside that she feared injuring. Then she placed the box next to the other two again on the shelf, in precisely the position it had been in when she'd first discovered it.

Disregarding the rain, she hurried from the Cody Arms and managed to hail a cab at the corner.

As she stepped over an oily dark puddle to enter the cab, she decided it was time to ask Hedra to move out of the apartment.

Sam could move back in. He was due back from L.A. on the red-eye flight, which had probably already landed, and he wasn't working today. He'd cab in from LaGuardia and soon be in his room at the Atherton. When she finished with her interview, she'd go to the hotel and talk to him.

21

Allie walked away from the interview without any special feeling that the job was hers. They would call and let her know, Mrs. Quinette, an assistant administrator, had told her. *Don't call us.* Allie figured the odds were long that she'd be given a chance, especially after they checked her references and came across whatever poison Mike Mayfair had spread. There was no hiding in the world of computers. But at least she'd tried, taken some control of her life again. It was a partial revival of the spirit. A start.

As was her decision to tell Hedra she must move out.

The rain had stopped and patterns of sunlight lay in stark planes and angles on the buildings. Allie felt so good she rode the subway beyond Times Square and walked several blocks to the Atherton to see Sam.

Sam stood before the full-length mirror mounted on the closet door and adjusted his sport

coat so it hung evenly on his thin frame. Posing at
a slight angle, he glanced quickly at himself, as if
he might catch his reflection by surprise with a
button undone or a shoelace untied. No chance.
He'd been surprised too often lately not to be on
guard, surprised even by himself and his emotions.

He turned from the mirror and looked around
the new, smaller suite he'd been given at the
Atherton. It was hardly more than a large room
with an anteroom and extra closet. But the paint
was fresh, the gray carpet was new, and it was an inside, quiet room away from the street. The only
sound now was that of a TV or radio, constant patter seeping faintly through the old thick wall from
the next room. It sounded like a game show, but
the voices were so indistinct he couldn't even be
sure of that.

Sam had done brokerage business with one of
the suppliers of the Atherton, Bram Bolton, for
years, and a little special treatment on commodity
information for Bolton had prompted the man to
put in a word for Sam. Shortly thereafter, Sam had
been told he could move out of his ninth-floor
room, which needed decorating, and into this
one, at a rate reduced to the point where it was
cheaper than rent for an apartment. He was the
conduit for what Bolton and Mellers, the Atherton's assistant manager, thought to be inside market information, so it was an arrangement that
worked beautifully. A phone call here and there
concerning news as soon as it came over the broad
tape, and all three parties were happy. Nothing
there for the SEC to complain about, either; if

Bolton and Mellers assumed they were getting inside information, that was their business.

For an uncomfortable moment Sam thought about Ivan Boesky, the convicted Wall Street manipulator who'd placed profit before ethics. But this was quite different, Sam thought. There was nothing illegal here, and it was very small-time. The motive was a better hotel room in a city where living space was precious, but this wasn't exactly the Helmsley Palace.

There was a knock on the door. He had to leave soon for a lunch date, and he didn't want to get mixed up in a long conversation with Mellers. He considered not going to the door, then decided that was silly. Mellers might see him leave the hotel later.

He crossed the room and opened the door.

Allie. She was dressed up, wearing a blue dress and high heels. He thought she looked especially beautiful in blue.

She stepped into his embrace and clung to him, then kissed him on the lips. He bent her backward with the strength of his arms, then removed his mouth from hers. He gently massaged the nape of her neck.

She said, "Surprised to see me?"

He grinned. "A bit, but it's a pleasant surprise." He stepped back and made room for her to come in.

"Miss me?" she asked.

"Do bears miss honey?"

She stood in the center of the room and looked around. "They told me down at the desk you'd switched rooms." She peered over his shoulder. "This one looks better. Not that it matters."

He studied her. There was something new in her eyes. A bright pinpoint of light he didn't understand. "Why doesn't it matter?"

She drew a deep breath and said, "I'm going to tell Hedra she has to move out."

Sam was surprised. "Why?"

"The other day a man mistook me for her on the street. He stopped me and came on sexually, then got mad when I didn't respond."

"He propositioned you?"

"No, he reminded me of a conversation we were supposed to have had about a proposed . . . sexual experience. Kinky sex, suggested by me."

"And you think it was actually Hedra who talked to him?"

"Sam, I know it was."

Sam couldn't conceal his confusion. "Well, Hedra's allowed a social life."

"Some social life. It turns out she's mixed up with this wild crowd down in the Village, doing drugs, I'm sure. And she's been using my identity. Even wearing some of my clothes. *Being me* in a way that scares the hell out of me."

He went to her and held her close, liking the warm length of her body pressing against his own. "It can't be as bad as all that," he told her.

"I looked in her closet today, trying to find some of my clothes. She's got a wig in a box on the top shelf. It looks exactly like my hair, Sam. When I say she's using my identity, it's more than simply using my name. It's . . . like she's stolen my life."

"You went to the police about the obscene calls," Sam said. "Have you told them about this?"

"No, I don't see how it's a police matter, even though it does explain the phone calls. I really don't care what Hedra does as long as she stops being me. That's why I'm going to tell her our living arrangement's over. I want to make her life none of my business, and mine none of hers."

"She'll think you're doing it so I can move in," Sam said.

Allie smiled. "I suppose that might even be part of it, but so what?"

He stepped back and cupped her face in his long hands. "Your mind's made up?"

"Uh-huh. And I won't change it."

"Okay, but I think we better wait a few days before I move in. I made a commitment on this suite that's more than a deal with a hotel. The manager's a client of mine, heavily into blue-chip stocks. I've gotta take this one slow."

She looked puzzled for a moment. Disappointed. Then she said, "All right, Sam."

He leaned down and kissed her forehead, somewhat ashamed of his influence on her. "It's only a couple of days. You understand, don't you?"

"Sure." She gave him an up-and-down look. "You look nice. On your way somewhere?"

"Lunch with a bond client who's big on tax-free mutual funds." He glanced at his watch. "He's supposed to meet me here any minute, in fact."

She took the hint. Moved close to him and kissed him lightly on the lips. He ran the backs of his knuckles lightly down her cheek. He said, "Call me tonight and let me know how things work out."

"Will you come over later?"

"I can't. Dinner with the same client. He and his wife are in town from Omaha. They're going back tomorrow morning, so there won't be any other opportunity to wine and dine them seriously for Elcane-Smith." He shrugged and shook his head. "Business. I'm sorry, Allie. Really."

"There'll be plenty of time for us," she said. She kissed him on the lips and went out, giving him a backward glance full of promise. The apartment would be their own exclusive playpen again. Like a couple of teenagers alone in Mom and Dad's house. Allie, Allie.

As she stepped off the elevator into the Atherton lobby, Allie stopped and stood still for a second.

A sweet, familiar scent, but one she couldn't quite place, floated on the air like a memory.

Then she realized it was a perfume she often wore. Someone wearing the same scent had just passed, or stepped into the other elevator to go up.

She walked on through the narrow lobby and exited on West 44th Street.

22

Hedra had taken the news of her eviction with surprising calm. A tremor of her lower lip, a brief and oddly different cast to her eyes. That was all.

She'd told Allie she understood and she'd move out the next day, which astounded Allie. How could Hedra have someplace to go on such short notice? In New York?

The next morning the phone woke Allie. She lay for a few seconds, listening. Between rings she could hear Hedra moving around in the apartment, gathering her possessions.

The phone was relentless, sending chilling, vibrating knives into her brain. She groaned and shot a painful glance at the clock; God, there was sand under her eyelids! A few minutes till nine. Allie wrapped the pillow around her head to deaden the shrillness of the persistent phone. She waited. Wasn't Hedra going to answer it?

Finally she realized Hedra was going to ignore the phone; she was moving out, after all, and she received very few calls anyway.

Allie released the pillow, scooted to the cold side of the bed, and dragged the receiver over to her. Each ring of the phone was like an electric shock; she didn't want a headache this morning.

For a panicky moment she suspected another obscene call. Then she realized the odds were against it at nine in the morning. There was a time for everything under the heavens—even sexual perverts. Nine A.M. wasn't it. She blinked at the brilliant slanting light and said, "Hello," in a strained, husky voice.

"Miss Allison Jones?"

Allie cleared her throat. She said yes, she was.

"Detective Kennedy here. Remember me?"

She sat up straighter in bed, her back against the pillow and headboard, and tried to focus her sleep-fogged mind. She felt a wary elation. "You found the credit cards?"

Kennedy laughed gently. "No, I'm afraid not. It's not actually the missing cards I'm calling about. I wondered if you'd received any more obscene phone calls."

"Since I've talked to you, not really." There was no point in stirring up the law; Hedra was the reason for the calls, and she was moving out. Allie briefly considered telling Kennedy about the man accosting her on the street, but there was an explanation for that, too. Hedra. Allie didn't want to get Hedra in serious trouble; that would only prolong the mingling of their lives. It was hardly wise to make any of this police business.

"Good," Kennedy said. "I thought we might need to put a tap on your line, find out who the weirdo is. But if he's not bothering you anymore, I guess that won't be necessary."

"Guess not," Allie agreed.

After a pause, Kennedy said, "You okay, Miss Jones?"

"Uh, sure. Why?"

"You sound . . . I dunno, different from when you were here at the station. A little depressed or something. You want me to come over there and we can talk?"

God, I must sound terrible, Allie thought. Or maybe Kennedy was simply doing his job and following up on a complaint, serving the public. She said, "It's because I just woke up."

"Ah. The phone wake you?"

"Yeah, but that's okay. I'm glad you called. Glad you cared enough to take the trouble."

"Like I said, usually an obscene phone call doesn't develop into any worse problem. On the other hand, it doesn't hurt to take precautions. You did the right thing in coming to the police, dear."

"I know I did. Thanks."

"You sure you're all right?"

"Sure."

"Okay. Any more calls like before, though, and you contact me personally. That a deal?"

"It's a deal."

"Sorry I woke you."

"That's okay, I had to get up anyway. You were my alarm clock." She tried to put some airy brightness in her voice, like a TV game-show contestant, to show Kennedy she was just fine. "Bye, Sergeant. Thanks again for calling." *It was fun even though I lost.*

He told her good-bye and hung up. The broken connection crackled in her hear.

Allie stretched out her arm and replaced the receiver.

After lying there motionless for about fifteen minutes, listening to Hedra scraping and thunking things around in the apartment, she got up, put on her robe, and left the bedroom. The floor was ice against her bare feet.

In the living room, Hedra had just set down a cardboard box of paperback novels by the door. Dust was stirring in the air from her activity; it tickled Allie's nose and almost made her sneeze. Hedra glanced at her and didn't change expressions. She said, "A cab's on the way. I'll have everything outta here by tonight."

Allie was suddenly ill at ease. She didn't know what to say to Hedra. She felt guilty and hated herself for it. Finally she decided to make small talk to hold back the silence. "You had breakfast?"

"Coffee and a couple of Danish," Hedra said. "I went out and brought it back from the deli. There's some left in the kitchen, if you want it."

"Thanks."

Hedra didn't answer. She walked back to her bedroom and returned with an armload of clothes from the closet. Then she draped them over the arm of a chair. Allie couldn't help thinking the pile of clothes looked as if they were from *her* closet. Clothes aren't really as personal as we think, or as distinctive or recognizable. Thousands of this, thousands of that, often tens of thousands, sewn on assembly lines. Unless you were into Paris originals, everyone's basic black dress was like someone else's.

Allie said, "You still working at that place over on Fifth Avenue?"

"Yeah, I'll be there awhile longer," Hedra said. Allie wasn't sure she believed her, but Hedra was getting money from somewhere. Maybe she dealt dope; Allie wouldn't be surprised. Not anymore.

Hedra put down her clock radio on the pile of clothes and looked at Allie. "If you don't mind my asking, how do you plan on making the rent here alone?"

"I won't be alone," Allie told her. "Sam's going to move back in."

Hedra nodded. "I kinda thought so."

There were three firm knocks on the door.

Hedra and Allie exchanged glances. Hedra said, "I'll stand over where I can't be seen. No point in giving ourselves away as roommates this late in the game."

Allie thanked her again. She waited until Hedra had stepped around a corner. Then she yanked the sash of her robe tighter around her waist, walked to the door, and opened it.

Graham Knox stood in the hall.

He had on impossibly baggy pleated black slacks, and his woolly gray sweater with the leather elbow patches. He was so thin he looked lost as a child inside his clothes. His unruly hair was damp and combed more neatly than usual, and he was sporting his lopsided grin. Graham was so obviously glad to see Allie that she felt cheered just looking at him.

She moved in close to the partly opened door and stood so he couldn't see Hedra's possessions piled nearby.

He said, "I thought I better drop by and explain about the tickets."

"Tickets?"

His face sagged like a sad clown's, then lifted again to hide his hurt. "You know, my play . . ."

Allie had forgotten he'd promised her free tickets. To . . . what was it, *Dance* something? "Of course," she said. "I've been waiting, wondering."

She was sure she hadn't fooled him, but he obviously appreciated her effort and forgave her. He held out two tickets he'd been squeezing in his right hand. Allie accepted them. They were damp from his perspiration and faintly warm. They felt good between her fingers; a friend's gift that meant something and required nothing in return other than her presence.

"They're center orchestra seats for the third performance. By then most of the kinks should be ironed out and the play should go smoothly. I want you and Hedra to see it at its best."

Without thinking about it, Allie tilted forward on her toes and gave him a peck on the cheek. It surprised him and surprised her. "Thanks, Graham. Really. I'll be there. I doubt if Hedra can make it, though."

He was grinning almost maniacally. "If you have to come alone, that's okay. Maybe we can go out for some coffee or something after the performance."

"Maybe," Allie said. He'd read something into that innocent kiss on the cheek. Too bad. "I'll be there either way, Graham."

Inside his baggy clothes, he shifted his weight awkwardly from one leg to the other; he wasn't a graceful man like Sam. Dear Sam. "I better go down to Goya's," Graham said.

"Okay. See you."

"Drop in sometime when things slow down after the lunch rush. We can talk."

"I'll do that. Bye, Graham." She eased the door closed and heard his faint, retreating footsteps outside in the hall.

When she turned from the door, she found that Hedra had moved back into the living room and was glaring at her. There was an irrational kind of fierceness in her stare that frightened Allie. Hedra had gone into the kitchen and was holding half of a cheese Danish that had become mush in her clenched fist. "He mentioned my name."

Allie said, "He lives upstairs. He knows we share—shared—the apartment."

"You *told* him?"

"No, he saw us together and overheard us talking in the hall one day. He guessed."

Hedra suddenly noticed she'd mutilated the rest of the Danish. She went into the kitchen to throw it away. Water ran in the sink as she rinsed off her fingers. When she returned she seemed calmer. "So who is this guy?"

"His name's Graham Knox. He's a playwright. That was what he wanted to see me about, to give us two free tickets to the off-Broadway production of his play. I told him some time back that I'd go."

"You meet him often at Goya's?" *What about Sam?* was in Hedra's eyes.

"He's a waiter there, Hedra. For God's sake, he's just a casual acquaintance."

"But he knows about me being here."

"He won't tell anyone. He's promised. Besides, what difference does it make now?"

"None, I suppose. But do you believe him? I mean, his promise?"

"Yes, I do. Besides, he's got no reason to inform on us. He's no friend of the Cody's management."

"But what if he tells someone else? I mean, like one of the other tenants?"

Allie couldn't understand this. "Hedra, why do you care? You're moving out."

"I care because I don't wanna be tracked down by Haller-Davis and told I owe back rent."

"I doubt if they'd do that." But Allie wasn't sure.

"They might, if this Graham guy tells the wrong person."

"He won't. He's promised about that, too. He told me he might need a roommate himself one of these days." Allie was getting irritated with Hedra's intense concern over Graham when it wasn't necessary. "Playwrights and part-time waiters aren't exactly high-income bracket; he understands the arrangement we had and he approves of it."

Hedra seemed to think about that. Finally she nodded. "Yeah, I guess I'm getting excited over nothing." She smoothed her skirt and walked to the window, then gazed down into the street. "Anyway, it's not life or death."

Her body straightened and she turned away from the window, starkly silhouetted for a moment in the morning light. "My cab just pulled up downstairs."

"Want me to throw on some clothes and help you carry this stuff down?" Allie asked.

"Why not?" Hedra said.

Allie made three trips with her and loaded the backseat and the trunk of the cab. Hedra said she'd be back that afternoon for the rest of her things, then slid into the taxi's front seat alongside the driver. "Good luck, Allie."

Allie suddenly felt as if she were betraying the trust of a helpless puppy; she told herself Hedra knew how to pull people's strings, change their perceptions of her almost minute to minute. "Luck to you too, Hedra. I'm sorry it didn't work out."

"It did for a while," Hedra said with a flicker of a smile. She closed the door and waited for Allie to move away before telling the driver her destination. As the cab pulled away, she didn't look back.

When the cab had been swallowed in traffic, Allie went back upstairs to the apartment.

She ate the Danish Hedra had left and drank a cup of coffee. Then she used the TV's remote to tune in *Donahue* and curled up on the sofa. The program was about unreasonable ordinances in the suburbs, laws that said you couldn't leave your trash can at the curb overnight. Or kiss in public. Or let your cat go outside without a leash and collar. That kind of thing. Donahue was outraged, stalking through the audience with his microphone and wobbling his head. Seeking soul mates or conflict.

It didn't interest or concern Allie in the slightest, but she watched it anyway. It was something on which to fix vague attention while she blotted out what was happening in the suburbs of her mind.

23

Two days later Sam was living in the apartment. Their world within the four walls fell into place as if time hadn't passed and Hedra hadn't moved through Allie's life. The first night seemed to Allie a fresh start almost from before the nighttime phone call that had prompted their first argument and Sam's leaving. The crushing, painful call that had caused her to place the classified ad that had drawn Hedra to her.

Sam was across the breakfast table from her again, hurriedly dressed for work and spooning diet yogurt into the mouth that she loved, that had been on her last night.

Allie had found part-time work as a computer programmer for a small camera store on Sixth Avenue. She was busy during the day setting up a program that would keep a running inventory on thousands of lenses, filters, and accessories. She hadn't realized there were so many ways for a professional photographer to change and shape what appeared in the viewfinder, so many ways to bend reality to a purpose.

She'd finished her coffee and was about to leave with Sam. An old sensation was back; it gave her a secret thrill, the way they were lovers inside the apartment but had to act like strangers the minute they stepped out into the hall. Was that the sort of emotion that might disappear with marriage?

He'd stood up and was shrugging into his suit coat. He scooped up his attaché case. Prince of commerce in a hurry. She smiled and placed a hand on his chest to stop him, then kissed him on the lips. She didn't mind the taste of yogurt.

"What brought that on?" he asked.

"I love you. I'm happy. I want you to know."

He gave her a quick hug. "I'm happy, too, Allie, but neither of us'll be quite as happy if I'm unemployed."

"You leave first," she said.

He nodded, then opened the door to the hall and glanced in both directions. He blew her a kiss and stepped outside and closed the door, all in one nimble, graceful motion.

Allie counted to fifty, listening to the humming silence of the apartment, then followed.

By the time she reached the lobby, he was nowhere in sight.

A shipment of Nikon accessories hadn't arrived at the camera shop that morning as scheduled, and the shop's owners, two implacable brothers of Iranian descent, gave Allie the afternoon off rather than pay her for doing drone work.

The weather was glorious, so she walked up to Central Park, past the lineup of bored and patient horses waiting to pull tourists in carriages along the congested streets. She entered the park and sat in quiet coolness on a hard concrete bench near the lake. Beyond the trees she could see the reach of skyscrapers, the newer ones with squared-off tops that seemed to flatten against the sky, the older ones piercing the blue like needles, or curving gracefully in Art Deco elegance. A trio of young men pedaled past on the new, thick-tired bicycles known as mountain bikes. Chains clinked against metal guards, and gears ticked and whirred in the quiet afternoon. On the grassy slope near the lake, a man and a woman lay on a blanket with their heads close together, talking. The woman had red hair and was rather stout. The man looked younger and was wearing a white shirt and red tie. A business type, like Sam. Every once in a while the woman would laugh and grab the tie and flick it in his face. The musical sound of her laughter floated on the bright, clear air. Allie watched them for a while, thinking about Sam and the way the fragments of their shattered lives had so seamlessly fit back together.

The breeze picked up and carried exhaust fumes from nearby Central Park South into the park, reminding Allie that she'd been sitting for almost an hour and her world waited just beyond the trees.

She surrendered the park to pigeons, dope dealers, the homeless, cyclists, joggers, and lovers, and got up and walked back to the street. Vital and diverse New York, she decided, maybe wasn't such a heartless place after all.

If she and Sam were frugal, money should be no problem. She rode a subway instead of a cab back to West 74th. As she walked past Goya's toward the Cody Arms, she peered in the window but didn't see Graham Knox.

When she entered the apartment, the living room window was open and a cool breeze was sluicing through. Allie didn't remember leaving the window raised but was glad that she had. She slipped off her high-heeled shoes, sat down in the wing chair, and massaged her feet. Concrete against flesh, separated only by a thin slice of leather, could take its toll. She was getting a blister on the bottom of her left big toe. A bandage wouldn't be a bad idea.

She stood up and padded barefoot toward the bathroom, limping slightly and carrying her shoes.

She was five feet from her closed bedroom door when she heard a noise. A soft creaking sound. Then another.

Another.

A rhythm old as time.

Her heart expanded painfully in her chest. Her throat tried to close, and she was having difficulty breathing.

Silently, she edged forward.

She heard a soft, regular moaning. What she'd known in the back of her mind leaped like something uncaged to the front. She stepped forward and pushed open the door.

They were on the still-made bed, both of them nude. Hedra was straddling Sam, her hands propped on her hips. Only Allie didn't know at first that it *was* Hedra.

It was the wig. Hedra was wearing the blond Allie wig.

She and Sam were both perspiring and Hedra was grinning down at him with an intense expression though her eyes were half-closed. So preoccupied were they that they didn't notice Allie at first.

Then Hedra sensed something. She stopped grinning, stopped the rising and falling contortions of her glistening body, and turned toward her.

A needle of fear penetrated Allie's shock and rage. Hedra stared insolently at her as if Allie didn't belong there. As if Allie were trespassing in her own apartment.

Sam had seen Allie now and was staring at her dumbstruck with his mouth hanging open.

Hedra glanced down at him, then back at Allie. She was grinning again. She said, "Oh, hi, Allie."

When they were both gone, Allie sat paralyzed on the sofa. The breeze crept in through the open window and rippled coolly around her bare feet like chilled water. Hedra and Sam. Sam and Hedra. Oh, Jesus! She knew she shouldn't be surprised. Some far corner of her consciousness had known but hadn't admitted the possibility that her lover and former roommate were deceiving her. If Hedra—sick, conspiring Hedra—envied everything else about Allie, why *wouldn't* she want Sam? It was logical, insofar as logic could be applied to Hedra, but Allie simply hadn't wanted to believe it.

This . . . abomination, this *unfairness,* was sinking in, altering her world forever. The hum of traffic from outside grew louder and became a continuous roar, blotting out all rational thought. A beast devouring her mind.

Hedra had everything she wanted from Allie now. The rape and destruction were complete.

Oh, hi, Allie.

Allie dug her fingertips into her temples, harder and harder, wishing she could penetrate her skull and her mind and rip from them like raw matter the pain of what had happened to her.

The telephone rang.

She sat listened to it for a long time, then lifted the receiver and touched the hard, cool plastic to her ear. She didn't say anything.

A man's voice said, "Allie? Allie? Hey, Sweet Buns, it's me. Remember? Hey, I know you're there."

She lowered the receiver slowly, letting it clatter back into its cradle. She sat staring at the wall, wondering who she was, and what she had done.

24

That night, Sam described Allie's visit at the Atherton. It seemed the only way he could stop thinking about it; share it so it was halved. He knew that, with Allie, the final corner had been turned.

All the while he was talking, Hedra lay beside him in his bed in the Atherton suite. They'd made love. The room was totally dark and still smelled from their coupling. Hedra was smoking a cigarette, invisible to Sam except for the glowing red ember that now and then brightened like a beacon aimed his way, a warning to ships on a dark sea.

Hedra said, "Allie's imagination must have been rolling in high gear. Actually, I did use her name, but it was no big deal. It came to mind when some guy was getting too friendly and I didn't wanna give him my own name. He caught me off guard or I'd have given him the name of my third-grade teacher or somebody like that. The drug stuff is pure imagination. Unless . . .

"Unless what?"

"I offered Allie some tranquilizers once. She was almost bonkers after losing her job. Maybe that put the idea of me and drugs in her mind." Hedra drew on the cigarette, making its ember flare angry red in the darkness. " 'Nother thing. A couple of times I dissolved tranquilizers in her coffee or hot chocolate without her knowing it."

"You *what?*"

"Nothing strong, Sam, just some old prescription medicine. Now, don't get so excited. I did it for her own good. And tell you the truth, so I could live with the crazy bi—no, I shouldn't say that. She's under a strain. She's got this hands-off thing about any kind of drug, and I just wanted to help her through the rough times, till she could feel better on her own." Sam heard Hedra shift her body so she was lying on her side, facing him. He felt the mattress depress. She was still perspiring; he could feel the heat emanating from her. "I did it because I'm her friend, Sam."

A tangle of thoughts spun through his mind. He couldn't help asking, "Is that why you're here with me? Because of Allie?"

She was silent for a moment. He saw her cigarette flare. Heard her exhale and smelled the smoke. "I don't think so. What about you? Is it Allie you're really sleeping with?"

He was silent. He couldn't see her in the darkness, but he knew she was wearing the wig. *God! What kind of twisted creature have I become?*

"Never mind," she said. "Some things it's better not to think about, and we don't have to think about them, do we?"

"No," he said, "we don't. But it's eerie, what's

happened. Sometimes the way you talk even when we're *not* in bed, the way you dress, or motion with your hand or tilt your head, it's . . . well, so damned strange."

"Face it, the real thing turned out not to be the real thing. You regret this, Sam? Me and you?"

"Not at all." Was that a lie? he wondered. Maybe so, but what was the point of regretting what you couldn't change or resist? What was the use of hating a weakness in yourself if you knew you couldn't overcome it?

"Listen, I don't have to be here if you don't want me."

He thought about her not being with him and didn't like the idea. When he and Hedra were in the same room, it was as if each of them had swallowed half of a powerful magnet. He had to be near her, to touch her. Once he'd allowed their affair to start, he was caught up in a force ponderous and irresistible. Whatever he still felt for Allie was dwarfed and crushed before it.

The real thing turned out not to be the real thing.

"Believe it," he said, "I want you here."

He felt her hand glide down to his pubic hair and caress his penis. She did something quick and rhythmic with her fingers and immediately, almost against his will, he had an erection. He was struck again by the contrast between the Hedra he'd first met and this woman. In the dark, she was somebody else. Somebody else . . .

He heard a fizzing, sputtering sound, as with her other hand she dropped her cigarette in her glass with melted ice in it by the bed.

In an amused voice she said, "Another dead soldier," and climbed on top of him.

Allie almost lacked the willpower to climb out of bed in the morning. Sometimes she wondered what it would be like to "take to her bed and die" like the heart-stricken Victorian women in romantic novels. Self-pity, something she'd always despised in others, had attached to her like a parasite and wouldn't be dislodged by reason.

She had dreamed of Sam and Hedra, of them making love in *her* bed, where she and Sam had lain together. She heard their groans, the rocking and banging of the headboard. The keening of the bedsprings mingled with their own subdued moans. In the dream she tried to block it from her hearing, drifting to the window and staring out at the universe beyond the glass. She pretended what was going on in the bedroom wasn't happening. Couldn't be happening. But the relentless rhythm of their lovemaking was persistent, and she couldn't deny the extent to which Hedra had taken over her life, as the sounds coming from the bedroom crashed into her tortured mind. *My bed! Bed! Bed! Bed!*

When she awoke she thought she heard Sam singing in the shower, as he often did. Water gushed through the plumbing in the old walls, nearly drowning out his voice. "I'm takin' the A-Train," he was singing, giving it an exaggerated jazzy glide. For an instant there was nothing wrong in Allie's life and her dream had been a cruel fluke that had nothing to do with reality.

For an instant. Before she was entirely awake.

Then her depression wrapped itself around her. She had to use all her will to struggle out of bed, even though she had to relieve herself so badly she couldn't lie still. She commanded each leg to move as she plodded into the bathroom.

She didn't bother eating breakfast, opting instead for a cup of instant coffee, and it was an effort to spoon the dark granules into a cup of water heated in the microwave.

As she settled into the sofa to hold her cup with both hands and sip at the hot coffee, she was surprised to hear a knock at the door.

Even more surprised when she'd trudged to the door, opened it, and found the hall empty.

Then she glanced down and saw on the mat a long-stemmed flower on a folded sheet of white tissue paper. She stooped and picked it up. It was a dark orchid with petals the consistency of flesh. A small white card was Scotch-taped to the paper. In black felt-tip pen it read, "Thanks, Sweet Buns. Until next time."

Allie touched the thick, fleshlike petals and revulsion welled up in her. She flung the orchid on the hall floor. Then she backed into the apartment and slammed and locked the door.

25

Allie didn't leave the apartment for days. She ignored her temporary job at the camera store. The Iranian brothers must have called, she was sure, but she didn't bother answering her phone. By now they'd probably replaced her and not thought much about it. People did strange things in New York. People came and went for their own reasons, and life continued its raucous, zigzagging slide toward eternity.

She didn't call Sergeant Kennedy about the orchid and note she'd found by her door; the thought of more contact with the police repelled her. She wanted only to escape from unpleasant reality.

It scared her finally, the possibility that she was withdrawing completely from everything human, so she began to go out and take long walks, for the exercise, she told herself. But she knew it was really for the tenuous contact with people. In one way the press of Manhattan's humanity made her feel less alien, but in another it made her feel more lonely. Often she had the sensation she was invisible. Locked inside herself and invisible.

During one afternoon walk, on impulse, she stopped in at Goya's for lunch. It would help to talk to Graham; he at least thought she was real. She sat at her usual table. The restaurant was crowded with a mixture of neighborhood people, office workers on their lunch hours, and a few tourists who'd stopped to eat after wandering around the Upper West Side. The mingled, spicy scent of a kitchen going full tilt added to appetites. A grayish haze from the smoking section hovered close to the high ceiling, swirling ever so gently with the lazy rhythm of the two large and slowly rotating paddle fans. Goya's employees in black slacks and red shirts glided swiftly and efficiently among the tables, holding trays level above their heads and out of harm's way; the nonchalant balancing act of waiters and waitresses everywhere.

Allie expected Graham to appear any second, dodging tables and diners with his lanky sideways shuffle, wearing his lopsided grin and exchanging comments with regular customers. Her glance kept darting reflexively to the kitchen's swinging doors, like a reformed smoker's hand edging toward an empty pocket.

But a tall girl with wet-look red lipstick and dark hair in a frazzled French braid took Allie's order. The plastic tag pinned crookedly to her blouse said her name was Lucy. She was tentative and seemed new to the job.

"Is Graham Knox working today?" Allie asked.

"I don't think so," the girl said. "I mean, I just

started and don't know everybody yet, but the guy I think is Graham isn't in today."

Allie thanked her and watched her walk away.

Since Goya's was crowded, about twenty minutes passed before Allie's food arrived. Lucy smiled with only her glossy lips and said she was real sorry about the delay. As she placed the white plate on the table, Allie noticed her fingernails were long and painted to match her lipstick. About half the bright red nail polish had been chipped or chewed away.

Allie fell into a somber mood as she sat munching her pastrami-on-rye and sipping Diet Pepsi. A different waitress, this one middle-aged with hair going to gray, asked if she wanted her glass refilled, but Allie declined. She left immediately after finishing her sandwich.

For a long time she walked the crowded, noisy streets of the city, until her feet were sore and the spring was gone from her legs. Around her, steam rose from the sidewalk grates; the monster breathing. She sat for a while on a bench in Riverside Park before smelling rain in the air and starting for home.

The phone was ringing when she let herself into the apartment. She hadn't been using her answering machine because she dreaded having to deal with the kind of messages that might be left, so the phone kept ringing. She ignored it.

The ringing continued as she slipped off her blue blazer and draped it over the sofa arm. She sat down in the wing chair and stared at the ringing phone. She didn't move.

Finally it stopped ringing.

Allie walked into the kitchen and got a glass of water, then sat again in the wing chair and stared at the dusk closing in outside the window. The noise of the city was beginning to lessen with the advent of night and the threat of rain.

The phone began ringing again. Shrill and insistent.

It rang twenty-one times before it stopped. Someone wanted very much to talk to Allie.

Whoever it was, they kept calling back. Finally, on the third ring of the fifth call, she lifted the receiver and held it to her ear.

Hedra's voice said, "I know you're there, Allie."

"Yes, I'm here," Allie said. She wasn't even curious about why Hedra had called. Nothing about Hedra could surprise her now.

"Sam's going to be mine forever," Hedra said. "I've seen to that." Her voice sounded odd, flatter than usual yet with an undercurrent of excitement.

Allie almost laughed. "Don't try to tell me the relationship has only just been consummated."

"I wouldn't tell you that," Hedra said. "Anyway, I never liked that word 'consummated' when it was used to describe people. It sounds too much like soup, don't you think?"

Allie held her silence.

Hedra said, "Okay, crabby appleton, I know you're still on the line." A little girl's voice. Taunting. But still flat. "Listen, I didn't mean to hurt you, Allie."

"Then why did you?"

Instead of answering, Hedra said, "Are you lonely, Allie?"

"Yes," Allie said, "I'm lonely."

Hedra said, "I'm not."

"You have Sam," Allie said. "You deserve each other. You're both contemptible."

"*He's* contemptible. Otherwise he wouldn't have put his hands on both of us. He wouldn't have done what he did to us."

"He didn't do it alone, Hedra."

"He didn't *have* to do it at all, did he? What if I promised he'd never do it again?"

"I don't want your promises," Allie said. "I don't care anymore about either of you. Can't you understand that? There's no reason for us to have anything to do with each other."

"I hope you're right, Allie."

"Don't call me again, Hedra."

"I won't."

The connection broke with a click, and the empty line sighed in Allie's ear until the dial tone buzzed.

She hung up the phone and sat for a while thinking about the call, watching a large blue-bottle fly, later along in life than it thought, drone and bounce off the window, trying to escape into the drab, cool evening. The sky was darkening quickly now; it was getting dark noticeably earlier each day. Seasons changing.

What was Hedra trying to do? Why had she virtually taken over Allie's life, sapped Allie of herself and somehow *become* another Allie? She'd lived in Allie's apartment. Wore duplicate clothes, jewelry, and perfume. Sometimes wore Allie's clothes and jewelry. Used Allie's identity. Even some of her gestures and speech habits. Slept with Sam.

Envied Allie.

Had no identity of her own.

"She's ill," Allie said to the bluebottle fly. Hedra had mentioned being hospitalized as a young girl. Possibly she'd been kept in a mental institution, and she was still very, very sick. So gradually had the situation made itself evident that the seriousness of Hedra's problem had never registered on the unsuspecting Allie. Allie had misjudged the intensity of Hedra's inner fire and envy. It was clear now why she'd wanted Sam so desperately, and why she flaunted the affair in front of Allie. It was as if she were letting Allie know that now she, Hedra, had finally supplanted Allie, and Allie no longer was quite real. Allie had become the inhabitant of an empty life, the shadowy subleasing roommate in her own existence.

The terrible part was that Allie *felt* that way. She'd bought it. She'd been so involved with other problems in her life that she hadn't noticed danger creeping up from an unexpected quarter. And then it was too late.

It was Hedra, Allie realized, who must have stolen her credit cards and driver's license, so she could be Hedra *outside* the apartment as well as inside. Hedra, the thief who stole so much more than property.

Why had Hedra called tonight? What had she meant about making Sam hers forever? And why the strange tone of her voice? There'd been an odd, deranged quality to the way she'd sounded. On the other hand, why shouldn't there be? She'd certainly been behaving that way.

Allie remembered the blueberry cobbler recipe

she'd found in the shoe box in Hedra's closet, and the murder news item on its reverse side. There had been other newspaper clippings in the box, but she hadn't looked at them, assuming they were other recipes or cooking columns. But maybe the grisly homicide story on the back of the recipe didn't simply happen to be there. Maybe it was the *recipe* that happened to be on the back of the news item. Maybe the other clippings were about murders.

No, Allie told herself, don't let your imagination make a fool of you again.

But the longer she sat there, the more a kind of pressure built in her. Things Hedra had said and done over the months seemed to click into a pattern and became meaningful. Ominous. Imagination? Maybe.

Only maybe.

Allie walked to her purse and dug in it until she found the card Sergeant Kennedy had given her. Then she untangled and stretched the phone cord so she could rest the phone in her lap while she sat in the wing chair.

Listening to her own harsh breathing, she punched out the number on the card. She waited while the phone on the other end of the line rang, unconsciously twirling a lock of her hair around her left forefinger. It was a nervous habit she'd had as a teenager, and she wondered why she was doing it now. God, was she regressing? She jerked her hand away so abruptly she pulled her hair. Then she hung up the phone.

She had to give this some careful consideration before talking to Kennedy. For all she knew, her

call would result not in a quelling of her fears, but
in a uniformed officer knocking on her door
within minutes, then a ride to the precinct house,
where events would be dictated by emotionless
procedure. One phone call, and the blue genie of
police power would be out of the bottle and out of
control. The police would want something more
substantial than the anger and dread of a spurned
lover. And that was how they'd see Allie. Even
Kennedy would see her that way.

Allie thought again of the news item on the
back of the recipe clipped from the paper.

Right now, whether she liked it or not, she
cared a great deal about Sam.

She shouldn't care, but she did. And if Sam
knew what she knew about Hedra, he'd feel differently—not only about Hedra, but about Allie.
He'd *have* to feel differently.

She phoned the Atherton Hotel and asked the
desk to ring Sam's room. Then she waited while
the phone rang eight, ten times, until she was positive it wasn't going to be answered.

Allie hung up and glanced at the clock. It was
quarter past eight, but sometimes Sam worked
late. She remembered the number of Elcane-
Smith Brokerage and pecked it out with her finger
so violently she bent a nail.

Someone answered at Elcane-Smith, a harried-
sounding man who told her Sam had left at five
o'clock.

So where was Sam? Possibly on his way to meet
Hedra for dinner. Or in his room and not answering his phone. Maybe because Hedra was with him
and they were making love.

Reason left Allie. Only fear for Sam remained. Sam, who was in her blood forever.

What she really wanted most was to have him back. She didn't like knowing that about herself, so she shoved that sticky bit of knowledge to a dim corner of her mind where she could let it lie for a while before coming to terms with it. She heard again Hedra's little-girl taunt on the phone, and she understood the great truth: What we wanted, whom we needed, was wound and set like clockwork in us when we were children, infants perhaps, and after a while there could be no denial.

If Sam wasn't in his room, she'd find him no matter where he was and convince him Hedra was sick. Maybe dangerous. A woman who had no self, and who might be the collector of news stories about gruesome murders. The police would be interested. She and Sam could go to the police together and substantiate each other's stories, and Kennedy would listen. Together she and Sam could awaken from the nightmare.

She wanted to be real again. To be the only Allie Jones. *She was sure she wasn't imagining things.*

She strode to the hall closet to get her blue coat.

It wasn't there. Wearing only the blazer over her jeans and blouse, she rushed out into the cool night, risking rain.

26

In the Atherton Hotel's long, narrow lobby were a white sofa and chair in front of a large mirror and an arrangement of potted plants. Beyond them, the desk and the entrance to the adjoining coffee shop were on the left, the elevators on the right. A middle-aged Hispanic woman sat low and almost unnoticeable at the switchboard, idly plucking at a hangnail. Behind the long marble-topped desk, a tall gray-haired man was busy registering a young couple whose only luggage seemed to be the over-stuffed backpacks lying at their feet in a tangle of canvas strapping, like parachutes in case of fire.

One of the elevators was at lobby level. Its doors slid open immediately when Allie punched the UP button. She stepped in and pressed the button for the tenth floor.

On Five, the elevator stopped and an over-weight blond bellhop got in and smiled at Allie. He was carrying a clipboard under his arm and had a yellow pencil wedged behind his right ear. At Seven, he got off the elevator, and Allie was alone when it arrived at Ten.

She walked down the narrow, dimly lighted hall toward Sam's room. The carpet soaked up the sound of her steps. A TV was playing too loud in one of the rooms; the inane chatter of a game show seeped through the door as Allie passed, then was left behind in an outbreak of enthusiastic but diminishing applause. Somebody had won big. The humidity outside had inundated the hotel; the hall was cool and had a mildewed smell about it. The air was almost thick enough to feel.

The next room was 1027, Sam's room. Allie stood for a moment close to the white-enameled door. No sound came from inside.

She knocked.

No answer. Nothing.

She turned the knob and found the door was unlocked. In fact, it hadn't been closed quite all the way. Wasn't even latched.

Maybe Sam hadn't pulled it tight when he'd left to go out. He could be careless that way. Or maybe he was in the shower. Or sleeping so deeply her knocking hadn't awakened him. She prayed it was something like that, that the reason he hadn't come to the door was something innocent and explainable.

She swallowed, pushed the heavy door open, and stepped inside.

The smell that struck her was familiar, yet she couldn't quite place it. The lights were out in the room. The only illumination was from the picture rolling soundlessly on the TV near the foot of the bed; a car chase racing vertically as well as horizontally. The TV game show next door was barely audible through the wall. Sam's double bed was unmade, sheets and spread in a wild tangle.

She could see into the suite's adjoining room. It was also dark. The bathroom door was closed, but no crack of light showed beneath it.

Allie said, "Sam?"

The only answer was the muted, constant roar of traffic ten stories below, the background rush of noise that was always there and was itself a part of the city's silence and existence. A vital sign of life; steel blood coursing through concrete arteries.

Allie saw something on the floor near the television, at the foot of the bed. The flickering light from the screen had a strobelike effect and she couldn't make out what the object was.

She moved forward a few steps.

Stopped and gasped.

She wasn't seeing what she thought! It was a trick, a magician's prop!

It was a fake! Please!

But as she edged closer she knew she was looking at a hand that had been severed at the wrist.

Shaking uncontrollably, she lurched away and steadied herself on a small desk with a lamp on it. She switched on the lamp, but carefully avoided looking again at the severed hand.

She saw Sam's ankle and his black wing-tip shoe protruding from behind the bed and walked over there, staying near the wall, away from the hand. She tried not to think of the hand, lying there so still like some kind of pale, lifeless sea creature that had somehow worked its way onto land and then died.

She didn't want to look at Sam, either, but she knew she must. She'd come this far and there was no choice.

He was on the floor between the bed and the wall. Lying on his back with his eyes wide open and horrified, his arms bent out of sight beneath his body. His other hand was resting on one of the pillows on the bed, centered as if it were on display in a museum. His jockey shorts and pants were bunched down around his knees. Things had been done to him with a knife.

Something in the room was hissing loudly. Steam escaping under pressure? Then she realized it was her breathing.

Allie backed away, stepped on something soft—the hand on the floor—and whimpered. Leaped to the side and froze like a startled, terrified animal. She stared at the stained sheets and recognized the smell in the room as blood. Bile surged bitterly at the back of her throat, a burning column of acid. Her stomach contorted so that she actually felt it roll against her belt. She retched and ran bent over to the bathroom, flung open the door, and automatically switched on the light.

More blood!

On the tiles. The white toilet seat. The white porcelain tank. A smeared red handprint on the curved edge of the bathtub. Allie saw that a trail of blood led from the bathroom toward the bed. Her jogging shoes were stained red.

The stench in the bathroom was overwhelming. She gagged, sank down on her knees before the toilet bowl, and vomited when she saw feces and a pudding of clotted blood in the water. Sam must have been attacked while he was sitting there, during a bowel movement. That was how it appeared, anyway. So violently did she vomit that some of what was already in the porcelain bowl splashed up in her face.

Trembling, moaning, she scrambled to her feet and twisted the faucet handles of the washbasin. She scooped handfuls of cold water over her face, listening to the cool, pure sound of it falling back into the basin. She kept scooping water until, with great effort, she made herself stop. Then she washed her hands thoroughly with the small white bar of hotel soap, though they were unsoiled. She staggered from the bathroom, noticing that the carpet was soggy and gave beneath her soles. Her heart slamming against her ribs, she ran to the door.

She didn't remember dashing down the hall to the elevator.

Riding the elevator down to the lobby.

The Hispanic woman at the switchboard stared at her and frowned with black, unplucked brows. She was peering into Allie's eyes as if there were something disturbing behind them that she'd never seen before. The tall gray-haired desk clerk stopped what he was doing with some crinkled yellow forms at the far end of the desk and glided toward her, his features aging with each step and with his growing apprehension. He'd been around a long time and knew trouble when he saw it.

He said, "Miss . . . ?"

Allie leaned with both hands on the desk, her head bowed. She gave the desk clerk a from-down-under look and said, "Room Ten twenty-seven.

Dead." Didn't sound like her voice. Someone high, floating, imitating her.

The switchboard operator had stood up and was crowding the desk clerk, as if she might want to hide behind him. Didn't seem much taller standing. She said, "What? What'd you say, hon?"

Allie tried to speak again but couldn't. Her throat was constricted. She heard herself croak unintelligibly.

"Somebody dead in Ten twenty-seven?" the desk clerk asked in a distant, amazingly calm voice. As if dead guests were part of hotel-biz; one or two every night.

Allie nodded.

"You sure?"

She could manage only another nod.

He stared at her like a stern, impossible father about to ask an important question, warning her in advance that he wanted the truth but he didn't want to hear anything unpleasant. "You mean he died of a heart attack? Something like that? Right?"

"Murdered," Allie made herself say. "Cut up in pieces."

The switchboard operator said, *"Madre de Dios!"*

The desk clerk straightened up so he was standing as tall as possible and, still with his calm gaze fixed on Allie, called, "Will!"

An elderly black bellhop appeared. The old desk clerk casually reached into a side pocket and tossed him a key. It must have been a passkey. Its metal tag clinked against it as the bellhop caught it with one gnarled hand.

"Run on up to Ten twenty-seven," the desk clerk

said. "See what there is to see and then phone down."

The bellhop glanced at Allie. He had sad, very kind eyes. He said, "Got somethin' all over your shoes."

Allie heard herself say, "Huh? Oh, that's blood."

The bellhop's face got hard with fear and a kind of resolve. Or was it resignation? "Seen that before," he said, and walked over and got in the elevator she'd just ridden down. "Seen you before, too," he said as the door slid shut.

But he hadn't, she was sure.

It took Allie a few seconds to realize what he'd meant. And its significance.

It was Hedra he'd seen. Hedra wearing her Allie wig. Wearing her Allie clothes. Inside Allie's blue coat. Walking her Allie walk.

Not Allie! Hedra!

Within a couple of minutes the switchboard buzzed urgently and a tiny red light began blinking. An insistent code: *Murder! Murder! Murder!*

The Hispanic woman drifted toward it. Her eyes were brown pools of fear. The desk clerk shuffled over to stand by her. He leaned over with his gray hair near her dark hair, as if he wanted to hear firsthand what was being said on the receiver pressed to the woman's ear.

While they were standing facing away from her, Allie fled from the lobby and into the street.

27

She didn't realize until she was inside and had shut the apartment door that this wasn't shelter. She'd been stupid to come here. Sam might have something on him that would tell the police where she lived. Hedra might have seen to that.

Hedra! Would Hedra have returned here?

A few feet inside the door, Allie stood in darkness, listening. The apartment was silent.

Even if the police learned her identity and address, she was sure she had *some* time. She walked into the living room and switched on a lamp.

There was her empty cup where she'd left it on the folded *Village Voice* on the table. The remote control for the TV rested where she remembered, on the arm of the sofa. The phone sat on the floor next to the wing chair. Where she'd left it.

Everything seemed to be exactly as it was when she'd hurried out of the apartment.

She switched on more lights and moved toward the hall to the bedrooms. In the glow cast from so many sources, a dozen dim shadows moved with her. Her legs felt rubbery but she wasn't tired.

There was an engine in her chest; she was running on adrenaline.

She glanced in the bathroom and felt a sudden nausea, remembering the bathroom at the Atherton Hotel.

At the door to Hedra's old bedroom she stopped. She reached around the doorjamb, into the room, and groped across rough plaster for the plastic wall switch, found it, and flicked it upward.

The overhead fixture winked on.

Allie almost expected to find something hideous inside. Some further manifestation of Hedra's madness. But this room, too, was as she'd left it. There was, in fact, a special kind of blankness about it, as if, like Hedra, it yearned to be imprinted with personality.

Knowing her time inside the apartment was limited, Allie decided to pack some of her clothes in her carry-on and then get out fast. She'd fetch her red-and-white TWA bag down from her closet shelf and quickly stuff it with whatever seemed appropriate. She wanted only to get clear of the Cody Arms before the police arrived, to run and hide somewhere so she could take time and try to think this nightmare through, figure a way out.

Allie was having difficulty breathing, as if she were being crushed in a vise. She knew there was nothing of Hedra anywhere in the apartment. She felt like screaming, but she covered her mouth with her hand and willed herself to be silent. Slumped on the mattress, she sat with her elbows on her knees, meshing her fingers so tightly they ached. She sat paralyzed, still trying to fully comprehend what had happened, what it meant. On the opposite wall she saw a spider racing diagonally toward the molding up near the ceiling, seeking shelter in shadow.

Then something deep in her stirred to life. A quiet rage and a primal determination to survive. Ancient voices speaking.

She got up and located the canvas carry-on, crumpled and shoved to the back of her closet shelf, behind her folded sweaters. She grabbed a few clothes from the closet and stuffed them inside, ignoring the hangers that dropped to the floor. Zipped the bag closed, tearing a fingernail. She'd tend to that later.

Careful not to get Sam's blood on her hands, she untied her jogging shoes and worked them off her feet. The blood, russet-colored now, hadn't soaked through; her socks weren't stained. She put on her pair of almost new Nikes, then she slung her purse and the carry-on by their straps over her right shoulder.

After a brief detour to the kitchen to poke several granola bars into the carry-on, she hurried to the front door and let herself out into the hall. She kept straining to hear approaching sirens, but there were only the normal sounds of traffic. Once, sparking a moment of panic, she heard a distant siren that was obviously moving away and quickly faded.

She was ten feet from the elevator doors when she heard the thrum of cables and the oiled metallic grinding of an elevator arriving. Fear grabbed her again.

Hoping none of her neighbors would open an apartment door and see her, she ran down the hall toward the rear fire stairs, staying up on the balls of her feet so she'd make as little noise as possible.

As she was rounding the corner, she paused despite herself and glanced back, saw the elevator doors slide open. Four men filed out of the elevator. Two of them wore drab gray suits. The other two wore the old-fashioned blue uniforms of the New York City Police Department. None of them was smiling; they had somber, anxious expressions and moved almost with the precision of a drill team. They turned right, away from Allie, and didn't see her.

She decided against the fire stairs and rode the service elevator down instead. Didn't the police always have someone watching fire escapes? Waiting in the shadows?

The lobby was deserted, but she could see a patrol car parked directly in front of the building. A uniformed officer was sitting behind the steering wheel, and a pulsating haze of exhaust rose from beneath the rear bumper, like life escaping.

Allie's heart was double-pumping and her mouth was dry. *Back way! Back way!* Keeping an eye on the police car, she sidestepped to the oversized freight door, about twenty feet from the service elevator. She rotated the knob and pushed on the heavy door.

It opened only a few inches. She could see a glint of steel, a heavy hasp and padlock on the outside. No escape that way.

She stood there for a moment, light-headed, then ran down the hall to a room where she knew cleaning equipment was stored.

She'd intended to hide there until the police

left, but as soon as she was inside she saw a small, high window with steel mesh over it.

Standing on a square can of cleaning fluid that popped and twanged under her weight, she forced the old wooden window open. The steel mesh was ancient and rusted, but it looked strong. Allie inserted her fingers through it, gripped hard, and worked it back and forth, at first very slightly, then an inch or two each way.

It was installed to resist pressure from the outside, not designed to keep people in. The top of it gave. Then one side. Ignoring the pain in her fingers, she bent the mesh back against the window frame, then forward in wider and wider arcs.

And suddenly it broke free and dropped into the gangway alongside the building.

Allie got down from the can she'd been standing on and placed it on top of an upside-down metal bucket. Stood on the can again, carefully balancing herself, and managed to squeeze her head and shoulders through the window into cool outside air. *Freedom.*

She thrashed around with her right leg, found leverage with her foot, and pushed herself through the window to drop and lie on the concrete pavement. *Ouch!* Her elbow was on the sharp steel mesh she'd broken from the frame. There was a clanging noise as the bucket and can tipped over inside the storage room.

She struggled to her feet in a hurry, brushed rust and dirt off her clothes, and made her way along the gangway to West 74th. She emerged at the corner of the building, behind the parked police car with its motor idling.

Unless the cop behind the steering wheel happened to be looking in his rearview mirror, he wouldn't see her.

When he seemed to move his head to glance in the opposite direction, she put on a casual air, did a sharp turn out of the gangway, and walked quickly away.

Realizing she'd left her purse and the carry-on in the storage room.

28

Allie had no idea what she might do. Where she might go. There was no one to ask for help. None of this seemed real to her. Even she was beginning to doubt Hedra had ever existed. She had to keep reminding herself that her world had changed. She was a fugitive. Wanted for Sam's murder. Sam! Poor Sam. The fool she'd loved and still loved, still needed. They had both been seduced and victimized. Irony twisted her inside; now, after his death, she could better understand and forgive him.

She spent the next several hours wandering aimlessly around the Upper West Side, then walked down Central Park West and over to Fifth Avenue. A fine mist formed in the air; hardly enough to get her wet. Then the mist changed to flecks of snow that fell and disappeared magically on the wet sidewalk in front of her. She seemed to be walking toward a void that would eventually consume her, as if she were ephemeral as a snowflake. And maybe she was.

It finally occurred to her that she was cold and shivering. She stopped walking and was about to

enter a small Chinese restaurant, then realized
she hadn't any money. Through the steamed-over
window she could glimpse people eating in a
booth. Two men and a woman, well-dressed, talking animatedly between bites. The woman, young
and with a swirl of dark hair piled high on her
head, smiled and broke open a fortune cookie.
Allie had intended going into the restaurant to get
warm; now she realized she was hungry as well as
cold. There was nothing she could do about
hunger. Not right now.

For a moment she considered going down into
a subway stop to keep warm, but there was danger
there for a woman alone. She'd read in the newspapers about robbery, rape, and killing in the sub-
ways, seen tragic tape on TV news. And all the
time she'd been living with the woman who'd . . .
done those things to Sam.

The woman who wore her clothes.

Who had become her.

Allie realized she was near Grand Central Station. It would be warmer there. But would the police be watching for her, expecting her to try to
catch a train out of the city? Scenes from a hundred movie and TV shows tumbled through her
mind, bureaucratic authority figures instructing
their underlings to "cover the airport and train
station!"

But she knew there were too many murders in
New York for the police to be constantly on the
alert in all the stations, terminals, and airports
that provided means of escape. Besides, they still
might not even know what she looked like, and al-

most certainly hadn't had time to circulate her photograph. She should be safe at Grand Central for at least tonight.

Jamming her fists deep into the pockets of her blazer, she hunched her shoulders and started walking. The flecks of snow were getting larger. Heavier. She felt one settle and melt on her eyelash, another dissolve coldly on her lower lip.

She entered Grand Central from 42nd Street and took the ramp down into the cavernous main area. The place was busy but looked oddly deserted because of its vastness.

Allie ignored the stares of people who passed her. They *seemed* to be staring at her, anyway, as if there were something about her that marked her as different and desperate. Could they sense her terror? *See* it on her?

She found a clean spot on the floor, sat down, and leaned back against the wall. Letting out a long breath, she waited for the warmth to penetrate her clothes.

Nearby, a shabbily dressed woman with a torn Bloomingdale's bag sat and stared at her. A street person, Allie was sure, with no address, no hope, no perceived future beyond the hour. The woman seemed disturbed that she couldn't categorize Allie, who obviously was not waiting for a train, but was dressed rather well to be one of the army that walked the streets of Manhattan and sought places like this for shelter.

After a few minutes the woman seemed to lose interest. She settled back with her chin tucked into the folds of flesh at the base of her neck, lowered her puffy eyelids and appeared to nod off to sleep. One of her withered hands slid from her lap onto the floor, where it lay palm-up.

Like Sam's hands.

Allie looked away. Shook the vision. She'd read about people who virtually lived in Grand Central, moving around so the police never got a fix on them as vagrants. She decided she should be able to spend the night here, getting up and changing locations once or twice. She'd have to doze sitting up, like the old woman across from her, but that would be better than roaming the cold and dangerous streets.

A bearded man in a scuffed leather jacket hurried past, late for his train. He was munching a hamburger in a McDonald's wrapper. Allie caught the savory scent of the fried beef and onion. About twenty feet beyond her, he absently wadded the wrapper around the hamburger and dropped it into a trash receptacle. He picked up his pace and began to run, licking his fingers as if they were just-discovered popsicles.

Allie sat staring at the refuse can. No one seemed to be paying attention to her. The old woman with the Bloomingdale's bag was still asleep. The scent of the hamburger lingered, or might Allie only be imagining that? Hunger could make the mind play pranks.

Allie thought, Oh, Jesus! I'm really going to do this. She slowly stood up and ambled over to the trash container, as if she were going to throw something away.

Instead she reached inside, as if it were the sort of thing she and everyone else did every day, and her exploring hand sought the crumpled paper wrapper with the still-warm hamburger inside. It was like a live thing hiding from her, but at last her fingers closed on its vital warmth. She drew the aromatic prize out quickly, unable to keep her eyes from darting around to make sure what she'd done had gone unnoticed. But there was no way to be positive. Walking too fast, she returned to her spot on the floor.

She sat for a moment with her heart pounding. Then she told herself that for all anyone passing her knew, she'd bought the hamburger and was finishing eating it. She might be sitting here waiting for a train departure, or for a friend coming into the city to visit her. Might live on goddamn Park Avenue, for all anyone could guess. Not that it was any of their business, was it?

Bastards! she said to herself, hating them because she *did* care what they thought.

With exaggerated casualness, she peeled the wrapper away from the hamburger. She started to tear off the portion of bun marred by the man's tooth marks, then thought better of it.

Took a deep breath and bit into the hamburger.

There was cheese on it, along with onion and pickles. She'd never tasted anything that brought such sensation to the taste buds. She could almost see and feel the word "delicious."

Too soon, she finished the hamburger and was licking her fingers, as the man who'd thrown it away had licked his, only with more obvious greed and enjoyment. When she glanced to the side, the old woman still had her chin resting in the folds of her neck, but her slanted, rheumy eyes were open.

A look passed between her and Allie, for only a second, a spark of understanding that was like a lightning bolt to Allie. The woman had placed her at last in the hierarchy of humanity. They were one and the same, the look said. Outcasts and comrades in agony.

Allie quickly averted her eyes and wiped her hands on her jeans.

Hunger still clawed at her.

She'd never been so lonely.

In the morning she awoke to the shuffle and humming of the busy station. A godlike, echoing voice was making unintelligible pronouncements over the PA system: *"NOWREEING PRESSTO STAMFOR ONTRAREEESAAAN!"* No one was paying the slightest attention to Allie where she lay curled on the floor. Now and then an eye would glance her way and then quickly be averted, as if denying her existence. There was some charity in the world, however; a crumpled dollar bill and some change lay on the floor near her hand. Only the thousands of passing potential witnesses had prevented it from being stolen.

Allie sat up and tucked the money into a pocket. She worked her mouth to remove some of the sour taste that had accumulated during the night. A hint of onion from the hamburger still lingered. She was thinking more clearly now. Graham! He was someone—the only one now— who could corroborate Allie's claim that Hedra had shared the apartment.

If the police would listen to Graham and believe him. Allie had read about how the law hated and resisted evidence to the contrary in what, to them, was a murder with a known perpetrator. The prosecuting attorney was probably salivating while waiting for Allie to be arrested.

She braced her back against the smooth wall and used numbed legs to lever herself to her feet. Then she glanced around and saw a bank of public phones. Gripping the coins she'd scooped from the floor, she walked stiffly toward them.

Graham didn't answer his phone.

Allie called Goya's next, and was told that he wasn't working today, they had no idea where he might be reached.

Her heart fell as she hung up. She couldn't risk going back to the Cody Arms, or to Goya's. She'd have to wait and try to get in touch with Graham later.

She found that it was warmer outside. There was no accumulation of snow but the streets were still wet. People wearing raincoats and carrying folded umbrellas scurried along the sidewalks, on their way to work. Exhaust fumes hovered thick and noxious in the air. Stalled traffic on East 42nd was like a freeze-frame on TV, but with shouted curses and the frantic blaring of horns. Allie wondered why New Yorkers seemed to think that leaning on a horn might help clear a traffic jam. Many of them thrived on noise, she supposed. Maybe some people adapted to noise and then craved it.

Near the sidewalk a cabbie was leaning with his head and bare arm out his taxi window, chewing out a bicycle rider who'd gotten too close and scraped the cab with a handlebar. The cyclist was wearing a shirt that had KING MESSENGER SERVICE lettered across the back. "Both wheels up your ass . . . !" the driver was yelling, so angry he was spraying spittle. The messenger, a scrawny kid who looked about fourteen, was chomping a huge wad of gum or tobacco. He looked blissfully unconcerned.

Allie walked on. A few seconds later the messenger flashed past on his bike, whipping the vehicle from side to side between his legs, wove with breathtaking elegance between a car and a bus, and disappeared. Nonchalant survivor.

Allie knew where she was going now. She'd thought of it last night, slumped on the hard floor in Grand Central Station. Sleep had come to her only in snatches until almost three A.M. Seconds after closing her eyes, the dream would begin. Sam lying on his back with the stumps of his wrists at his sides. Sam staring at his hotel room ceiling with those wide and terrified eyes. Sam and the blood. Hedra and the blood. Sam, already dead, gazing at Hedra. Saying, "Allie . . ." The blood, blood, blood.

When she finally did fall asleep, it was into a red ocean where dead things swam.

A floor was a poor substitute for a bed. She still had an incredibly stiff neck. And she'd been mortified to find the money near her on the floor. Mortified but grateful to the stranger who'd mistaken her for one of the dispossessed and homeless.

Mistaken, hell! She was *one of the homeless.*

She'd conserved her change for the phone and used the dollar to buy a doughnut in a coffee shop in Grand Central. She'd made herself eat it methodically, so the counterman wouldn't realize she was starving, then washed it down with a glass of water. Half a hamburger for supper and a doughnut and water for breakfast. Surprisingly, as she'd hurried out of the station she felt satisfied. And she walked now with a sense of purpose.

She knew where Mike Mayfair lived, all by himself in his loft apartment in SoHo. He'd be in his office at Fortune Fashions by now, leaning back behind his desk and making life hell for his secretary. Or sitting in his car in stalled traffic. Either way, there'd be no one in his apartment.

Allie had become a beggar. Now it was time to be a thief.

29

Mayfair's apartment building was a drab gray structure that housed a flower shop and a bookshop in its ground floor. Allie walked around to the side of the building, where there was a narrow gangway that smelled of garbage and stale urine. She glanced up and down the street, then sidled around the corner and walked to the black iron fire escape that stair-stepped jaggedly down the side of the building.

She leaped up and grabbed at the gravity ladder that would lever down to street level, but her grasping fingers missed it by six inches. "Damn!" she said, so loudly she was shocked by the volume. But there were only a few low, dirt-caked windows on the sides of the buildings that flanked her; no one had heard.

Allie moved down the side of the building to a steel Dumpster overflowing with trash. She stood on her toes and peered inside, hoping to find a piece of rope or twine she might weight and toss up to snag the gravity ladder and pull it down. The sweet garbage stench of the Dumpster nauseated her, and all she saw were stained cardboard boxes, empty cans and bottles, and black and green plastic trash bags.

Backing away from the horrid smell, she noticed that the Dumpster rested on small steel wheels. She studied it. Though it had to be heavy, especially laden as it was with trash, she told herself it wasn't all that large. *Only about the size of a Volkswagen.*

Holding her breath against the sickening stench, she got behind the Dumpster. She turned and rested her back against hard steel, and pushed with her legs.

The wheels squealed and the Dumpster moved a few inches over the rough pavement.

She took a deep breath, smell or no smell, and pushed harder, felt the steel at her back move again. More than a foot this time.

And she knew she could do it.

Slowly, so the wheels would make as little noise as possible, she shoved the Dumpster beneath the fire escape. Then she closed its steel lid and climbed up on it.

She easily reached the counterweighted fire escape ladder and pulled it down to her. It squealed, too, but in a lower octave and not as loud as the Dumpster wheels.

Though SoHo had become gentrified and quite expensive, it was still the kind of neighborhood where no one would pay a great deal of attention to someone ascending a fire escape in broad daylight. And most New Yorkers, if they did see Allie, would shrug and go on their way. It didn't pay to get involved with strangers climbing fire escapes. Besides, they would conveniently reason, she probably lived or worked in the building and had forgotten her key.

She was careful at each window, but most of the shades were pulled, or the glass looked in on empty offices or apartments being readied for refurbishing.

When she reached the top floor, she found the window to Mayfair's loft apartment locked.

She removed a shoe, then she looked around and gave the glass pane a tap with its soft heel. Nothing happened. She struck again, harder, and the upper-left corner of the glass fell neatly into the apartment and shattered on the kitchen floor.

Cautiously, she angled her arm in and found the window lock. It didn't move easily, but she managed to twist it until it wasn't clasped. She hastily slipped her shoe back on, then she slid open the window and ducked inside.

The glass on the tile floor crunched beneath her feet.

She stood poised to scramble back out the window, but Mayfair's apartment *felt* empty. The air was still. Traffic sounds were barely audible. A tension in Allie eased.

All the kitchen appliances were white and new-looking. The table had a glass top and white metal legs. The chairs were white metal with padded gray seats. The walls were white. Faucets and stove hardware gleamed silver. There was not a sign of a dish or a pot or pan or kitchen utensil; everything was in the neat white cabinets. Allie thought the kitchen looked like the kind of place where autopsies were performed.

She left the kitchen and found that the rest of the apartment was one large room with a sleeping area set off by a folding screen. One wall was mirrored floor to ceiling, and modern sculpture rested here and there on glass-topped, sharply angled tables with stainless-steel legs. The wall behind the low-slung, green leather sofa held a vast unframed canvas coated with thick white oil paint except for an olive-drab square near the upper-left corner. Allie doubted if Mayfair was a collector; probably he'd hired a decorator. Probably he'd attempted to seduce her before paying her. If he ever *had* paid her. The asshole!

Allie moved forward slowly, her jogging shoes sinking into the deep-piled carpet that covered most of the apartment. What did he have beneath the stuff—a water mattress? To her left was a small dining area with a bleached pine table and chairs, a matching hutch, and a grotesque and angular silver chandelier that was itself like a piece of bad sculpture. Some taste, Allie thought; maybe the decorator deserved to get screwed.

A ribbon of sound from the sleeping area made her stop in midstride. She felt a chill and her heart began banging as if trying to break through her ribs.

Music was seeping from behind the folding screen.

She forced herself to move forward, careful not to make the slightest noise. If it weren't for the deep, sound-muffling carpet, she'd have turned and run from the apartment.

She edged closer, leaned forward, and peered around the screen.

Mayfair's sleeping area was unoccupied. The round bed was unmade, its floral-print spread lying in a heap on the floor. On a shelf behind it a stereo system was glowing like the control panel of an airliner. A homogenized version of the old Doors hit "Light My Fire" was oozing softly from the speakers. Wadded white underwear and a pair of black socks also lay on the floor. A glass with an amber residue at the bottom was on the night-stand, alongside an ashtray overflowing with ciga-rette butts and ashes. A book by Jackie Collins lay open on the bed. Christ! Allie thought.

She remembered seeing a door that must lead to the bathroom, and wondered if Mayfair might be in there.

She went to it and cautiously looked inside. She could see into a blue-tiled shower stall. A large white towel was wadded on the floor near the toi-let bowl. She moved in close. A white bar of soap lay near the drain on the floor of the stall, its cor-ners worn smooth; the brand name engraved on its blanched surface reminded Allie of carving on a tombstone.

Apparently Mayfair had simply gone to work and neglected to turn off his stereo. Or maybe he'd left it on to discourage burglars, make them think someone was in the apartment. Allie smiled at that one, as she stood wondering what the stereo might be worth if she took it to a pawnshop down in the Village.

Then it occurred to her that she might attract a lot of attention leaving the building with a stereo system.

She went back to the sleeping area and Mayfair's dresser. There were a crumpled dollar bill and sixty-five cents in change on top, among a stack of papers that turned out to be nothing but laundry tickets and some charge receipts for clothes and a stay at a motel in New Jersey. An empty condom wrapper with some kind of lubricant on it lay near the dollar bill. Yuk! What a life this scuzzball led. She began searching through the dresser drawers. The top ones contained folded underwear, shirts, and socks. The bottom drawer was filled with an extensive collection of pornography.

Allie opened the huge bleached pine wardrobe to an array of exclusive-label suits and sport coats. Not a place for polyester. A rack on the door held dozens of ties. One side of the wardrobe consisted of narrow drawers, which she examined.

Ah, this was better. The shallow top drawer held Mayfair's jewelry. An expensive Movado dress watch, three heavy gold chains, and a man's gold-link bracelet with Mayfair's initials engraved on it. Three rings, one of them set with a diamond. Some onyx and gold cuff links. An aged and cracked photograph of a young blond woman in a twenties-style feathered hat; the photo was in a beautiful and obviously expensive silver filigreed frame. Allie studied the woman in the photo and wondered if she was Mayfair's mother. She felt a stab of guilt, then she had to smile. She was wanted for murder and was feeling uneasy about stealing.

Then she remembered how Mayfair had manipulated her, and she stuffed the jewelry into her pockets. She left the photograph, frame and all, in

the drawer, out of deference to the might-be-mom.
That made no sense, she realized, but what in her
life had made sense lately? What truth hadn't
fallen in fragments?

She walked from the sleeping area and noticed
another door on the other side of the apartment.
At first she thought it might lead to a hall, but
when she opened it she found it was to Mayfair's
home office. More goodies? She stepped inside.
The office contained a wide cherrywood desk, a
table with a copy machine, and several file cabinets. A large glossy photograph of a nude woman
reclining on the hood of a red sports car was
framed and hung on the wall. The line of her hip
and thigh was exactly the same as the line of the
front fender. This one probably wasn't Mayfair's
mother.

On the desk was a Zenith portable computer, a
laptop job with a backlighted screen and plenty of
storage capacity. Allie was familiar with the model
and knew what it was worth. She knew also that it
folded into a neat and compact carrying case that
would attract little attention. She smiled and stepped
over to the desk.

She decided to leave Mayfair's apartment the
way she'd entered. In the kitchen, she noticed for
the first time a used coffee cup in the sink. On one
of the kitchen chairs was a folded *New York Post*.

Allie felt strangely secure in the apartment, and
for a moment considered sitting down at the table
and reading the newspaper. An interlude of nor-
malcy.

Then she reminded herself that Mayfair might
have a cleaning lady due to arrive. Or for that mat-

ter a friend, or Mayfair himself, might walk in the door any second. This would be more than mere embarrassment. After all, she was trespassing. Burglarizing.

And wanted for murder.

She got a block of cheese and an apple from the refrigerator and poked them into her blouse with some of the stolen jewelry.

Carrying the computer case in her right hand, the newspaper tucked beneath her arm, she climbed back out onto the fire escape and made her way down.

On a bench in Washington Square she ate the cheese and apple while she read the paper.

It had been folded out of order on the table in the apartment. When she straightened it out, she found that Sam's murder was front-page news in the *Post* because of its sensational nature. "Grisly Sex-Slaying at Midtown Hotel," shouted the headline. There was an accompanying photograph of police cars and an ambulance in front of the Atherton. The desk clerk at the hotel remembered a blond woman in a blue coat with a white collar, whom he'd seen often with the victim. The woman had hurried from the hotel the afternoon of the murder, and the desk clerk and a bellhop remembered several large red stains on the coat but hadn't thought much about it. That evening, when the woman returned, spent time upstairs, and then came downstairs and reported that the victim was dead, she hadn't been wearing the coat, but she still had on bloodstained shoes. There was speculation that she'd returned to the scene of the crime to retrieve something she'd left in the victim's room, or perhaps to pretend to discover the body and divert suspicion from herself.

From items found in the dead man's room, authorities soon identified the woman as Allison Jones of 172 West 74th Street. A quiet woman, neighbors said. Kept to herself. *Didn't they all? The ones who exploded into violence?*

She'd disappeared after the murder and was now being sought by the police.

The news story didn't say where the blood-stained blue coat was, but Allie knew. She remembered it draped over a hook in her closet. Where Hedra had put it after killing Sam, then phoning her and watching her leave the Cody Arms. And she'd played into Hedra's hands by being dumb enough, and upset enough, to leave the blood-stained shoes behind in the apartment before fleeing from the police.

Of course, the news account didn't mention Hedra. Hedra the elusive, who had moved through Allie's life like an evil illusion, a trick of the light that had left no trace.

As Allie set the newspaper aside, she was astounded to see Graham's photograph. She snatched the paper back up, smoothed the fold hard against her thigh, and stared. Graham was sitting in what looked like an untidy office, looking directly into the camera, his lopsided smile so radiant it seemed to jump from the black-and-white photograph in three dimensions. But this couldn't be Graham Knox! Not the Graham Knox she knew! Because the caption beneath the photo read "Playwright

Struck and Killed by Taxi." This couldn't connect
to her or Graham's life. There'd been some sort of
mixup; why should she even be interested in this?

But she sat forward, hunched over the paper,
and read about the other Graham's death. On the
successful opening night of his play, *Dance
Through Life,* he'd been standing outside the theater in a crowd and tragically slipped from the
curb and been struck by a taxi that was unable to
stop in time on the wet street. There was a quote
from a *Voice* critic, comparing Graham's work with
that of the young Tennessee Williams.

By the time Allie finished reading, it was the
Graham she knew. Had known. The one who lived
upstairs and who sneaked her free Diet Pepsis at
Goya's, the lanky, friendly terrier.

And suddenly Allie realized what Graham's
death meant. Now no one could corroborate her
claim that Hedra had shared her apartment. A
slab of ice seemed to form in her stomach, and
she shivered and wondered if Graham's death
really *had* been an accident. Was it possible Hedra
had murdered him as she had Sam?

Either way, Allie now had no way of proving
Hedra had ever existed. Sometimes even she
doubted if there'd ever really been a Hedra Carlson.

Allie had tried to learn about Hedra before
choosing her as a roommate. Afterward, *Hedra*
must have thoroughly researched *Allie,* probing
for information and answers, learning that she
had no surviving family, no one she would have
confided in. No one to help her now by at least be-

lieving in Hedra's existence. The only way to prove Hedra existed, Allie knew, was to find her.

But find her how?

Allie hurled the apple core away, frightening half a dozen pigeons into frantic, flapping flight, and stared at the ground between her feet. The grass was worn away by the feet of people who'd sat there; the earth was dry and cracked, half-concealing the curled pull tab from a can of soda or beer. She was aware of people walking past her, nearby, but she didn't look up.

After a while she remembered something. The man who'd accosted her on the street, mistaking her for Hedra, had mentioned a place called Wild Red's where, supposedly, they'd seen each other and talked. Perhaps made some kind of sexual covenant.

Leaving the newspaper on the bench, Allie left the park and walked until she found an office building with a public phone and directory.

Wild Red's was listed, with an address on Waverly Place in the Village.

The Village. Well, she was in the Village already; she wouldn't have to spend Mayfair's money on subway fare. And the Village was where she wanted to sell Mayfair's computer no-questions-asked.

She dug in her pocket for the change she'd stolen from Mayfair's apartment and shook it so it jingled in her hand. It felt good rattling against her palm.

You never could tell about men. All it had taken was a little breaking and entering, and Mike Mayfair was turning out to be her best friend.

30

Allie sold Mayfair's laptop computer at a place that repaired and sold used electronic equipment down on Houston Street. A narrow shop with a door below street level and a blue canvas awning that had been torn by wind or malicious hands.

She got only eight hundred dollars for the computer, though she knew that even secondhand it was worth twice as much. The smiling old man behind the counter had suspected it was stolen, she was sure. She'd probably confirmed that suspicion by accepting such a low price, but she didn't care. Within days the computer would probably be sold again for less than the going rate, also to somebody who knew it was stolen, and it would be in no one's best interest to inform the police.

The police.

After leaving the shop, Allie found a phone booth on the street. It wasn't a booth really, but it did have a curved Plexiglas shield to deflect traffic noise. She remembered how in the movies the police often reasoned out where a call had come from by the background sounds. Before dialing, she stood for a moment and listened to make sure there were only the usual Manhattan noises: roar of traffic, rush of thousands of soles on concrete, echoing car horns and distant emergency vehicle sirens, millions of hearts and hopes breaking.

She nestled into the booth as close as possible to the phone and fed coins into the slot, then held her cupped hand next to the receiver's mouth-piece to make sure she could be heard.

Allie was told by a desk sergeant that Detective Kennedy had been on vacation but was due in this afternoon around three o'clock. He asked her who was calling and could anyone else help her. She hung up.

She stood on the sidewalk in bright sunlight, her fists propped on her hips.

With money in her pocket she felt different. She'd regained her status as a human being, at least in the eyes of those who passed her on the street. She was a little ashamed by how much dif-ference a wad of hundred-dollar bills could make in the way she and the world saw each other. Something was wrong here. How must it be to live month after month penniless on the streets, as so many did? The invisible people of the city, the ones most of us didn't like to see because the vi-sion and what it suggested made us vaguely un-comfortable. But only vaguely; that was the true horror of it. Allie knew she'd never be blind to the dispossessed again; she'd learned how it felt to be without tooth and fang in the jungle.

She bought a pair of dark-tinted sunglasses from a sidewalk vendor. Not much of a disguise, really, though they did change the way she looked, with their uptilted black frames. She thought they gave her a devilish yet somehow sad expression. Wearing the glasses, she walked idly back up to Washington Park.

The benches and open spaces were lined with winos and the drug-wasted, as well as neighborhood people and tourists. A uniformed cop strolled on a course perpendicular to Allie's but paid no attention to her, nodding to a couple of kids on bikes who veered onto the grass to avoid him. Her blood beat a drum in her ears and she was ready to run if he even glanced her way.

He paused, stretched his arms, and ambled off toward the street, his nightstick, walkie-talkie, and holstered revolver jouncing on his hips and causing him to swing his arms wide, lending him the swagger of cops everywhere.

Watching him, it struck Allie that there was probably no better city in the country in which to be a fugitive. So ponderous and hectic was the press of people, and so infrequent was eye contact, that the likelihood of someone in New York happening to see and recognize anyone accidentally was extremely slim.

But not impossible, she reminded herself.

Near the pigeon-fouled statue of Garibaldi, she stopped and watched a squirrel take a circuitous route up a tree and disappear among the branches. A yellow Frisbee sailed near her, and a Hispanic girl about twelve ran and retrieved it from where it was lodged like yellow fall fruit in some bushes. The squirrel ventured halfway down the tree to see what was going on, switching its tail in anger or alarm.

Allie was tempted to spend hours in the park, but she knew that would accomplish nothing. And it might not be as safe here as she assumed.

Next, she decided, she'd find a place to stay. She smiled. Why not a plush hotel? One of those bordering Central Park? Maybe the Ritz-Carlton. Why not a mint on the pillow, and room-service meals? First class made the most sense for those who didn't intend to pay.

The idea gave her delicious satisfaction, until she realized that without identification or credit cards, she'd have to pay in advance. Plastic was needed to establish reputableness and pave the way for cash. She hadn't quite regained her full measure of Manhattan humanity.

She rode the subway to 42nd Street. Then she walked around the Times Square area and theater district until she found a hotel that looked seedy enough to be cheap and anonymous, but was still bearable.

The Willmont, on West Forty-eighth, wasn't the Ritz-Carlton. The entrance was an ancient, wood-framed revolving door, just inside of which the doorman, if that's what he was, dozed in a metal folding chair with a newspaper in his lap. The lobby was small and dim, with dusty potted palms, peeling floor tile, and two old men slumped in threadbare armchairs and gazing speculatively at Allie. She told herself they probably stared at everyone who came in. On the wall near the desk was a vast, time-darkened print of Custer's Last Stand. Custer stood tall in the middle of the melee, aiming his pistol at an Indian, like a man about to die. Taped beneath the faded gold-leafed frame was less ambitious artwork, a sign declaring the elevators were out of order. Its corners were curled and it looked as if it had been there a long time.

The desk clerk was a girl about twenty with a purple and orange punk hairdo and a nose that appeared to have been broken one more time than it had been set. She told Allie yes, there was a vacancy, and the rate was forty-six dollars a night. Ridiculously cheap by New York standards.

Allie registered as Audrey James from Minneapolis and paid in advance for a week. The girl didn't even ask if she had luggage or needed a bellhop, merely handed her a brass key on a plastic tag and said, "Two-twenty, up at the top of them stairs."

Allie accepted the key and walked toward a steep flight of stairs covered with moldy blue carpet. The old men were still staring. An equally old black man with a broom and one of those dustpans with a long handle nodded to her and smiled wide and warm as she went past. There was graffiti on the stairwell walls, but it had been crossed out with black paint and was unintelligible except for where the word FUCK had been crudely altered to read BOOK. BOOK YOU. Fooled no one, Allie thought, trudging up the creaking steps.

Was she fooling anyone?

The hall at the top of the stairs was a littered horror, but the room was better than she'd imagined. The walls were pale green and needed paint. The maple furniture was old but in good shape. Might even support her weight. The drapes were a mottled gray to match the carpet. Near the foot of the bed was a TV bolted to a steel shelf that was bolted to the wall. Allie saw only one roach, but a big one, scurrying for darkness on the wall behind the dresser. The room smelled like Pine-Sol disinfectant, which was probably better than the alternative odor.

A toilet flushed somewhere and water gurgled in a pipe buried in the wall. A man was yelling, very faintly, possibly from the room next door or directly above, "Get 'em off, get 'em off!" Allie wasn't sure what he meant and didn't want to find out. Thanks to the thick walls, he wasn't making enough noise to disturb her.

She walked to the bathroom and found that it, too, was clean, though the fixtures were old and yellowed porcelain. The tub had claw feet, and a crack in its side that had somehow been repaired and painted over with white enamel so that it resembled a surgery scar. There was a makeshift shower with a plastic curtain. The curtain was green with a white daisy design, and looked old and brittle enough to break at a touch. Green tile ran from the floor halfway to the ceiling; a few of the squares were missing to reveal ancient gray ridges of cement. There was a single small window, open about three inches and caked with layers of paint so that it would remain open about three inches today and tomorrow and far into eternity. A plank of cool air pushed in through the window, but the pine disinfectant smell was even stronger in the bathroom.

Allie locked the door and lay down on the bed, which was soft enough to aggravate any spine problem. She saw that the ceiling was cracked and water-stained. There was another roach up there, not moving and probably dead. She stared hard at it, thought it might have moved slightly, but she couldn't be positive. Vision itself wavered. The eyes played games with the mind.

She forgot about the roach and laid her plans.

Wearing her sunglasses, she'd go out and get some lunch, then buy some junk food to bring back to the hotel. Then she'd buy some new clothes—jeans, a blouse, a Windbreaker, some socks and underwear—and return to her room and treat herself to a long, hot shower. Maybe take a nap, if she could sleep. She didn't feel completely secure here at the Willmont, and it wasn't only the police she feared.

This evening she'd phone Kennedy again from a booth, then go to the Village. To Wild Red's, and see if anybody there remembered Hedra.

Springs twanged as she got up from the bed. She walked into the bathroom and moaned when she looked at herself in the medicine cabinet mirror. Her hair was greasy and plastered close to her head. Her face was pale. Her eyes, haunted and wide, stared back at her like those of a creature that had just sensed it was merely a link in the food chain, wild and cornered and resigned to death.

Hedra had done this to her. Turned her into this.

She washed her face and used her fingertips to do what she could with her hair. A comb and makeup; something else she needed to get while she was out.

After about ten minutes she again studied herself in the mirror. She was satisfied. Her reflection looked older, with eyes still haunted, but it wouldn't frighten children.

Most children.

Though she was exhausted, sleep was impossible. Allie climbed out of bed at six o'clock that evening and discovered she was hungry. After relieving herself in the bathroom that smelled like the Canadian woods, she unwrapped and ate one of the cheese Danishes she'd bought earlier that day, washing it down with a can of fizzy, warm Pepsi. Later, maybe, she'd take time to eat a more traditional supper.

After dressing in her new jeans and blue sweater, she slipped into her black Windbreaker and went downstairs. It buoyed her spirit, wearing new clothes, even if the ensemble's style had turned out to be Paris-punk.

The two old men in the lobby had been joined by a third. They all stopped talking and stared at her as she walked out to the street. What am I doing? she wondered. Swinging my ass? Sending out vibes? Are they expecting me to return with a man? She didn't much care if they thought she was an innocent prostitute and not someone wanted for murder.

She walked for a while on Seventh Avenue, lost among the thronging tourists taking advantage of a clear night. Then she used a phone in a Brew Burger at 52nd Street to call Kennedy.

"I'm afraid you're in some trouble, dear," he said when she'd identified herself and been put through to him.

Allie was soothed by his gentle, amiable voice. She pictured the bulky detective leaning back in his chair with his big feet propped up on his cluttered desk, a row of cigars protruding from his shirt pocket. She searched for words, then said simply, "I didn't do it." That sounded hollow even to her.

"'Course not, dear."

"It was something done *to* me. Something I let happen. It won't be easy to believe; I know that."

"Ah! I'm listening, though."

And in a rush of words she told him about Hedra and Sam, and about Graham, and what had actually occurred at the Atherton Hotel.

Kennedy waited until she was finished and said, "Your neighbors at the Cody Arms told us you lived alone. They never saw this Hedra."

"But that was the idea!" Allie said in exasperation. "Her being there was a violation of the lease. I had to *pretend* I lived alone."

"Well, it's a big and impersonal kind of place, all right, so what you say's surely possible. Tell me, dear, is there no one who could verify that you had this roommate?"

"No, there isn't. The only two people who could are dead. That's *why* she killed Sam! And maybe she even murdered Graham."

"So she could impersonate you without interference?"

"Yes. I think she planned to kill me, but then it wasn't necessary. She just blamed Sam's murder on me and saved herself the risk and trouble. She thought I'd be arrested and out of her way. I think she's spent time in a mental hospital. Maybe she's done it before, killed other women she's lived with."

"What makes you think she's killed other roommates?"

"There are all those newspaper clippings about murders."

"But didn't you just tell me you saw only one such clipping, on the back of a recipe?"

"Well, yes."

"Then you're not really sure about the others."

"No. Yes! God, I don't know. If you'll look for her we can find out."

"But why would she want to impersonate you?"

"She didn't just want to impersonate me—she wanted to *be* me! Psychiatrists probably have a word for it, like they do everything else. It was as if she didn't have a personality or an identity of her own, so she needed mine to fill the vacuum. She's mentally ill. Twisted. Do you understand?"

"I'm trying to, dear. Be patient with me. And you really think she killed this Graham Knox, too?"

"I don't know. I—" Allie suddenly drew in her breath. "You're trying to keep me talking so this call can be traced."

"Don't be so romantic and excitable, dear. That kind of thing happens mostly in movies and mystery novels."

"Don't call me 'dear' again!"

"All right, if you don't like it. What would it be, then—Miss Jones? Allie?"

"You! You're just a cop, like the rest of them."

"I'm a cop, dear. I never pretended to be otherwise. You must admit that. Some problems are too big to shoulder alone. I think you should come here so we can talk in person. I promise you—"

Allie slammed down the receiver and walked quickly away from the phone, out of the restaurant onto 52nd Street. The cacophony of nighttime Manhattan rushed over her in a deafening wave, intimidating her. She felt like hurling her troubles to the pavement and running as fast as she could away from them.

But she knew that wouldn't work.

Across the street several cabs were queued up to collect passengers at the Sheraton Centre Hotel. She waved to one of the drivers, and the cab eased out of the line and waited for her, blocking traffic. Horns blared, but the driver, unconcerned, slung his arm over the seat back and waited for Allie.

She climbed in and gave him the address of Wild Red's in the Village.

31

Music was pulsing from inside, and when she opened the heavy wood door it was deafening. Raw sound tumbled out onto the sidewalk, as if it had weight and substance, and might envelop her.

Wild Red's was long and low-ceilinged, with a polished mahogany bar that ran the length of one wall and disappeared in dimness and a haze of smoke as if into another dimension. The place was decorated in a motorcycle motif, with wall posters of leather-clad riders slouched on sleek mechanical chargers. One of the riders was a smiling young woman, nude except for black leather boots with high heels, and with incredibly tattooed breasts. The front end of what looked like a real motorcycle was mounted on the wall behind the bar, as if it were a moose head. A plaque beneath it read "Harley-Davidson" in flowing chrome letters. Allie stood just inside the door and waited for the pungent smell of marijuana to hit her, but the only scent was a mingling of stale liquor and ordinary tobacco smoke.

The music was blasting from large box speakers mounted at precarious angles high on the walls, aimed sharply downward like weapons for maximum volume. The song was one Allie didn't recognize, but it featured a strong steel guitar and a driving background beat.

Half a dozen people sat at the bar, two women and four men. One man was wearing a business suit, the other three had on leather jackets and boots. One wore leather pants to go with his outfit, and a long white scarf draped around his neck, as if he were a kamikaze pilot living it up before his brief flight to oblivion. Maybe that was what it was all about, Allie thought.

The two women seemed to be together. The nearer of them was a hefty redhead and had on a tan Windbreaker and jeans. Her thighs were so thick and muscular they visibly strained the jeans' stitches. On her jacket was a gold pin, a miniature set of handcuffs. Her companion was a petite brunette with squared bangs and a face like a leprechaun, wearing a studded Levi's jacket and baggy camouflaged fatigue pants. The pants were tucked into what appeared to be highly polished army boots. She looked like a tough orphan who'd been drafted by mistake.

There were a couple of people slouched at tables along the wall opposite the bar, mostly dressed in leather. They were drinking and talking softly. A man wearing what looked like a World War I flying suit, complete with leather helmet and dangling goggles, was dancing swing with a woman in a tight blue jumpsuit with BEYOND BITCH lettered on the back. The impact of their boots on the hard plank floor could be heard as an echoing beat under the music. Whatever the uniform at Wild Red's, boots seemed to be in fashion.

Without moving their bodies a millimeter, the three men at the bar turned their heads and stared at Allie. She ignored them and walked over to the bar and sat perched on the end stool, near the door. There was an empty glass in front of the stool next to hers, and a wadded white paper napkin with lipstick on it. A similar red-smeared napkin lay on the floor.

The bartender was a wiry young guy with a neatly trimmed mustache and beard. Moving lightly, as if he had much more energy than weight, he came over and said, "Yes, ma'am?"

Allie told him she wanted a Scotch and water on the rocks.

When he brought the drink, he said, "Been a while."

"From when?" Allie asked.

He looked puzzled. Then he put on a smiling but vacuous expression. Instant department-store mannequin. "Sorry. Thought you were somebody else. A regular."

"Who would that be?"

"Well, I couldn't really say. You know how it is, something struck a note in my mind."

Allie said, "Has Allie Jones been in lately?"

The bartender smiled. "I don't know many customers by name. What's she look like?"

"Something like me, they say."

He grinned, genuinely this time, crinkling the flesh around his eyes and making him look handsomer but ten years older. "Which explains why you looked familiar, I guess. Now I think I know the woman you got in mind. Not that you look a lot like her in the face; it's more the way you carry yourself or something. Just . . something, but strong. Your gestures and all. But like I said, it's been a while, even if we're talking about the same person."

"Know anybody who could tell me where to find her?"

"Don't know anybody who would, even if they could. This isn't the kind of place that acts as a referral service, you know?"

"Sure." Allie sipped her Scotch. It was surprisingly potent, or maybe she was light-headed from all that had happened to her. The bartender wandered off to see if anyone needed a fresh drink. Glad to get away from her, she thought.

She sat there awhile, watching, waiting. The other drinkers were studiously ignoring her, she was sure. They had the instincts of herd animals. There was something about her not setting quite right with them, throwing the night slightly out of sync. Danger at the waterhole.

The blaring music stopped and a softer, slower song came over the speakers, a number by Sade with a hypnotic Latin rhythm. The two guys in leather swiveled down off their stools and started to dance. They were good. What they were doing looked like a slow, grinding cha-cha in perfect time to the syncopated beat. The gamine brunette in the fatigue pants and studded jacket stared openly at Allie, grinned, and stuck out her tongue and wriggled it. The guy in the business suit said, "Stop that, Laverne." Laverne said, "Fuck you,

Cal!" but not as if she were mad. They were friends, Laverne and Cal.

Allie got up and carried her drink over to where Cal sat with his elbows propped on the bar. He was slightly overweight, in his forties, and had very blond unruly hair and a pleasant moon face. Like a grown-up Huck Finn, Allie thought. Though it was unlikely Twain had ever imagined Huck frequenting a leather bar. Where was Becky Thatcher?

Settling onto the stool next to him, Allie said, "I'm looking for Allie Jones. Know her?"

Cal smiled. A beatific smile despite crooked teeth. "Not as I can recall. Wanna dance?"

"No, thanks. You ever heard the name before?"

"Allie Jones? Yeah, I think so, but I couldn't be sure where. Hey, whoa! Aren't the police looking for an Allison Jones?" Tumblers in his mind had obviously clicked into place. Without waiting for her to answer, he said, "Yeah . . ." Looked apprehensive. Then his open, pale features went as blank as if a lamp inside him had been switched off.

At first Allie was afraid her photo might have been in the papers or on TV and he'd recognized her. For a crazy instant she considered running for the door.

Then she realized he probably thought she was an undercover cop, searching for . . . herself. Well, that would make a kind of sense from his point of view.

She thought, the best defense . . . Said, "Still like to dance?"

"Uh-uh. Sorry, gotta go." He turned away from her and dropped a folded five-dollar bill on the bar, then got down off his stool and walked outside, moving fast but trying not to hurry.

The two leather freaks on the dance floor had been snorting something from a white handkerchief while they swiveled their hips to the beat. Probably butyl nitrate. One of them had been watching what went on at the bar. He blew his nose in the handkerchief and stuffed it in one of his jacket's many pockets. Innocent guy with a cold, that's all he was. Sure.

Allie decided hanging around Wild Red's any longer was useless. She paid for her drink and got down off her stool.

As she was walking past the two women at the bar, the redhead in the tan windbreaker said, "C'mon back sometime when you're not lookin' for that dumb cunt Allie. You don't really wanna find her anyways; girl's sicker'n sick."

Laverne said, "Speakin' of dumb cunts, shut the one under your nose."

The redheaded woman smiled and shrugged. Allie nodded to her and went outside, wondering if the stares she felt would leave holes in the back of her jacket.

She was glad to be on the sidewalk. Breathing fresh night air.

She'd taken only a few steps when a man's voice said, "Hey, Allie, you in the deepest shit, girl!"

She turned and was facing a husky black man with a full beard and a dangling gold earring. He'd been hurrying toward her, but now he stopped in midstride. A surprised, suspicious look washed over his blunt features. He frowned, calculating. There was something wrong with his face, a puckered scar beneath his left eye, almost like another, squinting eye.

He said, "Sorry, Miss, had you wrong," and turned to walk across the street.

"Wait a minute!" Allie said, starting after him.

He shook his head without looking back. "Ain't got a minute."

He obviously knew Allie was wanted for murder, and thought it more than coincidence that a woman who so much resembled her—Hedra— had emerged from Wild Red's. He didn't want to talk to her, didn't know her and didn't want her to link him in any way to the Allie Jones he did know.

"Dammit! Need to talk!" Allie called, as he picked up too much speed for walking and started to jog.

She began chasing him, and he glanced back and broke into a flat-out run, crossing Waverly diagonally. He'd decided she was trouble he could outdistance.

He was bigger, faster. But Allie was desperate. *Damn him!* She lengthened her stride, feeling the strain in her thighs. Tried to breathe evenly through her nose, the way she'd been taught in gym class in high school, so she could regulate the flow of oxygen to her lungs and wouldn't get winded too soon.

The man ahead of her could run; he had an easy, athletic stride despite his bulk. His arms swung loosely and rhythmically and his shoulder muscles rippled beneath his tight brown jacket.

He gave the impression he had strength in re-
serve.

He cut around a corner, using some of that
strength to run faster. Allie tripped over a raised
section of sidewalk and almost fell. She stumbled
forward half a dozen lurching steps before regain-
ing her balance.

By the time she'd rounded the corner, he was
well ahead of her. Pulling away. She was sure she
was going to lose him.

But at the next corner a cluster of pedestrians
waiting to cross the street slowed him down.

He glanced over his shoulder, saw Allie gaining
ground, and elbowed people aside. Tires screeched
and a horn blared at him as he interrupted the
flow of traffic.

By the time she reached the intersection, the
light had instructed the waiting throng to walk.
She crossed the street at a run, bouncing off a
heavyset woman who cursed at her. A female voice
said, "Rude bitch!" Somebody laughed. Allie didn't
apologize or break stride, only ran faster.

She'd lost sight of the man, but she held her
speed for the next block. Ahead she glimpsed a
dark figure swinging around an iron railing and
diving down the steps of what appeared to be the
entrance to a basement apartment. Like a hunted
animal going to ground.

Allie sucked in a harsh, rasping breath that
seared her lungs and ran hard for the iron railing.
A throbbing ache flared in her right side, threatening to buckle her body and make her slow to a
bent-over walk. *Keep running! Push!*

She swung around the corner rail, as she'd seen

her quarry do, cutting her hand on a sharp spur of wrought iron. She lunged down two of the concrete steps and then stopped, gasping for air.

A Hispanic boy about fourteen was standing hunched in the shadowy corner of the entrance-way. He had his narrow back to her, but his head was twisted around so he could see her, the glow from the street catching his smooth features. Allie could hear the spattering of his urine on concrete; she breathed in the ammonia stench of it. He continued to gaze insolently over his shoulder, light from above causing the white of one eye to glitter. "What the fuck you want, lady?"

She didn't answer.

He turned his body toward her and stood with his feet spread wide, zipping up his pants. Grinned.

Allie bolted and ran across the street, then walked back the way she'd come. She looked behind her several times to make sure the boy wasn't following.

After a few blocks, her breathing evened out and the pain in her side faded away. But her thighs still ached and her knees felt weak. She walked slowly, trying to collect her thoughts.

At least she'd met people who'd seen Hedra pretending to be her. Hedra using her name and clothes and mannerisms. Not the sort of people who'd talk to the police, though, even if they might be believed. Even if the police could locate most of them.

But what did it all actually prove? The police would think it had been Allie herself who'd frequented Wild Red's, dressed and made up for picking up men, then, in less extreme clothes and makeup tonight, she hadn't been recognized. Certainly that's what a prosecutor would maintain in court.

And it sounded plausible, she had to admit. More plausible than *her* story.

Again, Allie found herself wondering if Hedra really existed.

32

The next morning, in her room at the Willmont, Allie counted her money. She still had enough to meet her needs for a while, but even living as she was, Manhattan proved expensive. It was a city where money talked, growled, and laughed, and would step over you for dead. Even the air was expensive; a doctor would tell you that. Trading the computer for cash had been no problem; deal enough with computers and computer people, and you learn where hardware and software might be bought and sold cheap and without questions. But stolen jewelry was another matter. She had no idea where to exchange it for cash.

From the brown envelope she'd stuck behind the bottom dresser drawer, she got out one of Mayfair's gold chains, a thick, eighteen-inch one lettered 14 KARAT on the clasp. There was also an *M* engraved there; Allie assumed that was merchandise or manufacturing coding and not Mayfair's monogram. And even if it was a monogram, so what? Plenty of people whose last names began with *M*. She hefted the tangled chain in her hand, closing her eyes as if that would heighten her sensitivity. It was surprisingly heavy and should be worth more than the others.

She returned the envelope to its hiding place behind the drawer. Then she slipped into her jacket, dropped the chain in a pocket, and left the hotel. Eyes in the lobby followed her, as if the chain were visible and everyone knew it wasn't hers. She almost laughed. A murderer worried about being branded a thief.

Selling the gold chain was easier than she'd imagined. She'd walked down Forty-seventh Street between Fifth and Sixth, the diamond district. Here, during the day, millions of dollars' worth of diamonds in all kinds of settings were displayed like mere baubles.

Halfway down the block, Allie had gone into a small shopping arcade lined with tiny shops, chosen the smallest, and told the man behind the counter she wanted to sell her husband's gold chain. He was a tiny man with a black beard and had a skullcap perched on the back of his head like a dark bald spot. He studied Allie for a few seconds, then examined the chain briefly with the jeweler's loupe that was dangling from a red string around his neck. He held the chain up to the light, then let it coil gently down into the small metal cradle of a scale.

In a thick Yiddish accent he said, "I can give you five hundred dollars, no more."

Allie didn't want to seem eager. "Can't you make it seven hundred?"

The man shrugged. "So I'll make it five-fifty. And I mean no more. Really. Final. *Finis.* Check the price of gold, figure my profit margin, you'll see that's more than fair."

"Cash?"

The man played the chain like liquid through his fingers, thinking about that. Though he was small, he had long, elegant fingers. "Sure, cash," he said. He handed the chain back to Allie, said, "Wait here," and disappeared beyond a thick hanging curtain that soaked up light like velvet.

He came back a few minutes later with eleven fifty-dollar bills. No receipt was offered or requested. There was no paperwork. This was a simple transaction between buyer and seller, what had made the world work for centuries.

"If you're in possession of any other such items, bring them in," he said, smiling. He'd chosen his words carefully, hadn't said "If you own" or "If you have." "If you're in possession of," was what he'd told her. As if it didn't matter whether she was the legal owner. She wondered if anyone in the world was actually honest.

Allie smiled back, nodded, and left the shop.

Sunday morning she heard about a theft in the Willmont; an old man's cash from his Social Security check had been stolen when he was out of his room. She wondered if she should keep the rest of Mayfair's jewelry where it was hidden behind the drawer.

She decided the smart thing would be to sell all of it as soon as possible where she'd sold the gold chain, then keep the money with her.

She was there a few minutes after the shop

opened Monday morning. The same man, wearing his yarmulke skullcap, was behind the counter, methodically setting out velvet-lined display cases glittering with diamonds.

Allie smiled at him. "Remember me?"

He tilted his head, narrowed his eyes. "Ah, sure, the gold chain. I trust you spent the money well."

"I did, but I could use more to spend just as well. I brought some other jewelry. Will you look at it? Make an offer?"

"Of course. That's my business. Just let me finish setting out these displays."

While Allie waited, he made several more trips to the room behind the curtain and emerged with diamond jewelry on display trays.

He held up a long forefinger, as if to say "One more," and spent several minutes behind the curtain.

Allie thought he might have forgotten her, but finally he emerged with another black velvet case and placed it in the display window. He stepped back and brushed his hands together briskly, as if slapping dust from them after hard physical work. Maybe he'd been doing heavy construction behind the curtain.

"Now," he said, smiling, "let's have a look at what you've brought me."

Allie scooped the jewelry from her Windbreaker pocket and laid it on the glass-topped counter. All of it. More gold chains, the rings, gold-link bracelet, wristwatch. All tangled together from being jostled in her pocket as she walked.

"Ah," the jewelry merchant said. He studied the rings and set them aside, then he sorted through the twists and kinks of the remaining intertwined jewelry. "Interesting. The watch runs?"

"My husband says it keeps perfect time."

"Of course. Or you wouldn't be selling it." He slowly and carefully lifted and examined each piece, then set it gently in the scale's basket, made notations on a folded sheet of white paper. The last piece, the gold bracelet, he lifted and then placed back on the counter. He said, "I'm sorry, miss."

Allie was confused. "Sorry? You don't want to buy?" Then she saw the man's sad dark gaze focus over her right shoulder.

"I'm sorry, too," a deep and gentle voice said.

She whirled and was looking at Sergeant Kennedy. A somber but alert uniformed patrolman stood next to him. Two more blue uniforms were just outside the shop's door. Two more serious, apprehensive faces, peering in through the glass at her like ritual masks. And they really were part of a ritual—the one that had been in her nightmares since the night Sam was killed.

In a rush she realized it must have been the gold chain with Mayfair's initial that had raised suspicion and drawn them here, probably photographs of her the police had circulated among shops like this. The police worked in ways that mystified civilians. And now they were actually arresting her, thinking she was Hedra. Or did they think Hedra was Allie? Did it really matter anymore? Hedra, Allie . . . The two personalities were finally and irrevocably linked. Merged. She was ready to accept that she was the weaker and less fortunate of the two components and would soon fade and no longer matter. Like a Siamese twin doomed from the moment of conception. The way Hedra had planned it.

Allie was under arrest for murder. This was how it felt.

But *what* was she feeling? She couldn't be sure. Was this actually happening? *Was it?*

She heard the shrill *Whooop! Whooop! Whooop!* of a siren in the distance, forging through congested traffic. It sounded like an exhilarated beast closing in for the kill. She was having difficulty breathing. Standing. Her legs began an uncontrollable trembling and she feared she might wet herself.

"Just relax now," Kennedy told her soothingly, smiling. "I'm going to read you your rights, dear."

33

Lawrence gathered up the breakfast dishes while Hedra read the *Times.* She was absently chewing on a piece of toast with strawberry jam on it, smiling.

So the police had arrested Allie. Charged her with murder. The story was no longer front-page news in the *Times,* but Hedra had been following the case in the papers and on TV and was waiting and watching for this inevitable development. She was sure the coverage in the *Post* would be more detailed, and probably on the front page, complete with photographs and a rehash of the murder. After breakfast, she'd go out and buy several papers and learn all she could. She used a forefinger to wipe jam from a corner of her mouth and licked the finger.

There was a clanking roar behind her: Lawrence running the garbage disposal. The roar became a growl and then ceased abruptly.

Lawrence said, "Shit! Fucker's stopped up again."

Hedra swiveled in her chair and watched while

he probed the disposal with a wood-handled ice pick. Stabbing at whatever was caught there as if he were chipping ice. Something in the disposal smelled like rotten eggs; she wished he'd get the thing unclogged as soon as possible. *Phew!* It was getting stronger.

Lawrence was a twentyish black man with the face of an aesthete and the body of a twelve-year-old boy. He was wearing only his white Jockey shorts, and he looked ridiculous standing there playing plumber.

He bent to reach beneath the sink, punched the red reset button, and the disposal rattled and roared again. He turned on the tap water to wash the mechanism free and beamed at Hedra as if he'd accomplished something important.

She said, "Well, aren't you some pumpkin?"

He looked unsure about how to take her remark. Instead of answering, he busied himself again with the breakfast dishes, rinsing and scraping them before propping them in the dishwasher. Now and then the knife he was scraping with screeched against the surface of a plate, like a creature in pain.

After a few minutes he glanced over his shoulder and said, "You sure we got enough stash laid in?"

Focusing her attention again on the paper, Hedra said, "Don't worry about it."

"Gotta worry. Stuff's gettin' impossible to steal at the hospital. Locks, record sheets, sign in, sign out. You wouldn't believe the shit they make everybody go through so nobody can walk out

with a thing. I mean not even a fuckin' tongue de-
pressor leaves that place."

"You don't need it from there anymore," Hedra
reminded him. "Don't need a bit of it from there."

"Good fuckin' thing," Lawrence said, clinking
knives and forks into the dishwasher's flatware
basket.

She'd lived with Lawrence Leacock in his tiny
apartment in the days since Sam's death, seldom
going out. She hadn't even been inside a church
since the incident at St. Ambrose's. She'd waited
until after mass and attended confession, not out
of guilt but as a plea for understanding. She
should have known better. She could still hear the
gasp of the priest on the other side of the confes-
sional screen before she'd fled. She was sure he
hadn't gotten a good look at her. She'd been careful about that, even while entering the confes-
sional, perhaps anticipating his reaction.

Lawrence, a kinky lab technician and coke addict she'd let pick her up in a bar up near Harlem,
was only too glad to take care of her. After all, she
took care of him, and almost every night. A girl
had to do what a girl had to do.

Hedra flicked a glance at Lawrence and then
continued to read. The *Times* speculated that,
given the nature of the crime, it was possible Allie
might plead insanity. That irritated Hedra. She
knew Sam's killer wasn't insane. Allie'd had to kill
him, as well as that obnoxious snooping playwright. Sometimes Fate took control, grabbed
people by the short hairs and dragged them, leaving no real choice of direction or destination.

"You want another cup of coffee, Allison?" Lawrence asked.

Hedra shook her head no, not looking at him. You could take only so much of a kitehead like Lawrence. She continued staring at the paper, now only pretending to read it. Thinking.

No, she wasn't insane. Not anymore. If she'd *ever* been. They'd never really made up their minds about her anyway. Their own minds that circled like pale vultures so high above hers, so far above suspicion. One of the white-coated fools had even suggested she might be a multiple personality. As if everyone didn't have more than one side. Hedra had overheard them talking about her overwhelming and formative need to escape reality, as if that, too, were unique. Tell me about it, she thought. Explain how I'm different from the millions of people who use drugs and alcohol regularly to escape from this shitty world for a while. Explain why I shouldn't want to forget the past, after what my father did to create that kind of past. Night after night in my bed, putting his hands on me again and again. Dream after dream that was real. "She wants desperately to be someone else," they'd whispered, trying to keep it a secret, but she'd heard it through the walls. "Poor child never really developed a center," her mother, poor mother, had said, quoting another white coat. "Doesn't have a sense of self-worth or identity. Wants to be someone else, anyone but who she is. My fault, my fault. Wants to be someone else."

Not anymore, Hedra thought, spreading strawberry jam on her third piece of toast.

Now I know who I am.

Lawrence had picked up the long-bladed knife he'd used to slice bacon and was placing it in the dishwasher. Hedra thought about asking him to bring it to her, then she changed her mind. She couldn't imagine why the thought had occurred to her.

34

Hedra had watched and waited, and when the time was right she met a Haller-Davis rental agent at the Cody Arms, a woman named Myra Klinger who was blocky as a soccer player and wore a pin-striped blue business suit complete with a yellow power tie and cuffed pants. Unexpectedly, Myra had a martyred nun's face with brown, injured eyes.

As she unlocked the door to apartment 3H, she looked oddly at Hedra. Hedra had dyed her hair red and styled it in a graceful backsweep, and with her altered makeup and deliberately added weight she had no fear of being recognized by any of the tenants. And even if she were recognized, it would merely be as someone they'd seen before in the building; they wouldn't connect her with Allie, whose own presence they'd only vaguely acknowledged. New York anonymity was a curse for some, for others a proper blessing.

Myra said, "Strange, you being named Jones. The woman who lived here last was named Jones."

Hedra smiled. "Common name. That's why my parents named me Eilla. Eilla Jones."

Myra swept open the door and stepped aside so Hedra could enter. It was all one smooth and expectant motion, like someone introducing a celebrity to an audience.

The apartment looked shockingly bare, and the traffic noises from outside seemed louder and more echoing than Hedra remembered. The scatter rugs were of course gone; there wasn't the slightest clutter in the place, and that changed its character entirely. But it could be furnished almost exactly the way it had been the day Hedra moved in. Standing and staring, Hedra could see it, all the furniture in place, the television playing and a book lying on the sofa, and there was a cup of hot chocolate resting on the fat sofa arm.

Home, she thought. I live here. I'm who I am, so there's nowhere else I should be, nowhere else *I could be.*

The air stirred by the opening door had settled back down; the atmosphere in the apartment was hot and close, thick enough for Hedra to feel lying smooth and heavy as the softest velvet on her bare skin.

She knew she was expected to react to the apartment, to say something, so she said, "Spacious, but it could be cozy, too." She walked down the hall, glanced into the bathroom as if looking at it for the first time. She nodded with approval. Nice touch, that. She peeked into the bedrooms and smiled.

"The place'll be painted," Myra assured her.

Hedra faced Myra Klinger and said, "No, I love it exactly the way it is. I wouldn't change a thing."

"You sure? It can be painted the same colors."

"I'm sure. And I can pay you three months' rent in advance. I'm promised a good job here, have been for months and now it's been confirmed, so money's no problem." Hedra told her about a job as a computer programmer. She gave Lawrence's phone number as the company number, in case Haller-Davis decided to check. She didn't think they'd bother, with a three-month advance plus a security desposit. And it was such a convincing story; she was so good at manipulating people like Myra Klinger, at sizing them up and then using them. It was, after all, their hearts' desire.

Myra was thinking hard about the situation.

"To tell you the truth," Hedra said, "this is the last apartment on the list a rental service company gave me. If I don't get this one, I'm not sure what'll happen; I don't have any more apartments to look at."

"You could get a new list."

"The way property is in Manhattan, I doubt if that'd help."

Myra shook her broad head and frowned. "Yeah, it's a hell of a world sometimes. Hell of a city, anyway."

"Sure is."

"People get trapped in all kinds of ways."

"Don't they, though?"

"Even caring, affectionate people whose only real crime is being human."

"Or different," Hedra said.

"That, too."

Hedra locked gazes with Myra until she felt the subtle arc of current she'd expected. "Different people in particular get fucked over in this city, so they've gotta stick together, don't you think?"

Myra's breasts were rising and falling. "Are you positive you want this apartment, Eilla?"

"I *especially* want it," Hedra said. "And I'll do anything to get it."

Myra smiled. "Maybe there won't be any problem. I might recommend you get the apartment."

"Oh, God! Thanks, Mrs. Klinger!"

Myra looked as if her feelings had been stepped on. She said, "It's *Ms.* And remember I said 'might.' "

"Oh, sure. Sorry. There's one thing more, Ms. Klinger."

"It can be Myra."

Hedra grinned. She just bet it could be "Myra." "Fine. What I mean is, is there a storage area in the basement?"

"Why, yes, there is."

"Would it be okay if I took a look at it? I've got some stuff to store—boxes of books and a bicycle."

"I don't see why you can't have a look," Myra said.

Hedra rode to the basement with Myra in the service elevator. It was the sub-basement, actually, as the basement itself had long ago been converted to apartments.

In the time she'd lived at the Cody Arms, Hedra had been to the basement only once. She remembered being surprised by its dim vastness, as she was again now. Though it was warm beneath the octopus tangle of heating ducts and with the boilers nearby, there was a cold feel to the basement, as if it were a cave. And in a way, Hedra thought, it was a man-made cave. Far below street level.

The south end of the basement was partitioned into what might be described as stalls. Square, equal areas divided by thick slat fencing that ran from floor to ceiling. There were spaces of about two inches between the slats. Each stall had a section of slats that swung open to provide access. These were the "storage lockers" of the apartments above. The ones that had items stored inside—about a third of them—were equipped with heavy padlocks. There was a number stenciled on each locker, corresponding with an apartment number.

Myra knew her way around down here. She reached up with a stocky arm and yanked a pull cord, and a low-wattage bare bulb winked on and lessened the dimness in a limited area. She gripped Hedra's elbow tenderly and led the way down the corridor between rows of storage lockers, reaching up two more times to work a pull cord and shed light as they walked. From somewhere in the basement came a steady electrical buzzing, perhaps a transformer. The sound faded behind them.

Allie's locker was about halfway down the row. It was empty. Hedra was disappointed. She'd thought maybe some of Allie's things might still be down here, overlooked when Allie's possessions had been moved out. Directly across from Allie's storage space was the locker for 4H, Graham Knox's apartment. Hedra saw that it still contained what was left of Graham's possessions. In the shadows she could make out a dented file cabinet, and on top of it an old typewriter gathering dust. Probably the junk was tied up in probate court, Hedra thought, or maybe simply waiting to be hauled away.

"Damn," Myra said, fumbling with a large ring of keys. "I don't think I have anything that fits this lock, or I could open the door and you could get a better idea of how much space there is."

"Well, that's okay," Hedra said. She ran a hand across the slats. "I can estimate pretty well from here. What I got'll fit right in there."

"I'll get the key to you later, I promise."

"You don't strike me as the type that'd break a promise," Hedra said. A large roach ventured into the light, then turned and scurried along the base of a storage locker and back into darkness. "Or go back on a bargain."

"I'm not," Myra said in a strained voice. She rested a hand on Hedra's shoulder, near the base of her neck. "Are you?"

"No," Hedra said, smiling into the brown, agonized eyes. Not unlike Lawrence's eyes, only older. More resigned.

The two women left the dim basement and went back upstairs to the apartment.

35

Hedra hadn't said good-bye to Lawrence. Well, he hadn't known they were parting, so what did it matter? She'd given him some coke that was like none he'd ever snorted or smoked. The ultimate and final high. He lay curled in a corner of the bathroom while she'd methodically removed every trace of herself from his life.

Before leaving she'd looked in on him, and he hadn't moved. He'd probably never move again under his own power. "Lucky Lawrence," she'd said softly before walking out. "You got what you wanted."

Hedra moved into the Cody Arms and began buying furniture. She'd taken the largest bedroom; it had a better view and more closet space.

Her first night back in the apartment she'd sat on the bare floor where the sofa used to be, sipping hot chocolate, watching a mixture of sleet and rain smear the dark window and cause her reflection to waver. She was wearing her dark slacks and favorite yellow blouse, her brown sandals that were slightly too large for her but comfortable. She studied her other self in the flat and undulating window pane and she and her Other exchanged smiles.

Sitting in the dim warmth of the apartment, listening to the splatter of rain dripping from the gutters onto the gargoyle stonework, she felt a contentment she hadn't known since rare moments as a child. She was in a secret place, a place to hide, and in a way she could carry it with her wherever she went and it gave her an unshakable peace and confidence. It was her most precious possession.

The next morning she took a cab to a beauty salon on lower Broadway and had her hair dyed blond and trimmed in the old Allie fashion. It was also the first day of her diet.

No one in the Cody Arms seemed to pay much attention to her. If the pleasantly plump woman who'd just moved in on the third floor looked remotely familiar, it wasn't mentioned. At least not to Hedra's knowledge. And if it was noticed, the fact that she was rumored to be the previous tenant's sister accounted for any resemblance of clothing or gesture. Hedra and the other tenants played the New York game of studiously avoiding eye contact and stayed out of each other's lives. Random collisions of fate could cause problems.

When Hedra went out at night, she seldom drifted in the direction of the Village. In a city the size of New York there were countless places to go, countless men cruising for companionship. Looking for someone like Hedra.

Always she introduced herself as Allie Jones. The name had long ago faded from the news and caused no flicker of recognition and required no explanation. Allie Jones, one of the many on the make and available to be made.

At Apple of My Eye, a lounge on East 21st Street, she was picked up by a handsome young stock-broker. The Manhattan single girl's dream. He'd peered at her through the haze of tobacco smoke and the flashing, multicolored strobe lights and, talking loud to be heard above the music, said his name was Andy. She told him she was Allison but he should call her Allie. First names only. That was the protocol for places like this. They'd stay on a first-name basis while they explored each other and decided how far the relationship might travel.

Andy was tall and angular, with sharp and sensi-tive features and thick black hair that was parted with geometric precision and seemed never to get mussed. He dressed well, though a little too trendy; shoulders a shade too padded, pleated pants too tight at the cuffs. Narrow black shoes with built-up heels, made more for dancing than walking, added half an inch to his height, though he didn't need it. He must have bought the shoes for style. Or maybe he was some kind of dance buff. There were plenty of them around. Young Fred Astaires.

That first night at Apple he'd asked Hedra to dance, then guided her through a complex series of steps she didn't know. But she had no difficulty following his strong lead. She knew he was making them both look good. Fred and Ginger. The man could damn well move.

"You dance great," he'd told her.

"Hah! Anyway, I enjoy the challenge."

He raised his left hand, nudged her beneath the shoulder, and guided her into an underarm turn. Ballroom stuff, as if to demonstrate that he had class. That he thought *she* had class. When she came out of the turn, he was right there to pick up the beat. Maneuvered her toward the edge of the wide dance floor and began a lazy, circling step so they could talk.

He said, "It's tell-me-about-yourself time, Allie. You from New York?"

"Not originally. From Illinois. But I haven't been back there in years. Don't wanna go back ever."

"Why not?"

"Oh, no solid reason. Just a collection of slightly unpleasant memories, all connected with the Midwest." She felt a thrust of fury at the base of her mind. "They don't understand there that the different apple in the barrel isn't necessarily the rotten one."

"Hey, I know what you mean. You live in the Village, I'll bet."

"Nope. Upper West Side. You?"

"I'm from New Jersey. Teaneck. Too expensive to live in Manhattan for some of us." He led her through a neat turn to avoid a couple who'd danced too close, then resumed his rhythmic, hypnotic circling step. "How long you lived in your apartment?"

"'Bout three years. Did I say I lived in an apartment?"

"I dunno." He smiled. "Doesn't everyone in New York live in an apartment?"

"No, sometimes a condo or co-op."

"Same thing. You go in a door and down a hall before you get to your door."

"Yeah, I suppose so."

"Bet you have a nice place. Maybe I could see it sometime."

A quick hint of a smile. "Definitely. Sometime."

"Where'd you live before Manhattan?"

She moved closer and rested her head on his shoulder. A tingle of alarm played up the nape of her neck, like the very tip of a soft feather drawn over flesh. What was going on here? "How 'bout you? Where'd you live before New Jersey?"

He told her, but she barely listened. Someplace in Connecticut. Not that it mattered. No way to know if it was the truth. A thousand voices in Hedra were screaming for her to be careful. She'd heard those warnings before and ignored them, and regretted it later. Alcoholics and gamblers must hear those same unheeded voices.

She and Andy danced until closing time and agreed to meet there the next evening. He kissed her lightly on the forehead as they parted. Nothing pushy, but a promise. Subtle foreplay.

And the next evening she went. She couldn't stay away.

She waited until almost midnight and he didn't show up.

After turning down her tenth offer of a drink or a dance, she decided to leave. She threaded her way across the crowded dance floor and past a line of people waiting to get into the main room. A short man with a gray beard and a gold-flecked silk jacket turned away from the woman on his arm and winked at Hedra. She said, "Nice coat, but that's about it, asshole," and walked past him and out the door.

Zinging the bearded man had given her a great deal of pleasure, but she wasn't sure why. Maybe she'd made him a substitute for Andy. He was the same sex; that was close enough.

Midnight was too late for a woman alone to ride safely on the subway.

Alone. Not what she'd planned.

It wasn't unusual to be stood up, she assured herself, as she hailed a cab to take her back to the Cody Arms. That was how it went in the singles scene in Manhattan, a cruel and devious game, each partner playing with the softest part of the other. Hadn't she always known it?

Still, she'd liked Andy a lot. She'd wanted desperately for the voices to be wrong, for him to be who he said he was.

But was anybody who they said they were? Really?

During the cab ride through the dark and rain-slick streets, snow began to fall.

At the Cody Arms, she paid the driver and climbed out of the taxi, feeling a few cold flakes on the back of her neck as she bent down and slammed the rear door. The cab pulled away and left a swirling turmoil of blue-gray exhaust that held the glow from the streetlight, then drifted low and disappeared in darkness.

She turned up the collar of her new blue rain-coat and hurried across West 74th Street, listening to the *clack! clack! clack!* of her high heels spiking the pavement. She wanted to be warm. Safe. Home. Soon as possible.

There was no one in the lobby or the elevator. She rode up to the third floor, waited patiently for the elevator to go through its yo-yo act to minimize the step up. As the sliding doors hissed open, she strode out into the hall, already fishing in her purse for her key.

As soon as she closed the apartment door behind her, she felt much better. Calmer. And she realized she was very tired. Being stood up was a strain. *The hell with you, Andy, you inconsiderate bastard.* She'd have a cup of hot chocolate and then read herself to sleep.

She didn't notice them at first. Not until she'd hung her coat in the closet by the door and taken three steps into the living room.

Then her breath became a cold vacuum and she stopped and stood still. *Mother of God!*

What was going on here? Were they real, sitting so calmly and unmoving on her sofa? Staring at her?

Not real, she decided.

Not possibly real.

An illusion.

She dug her fingers into her palms and laughed nervously, startling herself with the high-pitched rasp that exploded from her constricted throat. When she inhaled she found the air thin and dizzying and felt as if she might suffocate.

The large, tweedy man holding the brown package and the dead cigar said, "Nasty out there, isn't it, dear?" And she knew he was real.

Real, too, was the figure next to him on the sofa.

Sitting in Hedra's place.

Allie Jones.

36

Hedra knew she was in a trap but had little idea of its tightness or dimensions. She had to feel this one out. Move carefully.

What could they know about her?

Actually *know*?

That she'd moved into the apartment under false pretenses. That she wasn't using her real name.

That was all, really; they couldn't possibly prove she'd lived here before. They knew nothing about her actions during that time.

They can't prove anything, she told herself. She'd obscured every track and neatly snipped every loose end. Just like in the mystery novels she read so avidly. *They can know but they can't prove. Don't let them bluff you.*

With an immense effort of will, she calmed herself. The fluttering in her stomach slowed and almost ceased. She managed to stare at Allie questioningly. *Who are you?* She said, "Whoever you people are, I think you have the wrong apartment. You damn well better have a believable explanation."

Allie parted her lips to say something, then she decided against it and remained silent. There she sat in the streaming lamplight, staring at Hedra accusingly and as if she couldn't quite understand her. But it was Hedra who didn't understand. What was Allie doing here? Why wasn't she behind bars awaiting trial?

The big man absently holding the snubbed-out cigar uncrossed his weighty legs, then extended them and crossed them again at the ankles. *I'm not going anywhere,* his actions told her. He was wearing huge wing-tip shoes, scuffed as if he'd been kicking rocks. Sighing like an asthmatic, he reached into a suit coat pocket and dragged out a small leather case and flipped it open. He made a show of extending it toward her. "I'm Detective Sergeant Will Kennedy," he said, "N.Y.P.D. This is Miss Allison Jones. She used to live here, in this apartment."

Hedra didn't bother examining the identification, as if she were uninterested. She wished Allie would stop staring at her and say something. Wished the bitch would stop regarding her with that mixture of cold anger and puzzlement. And something else: pity. Hedra said, "I read in the papers Allison Jones was in jail."

Sergeant Kennedy smiled with a strange sadness. "And so she was. Miss Jones here persisted in telling us an interesting story. One nobody believed."

"Was it one she could prove?" Hedra asked.

Kennedy ignored the question. He sighed

again. "She said a woman named Hedra Carlson had been her secret roommate and had . . . well, gradually taken over her life in a very real sense."

"Taken over her life? What's that mean?"

"Become her, you might say."

The acrid smell of his dead cigar drifted to Hedra and nauseated her. "Well, I'm Hedra Carlson, but I just moved into this apartment a few weeks ago. I never saw it till the rental agent opened the door."

"But you're using the name Eilla Jones. We wouldn't have noticed that on the computer printouts, except for the address. That made it kinda jump off the page at us. It was Miss Jones here who convinced us to get computer printouts on all rental units in Manhattan occupied since the date of her friend's murder." Kennedy shook his head in wonder. "All that kinda information's available these days almost at the press of a button. Amazing, isn't it?"

"I don't know anything about her friend's murder, but I admit I used guile to get this apartment. Of that I plead guilty, Sergeant, but I'm not sorry. You have any idea how difficult it is to get an apartment in New York?"

"Everything's difficult in New York," he said, as if commiserating with her.

"I'd read about this woman in the papers"—a glance at Allie—"just after she killed that poor man in the hotel. One of the news items mentioned her address. The Upper West Side was exactly the area I wanted. I knew that, unless she was tried and acquitted in record time, her apartment would be available as soon as her rent wasn't paid, so I kept an eye on the place and was first to apply. I was prepared to wait. Justice seldom moves swiftly, does it, Sergeant?"

"No, but it moves."

For an instant he reminded Hedra of Justice itself, a force as inexorable as the swing of planets. She reassured herself he was nothing more than a very human, overweight cop. Nothing for her to fear if only she kept her head. Did he know how she'd convinced Myra Klinger to accept her for the apartment? Aging, ugly Myra, so grateful for someone like Hedra. "I did what was necessary in order to get the lease, Sergeant. I took advantage of Allison Jones's predicament. That kind of thing's done all the time to get an apartment in this city. One person's misfortune is another's good luck." She stood very straight. "I'm not ashamed."

He studied his snubbed-out cigar intently, as if at any second it might be the beneficiary of spontaneous combustion. "No, I expect you're not."

"I've never before laid eyes on Allison Jones."

"Well, I can't agree with that," he said in a level, amiable tone, as if he were differing with her about the Mets' chances to make the play-offs. "She's here to positively identify you, which she's done. And she says you and she lived here together for several months. That little by little you stole her life, her lover, her identity. That only two other people knew about you. One was murdered. The other died, maybe in an accident, though I suspect not. And you disappeared, leaving behind a mutilated corpse and a murder charge that appeared to belong to her."

Hedra didn't bother feigning surprise. "And now I've come back here?"

"You thought the real Allie Jones was in prison, possibly for life. No murder had been committed in the apartment. No one suspected a woman fitting your general description ever lived here. So it figured you'd return. There was no reason for you *not* to, this time. You'd almost *have to,* wouldn't you, if you were Allie Jones?"

"'This time'?"

"You've assumed other identities, other personalities, before Allie Jones."

"But I told you, I only did what was needed to get the apartment. I never told anyone I was Allie Jones. I'm not Allie Jones."

He rolled the cigar between his fingers. "Aren't you?"

It was time for positions to be made clear. Hedra said, "This is all very serious. For you, if you can't prove any of it. Which you can't, because it isn't true. If this woman says it is, I think you better have her sanity tested. Or maybe she's sane as they come and she's cooked up a story to give her the best possible deal in court. And anyone who can corroborate it, or prove to you it *isn't* true, is conveniently dead. Doesn't that make sense? If she's under indictment for murder, what's she got to lose?"

"The indictment's been dropped," Kennedy said. "Her story's been corroborated."

Hedra felt her heartbeat quicken, the blood pulse in her temples. She should have anticipated this. *Don't let them bluff you.* "You said the only two people who could corroborate it were dead."

"And they are." Kennedy leisurely unwrapped the plain brown package he was holding. Peeled away the thick paper with maddening slowness, crinkling it noisily. He had fingers the size of sausages, with blunt, tobacco-yellowed tips and almost nonexistent nails. Allie sat quietly with her eyes fixed on Hedra. She was even thinner than before. There was a worn resignation in the limpness of her hands resting palms-up in her lap, the slope of her shoulders. But her eyes were bright, almost as if glowing with fever.

Inside the brown wrapping paper was a thin cardboard box that had contained typewriter paper. Kennedy set the crumpled wrapping aside and lifted the lid slowly, as if something alive were inside.

He said, "Miss Jones was convincing enough for me to do what you might call some exploratory police work. A woman was killed and mutilated with a knife six months ago in her apartment on the Lower East Side. Her name was Meredith Hedra Carlson. That prompted us to look a bit further into what Miss Jones had told us. It turns out the *Times* does have a record of Allison Jones placing a classified ad in their 'Apartment to Share' section. So we examined Graham Knox's possessions and found this." He nodded toward the box. "It contained notes, an outline, and the first several scenes of what was to be Knox's next play, based on material he acquired by listening through the ductwork at his vent in the apartment above this one. He titled it *SWF Seeks Same*. It's about a Manhattan apartment dweller and her secret roommate."

He set the box on the sofa arm and shifted his bulk so he could lever himself to stand. "You must be somebody, dear. Who are you?"

Hedra wasn't aware of making a decision. No more than a trapped animal consciously decides on a final, desperate burst for freedom. An effort of nerve and heart and muscle that allows for thought later, in sweet and silent safety.

She was at the door, flinging it open, hurling herself into the hall.

In the corner of her vision she saw fat Sergeant Kennedy struggling ponderously up out of the sofa, knocking the box and its contents to the floor. Heard him say, "Dammit, come back here! You trying to kill me, too?"

37

Allie sprang to her feet as she saw Hedra bolt out the door. *Not again!* Hedra was real! Here! Now! Allie couldn't bear the thought of her disappearing again. Ceasing to exist.

Kennedy was flailing away, trying to get to his feet; he posed no threat to the swift and panicked Hedra. Allie ran for the open door, banged her hand on the knob as she raced through, and wheeled, almost falling, to dash after Hedra.

As she rounded the final corner in the hall, there was Hedra standing inside the elevator. Her back was pressed to the metal wall and she was watching with strange and dreamy detachment as Allie ran toward her. Fear had rushed her from reality.

When Allie was fifty feet from the elevator, Hedra's eyes widened in mild alarm.

At twenty feet, the elevator doors began to slide closed. Hedra might have smiled.

Allie dived at the elevator like a ballplayer sliding headfirst into a base. She felt the carpet burning her elbows, her chin, her stomach where her blouse had twisted.

She managed to thrust an arm between the closing doors. Her wrist was clamped by hard steel beneath soft rubber. *An animal caught in a spring trap.*

She struggled to a kneeling position. Something smashed loudly against the inside of the elevator doors. Hedra kicking at the intrusive wrist and hand. Allie could feel the vibrations of each blow. A bolt of pain shot up her arm as Hedra's foot mashed the back of her hand. Her wrist felt sprained.

Writhing to a crouch, she'd managed to work her other hand into the crack between the doors and was prying them open. Hedra gripped a finger and bent it back. Pain! *Oh, God!* Through her agony Allie could hear Hedra's breath hissing fiercely inside the elevator.

Gradually, then all at once, the doors slid open. Allie flung herself inside.

She grabbed Hedra in a wild, brutal hug, feeling an incredible satisfaction.

Hedra was real, all right. Solid and reeking of terror and in her grasp at last. Hissing, "Let go, Allie. Goddamn you, let me *go!*"

Allie was aware of Kennedy chugging down the hall, running with a bearlike wobble. The blackened dead cigar jutting from his mouth, his thick legs pumping and his arms swinging wide.

The elevator doors were sliding shut.

He'd never make it.

Would he?

When he was ten feet away the doors met and the elevator lurched into its descent. Pain jolted through the right side of Allie's head as Hedra sank her teeth into her earlobe, whimpering in the ear like a lover in desperate ecstasy.

Allie tried to push her away and Hedra punched her in the stomach. Allie almost doubled over in pain and heard the breath whoosh out of her. She raised her right foot and stamped down hard on Hedra's instep. Again! The teeth loosened their grip on her burning ear.

Finding strength where she thought there was none, Allie shoved away the feverish, rigid body pressed against hers. Hedra slammed into the corner. Allie grabbed her hair, her blond hair like Allie's own, and slammed her head against the wall.

Slammed it again and again until Hedra went limp and slumped to the floor.

Hedra curled her arms over her head for protection, drew up her knees and began to sob.

Allie leaned back against the opposite wall, drained of rage. She stood surprised and awed by the sense of profound pity she felt. *This must be what a twin feels when its sibling's in pain.*

The elevator jounced to a stop, and Allie dizzily placed her hands flat against the wall to keep her balance.

Hedra was quiet now. Unmoving.

When the elevator doors opened on the lobby, two plainclothes detectives and two uniformed officers were waiting. In the background hovered the mesmerized pale faces of onlookers, silent, watching intently, their expressions unreadable, their thoughts and fears too deep to reach the surface.

Kennedy appeared, breathing hard and looking angry and concerned. He must have ridden down in the other elevator. He'd lost his cigar, and black ash was peppered over his white shirt front. "You okay?" he asked Allie.

"Okay," she said, pressing her trembling palm to her ear, aware of a trickle of blood snaking down her arm.

One of the plainclothes detectives, a tall handsome man with neatly parted dark hair, entered the elevator and helped Hedra to her feet.

She glared at him, an accusation of unspeakable betrayal in her eyes. Her lips quivered. Parted. "You're not Andy. You pretended."

He gave her a fading, lazy smile as he gripped her elbow and ushered her from the elevator, almost as if escorting her onto a dance floor.

He said, "What's in a name?"

Epilogue

Allie moved out of the Cody Arms the next month. Out of the city. She'd been offered a job in the actuarial department of a large insurance company in Rockport, Illinois. The company's real-estate division found her an affordable place to live, a small house on an acre of wooded land just outside of town.

It was always quiet there. Her mail was delivered to a rural box on a cedar post at the end of her driveway. Her nearest neighbors, a retired carpenter and his wife, waved to her whenever they saw her in her yard. Cars passed only occasionally.

Her old apartment in the Cody Arms was leased and occupied within days after she'd gone. To a pair of single women who said they were sisters.

AUTHOR'S NOTE

Where does a writer get ideas? This is one of the few times this writer can pinpoint the time and place the book was conceived. I was in a restaurant with my wife, Barbara, and overheard two women in the adjoining booth talking about placing personal ads in a small local paper to get dates. It struck me that they were taking chances going out with men about whom they knew absolutely nothing. Then one of the women mentioned a roommate, and it occurred to me that women placed personal ads for roommates—people who will abruptly move in and become part of their home and personal lives— knowing about as much about them as they might from an ad resulting in nothing more than a single lunch date or conversation over a cup of coffee.

Their personal lives . . . A threat from a stranger inside the walls. Surely good material for a novel.

A publisher agreed.

Then, before publication of the novel, a major film company agreed.

This one had a different feel to it. I had sold film options on books before, and usually what followed was a check and then silence. These people seemed serious from the beginning. Columbia executive Michael Besman contacted me with assurances that the studio would keep me informed of progress on the project. And the studio did. At one point early in the process, Michael even called to bring me up to date on the construction of the sets. Talented new screenwriter Don Roos was going to do the screenplay. Barbet Schroeder was to direct. Casting was soon under way. Jennifer Jason Leigh and Bridget Fonda—two of my favorites—would be the costars. (I was told later that they decided between them which roles to play.) This was beginning to feel like a major film that would actually be made.

Unlike my writer friends' descriptions about their experiences with the film industry, the pieces for this movie fell into place like dominoes in a row. I could read on their faces that gloom was what I should be feeling. So I was waiting for the usual to happen—something to undo this deal.

Shooting began.

My wife and I were invited to the shoot in New York. My writer friends said, "Don't go. You won't leave town without crying."

Not so. One of the first things I saw when walking onto the set was a director's chair with my name on it. Cast and crew couldn't have been nicer or more accommodating. I was impressed by the dedication and professionalism of *everyone* involved. Not to mention the money that was spent. I recall a lineup of parked trailers on a block in Harlem, each a dressing room for a star, but each with the name not of the star but of the character he or she played in the movie. I found that kind of exhilarating and . . . well, creepy. People I had invented, who were made alive and recognizable by the artistry of the film industry, might be right behind those doors.

As I saw it, my job on the set was to avoid knocking over anything or anyone valuable. Introductions were made to cast and crew. I was duly impressed and intimidated, especially by Bridget Fonda, who had a bloody and serious looking arm injury inflicted by the beautiful and intense woman seated on a stool at the edge of the set—the remarkable Jennifer Jason Leigh. She didn't look in the least sorry, and was well on her way to becoming MTV's villain of the year.

So we watched the pros work: Schroeder in total control, actors with complete command of their roles, enhanced by creative lighting, costume, camera work . . . And later, a perfect score by Howard Shore. Watching it all brought to life piece by piece. It became evident that films are team efforts. There are a lot of phases in production where the wheels might come off; some very talented people prevent that.

Sometimes even they can't prevent it, and a film simply doesn't work. *Single White Female* does work. It remains a top-notch thriller, has spawned offspring, including the 2011 remake *The Roommate*, and even become part of the language. When a woman is imitated too closely, or her clothes are secretly borrowed, or her boyfriend is stolen by a friend, she's been Single White Femaled. I still get a kick occasionally hearing people use that phrase. In a different way altogether, I've been Single White Femaled. It was terrific.

Sarasota, Florida, 2011

Read on for an extract from

Pulse

by

John Lutz

available now from

www.constablerobinson.com/crime

1

It gave Garvey the creeps, transferring somebody like Daniel Danielle. The sick bastard had been convicted of killing three women, but some estimates had his total at more than a hundred.

They were the women who lived alone and let their guards down because the sicko could be a charmer as a man or a woman. Single women who disappeared and were missed by no one. Those were the kinds of women Daniel Danielle sought and tortured and destroyed.

Nicholson was seated next to Garvey. Like Garvey, he was a big man in a brown uniform. Their job was to transfer Daniel Danielle to a new, and so far secret, maximum-security state prison near Belle Glade, on the other side of the state from Sarasota. It was in Sarasota where Danielle Daniel (he had been dressed as a woman then) had been arrested while crouched over the body of one of his victims, and later convicted. The evidence was overwhelming. As a "calling card" and a taunt, he had put his previous victim's panties on his present victim, panties he had apparently worn to the murder. He was damned by his DNA.

Daniel was all the more dangerous because he was smart as hell. Degrees from Vassar and Harvard, and a fellowship at Oxford. Getting away with murder should have been a piece of cake, like the rest of his life. But it hadn't been. When his appeals were exhausted, he would be executed.

No one was visible on State Highway 72. This part of Florida was flat and undeveloped, mostly green vistas streaked with brown. Cattle country, though cattle were seldom glimpsed from the road except off in the distance. Wind and dust country for sure. Dust devils could be seen taking shape and dissipating on both sides of the road. Miles away, larger wannabe tornados threatened and whirled but didn't quite take form.

The latest weather report said the jet stream had shifted. Hurricane Sophia, closing in on Florida's east coast, now had a predicted path to the south, though not as far south as the dusty white van rocketing along the highway. Taking time to replace a broken fan belt ten miles beyond Arcadia had slowed them down. They were still okay, if the hurricane stayed north. If it didn't, they might be driving right into it.

Now and then a car passed going the other way, with a Doppler change of pitch as the boxy van rocked in the vehicle's wake. Off to the east there were more dust devils, more swirling cloud formations. The insistent internal voice Garvey often heard when some part of his mind knew something bad was about to happen wouldn't shut up.

Suddenly it began to rain. Hard. Garvey switched on the head-lights. Hail the size of marbles started smacking and bouncing off the van's windshield and stubby hood.

"Maybe we oughta go back," Nicholson said. "See if we can outrun whatever's headed our way."

"Orders are to deliver the prisoners." Garvey drove faster. The hail slammed harder against the windshield, as if hurled by a giant hand.

The prisoner chained in the back of the van with Daniel Danielle was a young man with lots of muscles and tattoos under his orange prison jumpsuit. He was scarred with old acne and had a face like chipped stone, with a crooked nose and narrow, mean eyes. He was easy to take for a hardened ex-con, but he was actually an undercover cop named Chad Bingham, there for insurance if something weird happened and Daniel Danielle made trouble.

Bingham would rather have been someplace else. He had a wife and two kids. And a job.

The easy part of the job was just sitting there sulking and pretending he was someone else. But the way things were going, he was afraid the hard part was on its way.

The hail kept coming. Nicholson was on the edge of being downright scared. Even if it didn't make landfall nearby, Sophia might spawn tornados. Hurricanes also sometimes unexpectedly changed course. He reached out and turned on the radio, but got nothing but static this far out in the flatlands, away from most civilization.

Garvey could see his partner was getting antsy so he tried to raise Sarasota on the police band. The result was more static. He tried Belle Glade and got the same response.

"Storm's interfering with reception," he said, looking into Nicholson's wide blue eyes. He had never seen the man this rattled.

"Try your cell phone," Nicholson said in a tight voice.

"You kidding?"

Nicholson tried his own cell phone but didn't get a signal. Both men jumped as a violent thumping began under the van.

"We ran over a branch or something that blew onto the road," Garvey said.

"Pull over and let's drag it out."

"Not in this weather," Garvey said. "That hail will beat us to death."

"What the hell was that?" Nicholson asked, as a huge, many-armed form crossed the road ahead of them, like an image in a dream.

"Looked like a tree," Garvey said.

"There aren't many trees around here."

"It's not around here anymore," Garvey said, as the wind rocked the van.

The van suddenly became easy to steer. Garvey realized that was because he was no longer steering it. The wind had lifted it off the road.

They were sideways now, plowing up dirt and grass. Then the van bounced and they were airborne again.

"What the shit are you doing?" Nicholson screamed.

"Sitting here just like you."

The van leaned left, leaned right, and Garvey knew they were going to turn over.

"Hold tight," he yelled, checking to make sure both of them had their seat belts fastened.

The wind howled. Steel screamed. They were upside down. Garvey could hear Nicholson shouting beside him, but couldn't make out what he was saying because of the din.

The van skidded a long way on its roof and then began to spin. Garvey felt his head bouncing against the side window. Bulletproof glass came off in sharp-edged, milky strips, and he was staring at the ground. With a violent lurch, the van was upright again, then back on its roof. Garvey realized that as addled as his brain had become, his right foot was still jammed hard against the brake pedal.

The van stopped. Hanging upside down, Garvey looked out the glassless window and saw that they were wedged against one of the rare trees Nicholson had mentioned. He looked over and saw that Nicholson was dazed and wild-eyed. And beyond Nicholson, out the window . . .

"Looks like a kind of low ridge over there," he shouted at Nicholson. "We gotta get outta the van, see if we can burrow down outta the wind."

"Everywhere!" Nicholson yelled. "Wind's everywhere!"

Garvey unhitched both safety belts, causing the weight of his body to compress onto his internal injuries. Ignoring the pain, he leaned hard to his right, against Nicholson, and kicked at the bent and battered door. It opened a few inches. The next time it opened, the wind helped it by wrenching it off one of its hinges and flattening it against the side of the van.

"Wind's dying down a little," he lied to Nicholson, and then was astounded to notice that it was true. The roaring had gone from sounding like a freight train to sounding like a thousand lonely and desperate wolves. A hurricane-spawned tornado, Garvey guessed. Moving away, he hoped.

He wormed and wriggled out of the van. The hail had stopped, but rain was still driven sideways by the wind. Garvey was sore all over. Later he'd have to take inventory to see if he was badly injured. With great effort he could stand, leaning into the wind. Nicholson was near him, on hands and knees, his head bowed to Sophia's ferocity.

The overturned van's rear doors were still closed, though the roof was crushed and the wire-reinforced glass was gone from the back windows. A pair of orange-clad legs and black prison shoes extended from one of the windows, and a voice was screaming.

Inside the back of the van, Chad Bingham was cut and bleeding from the long shard of glass in Daniel Danielle's hand. Daniel was bleeding himself, from cuts made by sharp glass or metal. Bingham's scalp was laid open and his face was covered with blood. In the wild tumble of the van, Daniel Danielle had managed to wrench the .25-caliber handgun from where it was taped to Bingham's ankle. Bingham, with his outside-the-walls complexion, hadn't fooled Daniel for a second.

Daniel held the small handgun against Bingham's throat. Bingham's legs were twisted backward, under him. The steel rail both men had been cuffed to had broken at the weld. They were free, though their wrists were still cuffed.

It was Daniel's legs protruding from the van's window. Both men knew the gun had hollow-point bullets and would kill easily and messily at close range. Daniel dropped the shard of glass, then used the hand without the gun and rubbed some of Bingham's blood over his own face and into his hair. Both men had prison haircuts. Bloodied up as they were, they could be mistaken for each other. Daniel needed only a moment of mistaken identity, and he would act.

He dug the gun's barrel into Bingham's throat. "Yell that I'm dead, and you want outta here. Do it if you want to live," he said to Bingham. "Don't do as I say, and bullets start slamming around your insides."

Bingham's eyes rolled with fear. He knew Daniel's reputation, and knew the killer had earned it.

"It's me!" he yelled. "It's Bingham. Daniel's dead. Get me the hell outta here!"

All the time he was yelling, Daniel was kicking with his free lower legs.

It seemed a lot of time passed. He jabbed again into Bingham's neck with the gun barrel. "Hey!" Bingham yelled, "Help!" While Daniel kicked.

Finally Daniel felt strong hands encircle his ankles, exert pressure. Pulling, pulling. As his body began to slide out of the van he stared into Bingham's eyes and kept the gun pointed directly at his testicles. Bingham didn't make a sound.

And then Daniel was free—like a cork out of a bottle.

"Thanks!" he kept repeating, as he faced into the wind and gained his feet.

"You guys okay?"

"We're—"

Garvey shut up when he realized the mistake they'd made. Daniel stepped close and shot him in the forehead.

Nicholson wheeled to run and Daniel shot him twice in the back of the neck. He fell and the wind rolled him a few feet and then lost interest. Daniel bent low into the wind and made his way back to the van. Bingham was still inside, curled up and playing dead. Daniel shot him in the testicles and Bingham began to wail. Daniel knew no one would hear even if they were nearby.

Still cuffed, he began his search for keys.

Five minutes later Bingham watched through the van's distorted rear window as a limping Daniel Danielle disappeared into the rain and wind.

Within minutes the hurricane sweeping across the state hit the area in earnest.

Chad Bingham would later testify in his hospital bed that Daniel almost certainly died from his wounds or from Hurricane Sophia. There was no way he could have survived out in the open as he'd been, without any nearby shelter.

It was Bingham who died from his wounds.